AN EMPTY SWING

AN EMPTY SWING
N.J. HANSON

TATE PUBLISHING
AND ENTERPRISES, LLC

Published by Tate Publishing & Enterprises, LLC
127 E. Trade Center Terrace | Mustang, Oklahoma 73064 USA
1.888.361.9473 | www.tatepublishing.com

Tate Publishing is committed to excellence in the publishing industry. The company reflects the philosophy established by the founders, based on Psalm 68:11,

"The Lord gave the word and great was the company of those who published it."

Book design copyright © 2016 by Tate Publishing, LLC. All rights reserved.
Cover design by Joshua Rafols
Interior design by Manolito Bastasa

Published in the United States of America

ISBN: 978-1-68301-970-1
1. Fiction / Mystery & Detective / General
2. Fiction / Ghost
16.04.11

To Hope Hill

*Death, the undiscovered country from
whose bourn no traveler returns.*

—William Shakespeare,
Hamlet, act III, scene i

1

The black sky was cold with only the light of faint, distant stars, and the waning crescent moon to illuminate the earth. A small gust rustled the orange and red leaves on this otherwise quiet October night. Nevertheless, in all this darkness, one man was not still.

In an old playground, one where the equipment is still mostly metal instead of plastic, a man stood waist deep in the ground. With his shovel in hand, he embedded the metal tip into the earth and pushed it with his booted foot. With a grunt and a heave, he lifted the shovelful of dirt out of the hole, and tossed it on the growing pile. He stuck the shovel in the ground, and rested his hands over the handle as he admired his work. Yes, this was deep enough.

He tossed the shovel out of the hole before dragging himself over the edge and back on his feet. After doing so, he walked to the nearby parked SUV and opened the back hatch. Inside was a large black garbage bag. He grabbed it with both hands and lifted it out, carrying it on his back to the hole he's just dug. The wind picked up again, and the small carousel slowly turned, emitting a loud rusty squeak. The man stopped suddenly. His head jolted up, and he looked around frantically, his breath caught in his throat, listening for any other sound. Nothing else was heard.

After a moment, he remembered to breathe. He took the bag and heaved it down into the hole where it landed with a thud. Grasping the shovel again, he began to bury it.

Wednesday, October 22

Luis ran as fast as he could—his arms pumped back and forth, his legs burned, his black-framed glasses bounced on his face with every step. Craning his neck back, he stole a glance over his shoulder to check if Butch was still after him. He was. No matter how fast or how far he ran, that guy would not give up.

Butch, a bully with a weird personal vendetta against Luis, chased after him. With rage in his eyes and his fists clenched, he was gaining ground on his target. For as long as Luis could remember, Butch had always liked to pick on and make a fool of him. This aggression was not solely focused on Luis, however. Just last week, Butch punched Joey, another kid from school, in the face because he didn't like how the other kid looked at him. Now Joey has a broken nose and a couple of loose teeth, something Luis definitely did not want today.

"You're dead, Luis!" Butch scooped a handful of rocks from the ground and chucked them as hard as he could. Most of them missed, and a few bounced harmlessly off Luis's backpack. One, however, struck him hard in the back of his skull.

"Argh!" Luis clasped his hand over the welt on his head. He winced and groaned, but he still ran as if his life depended on it, which he basically felt it did.

Ahead of him was the playground; not one for the school, but one build by the city and located in the town park. It was surrounded by a chain link fence, which Luis jumped and climbed over. He ran into the playground, passed the carousel and the swings, with Butch still hot on his tail. He grabbed one of the swings and threw it back at his aggressor. Butch easily dodged, but it did buy Luis a few extra seconds.

Luis passed the tilted fun house, and Butch followed. He circled the fun house a few times, with the bully always at least one turn behind him, until he threw open the door and ran inside. He braced himself against the other side as hard as he could, his heart still pounding in his chest. He was gasping for breath so hard he was afraid he might faint. Outside, he heard Butch continue to run circles around the fun house.

The footsteps outside came to a stop right on the outside of the door. Luis lowered himself quietly to the floor, lay on his side, and pressed himself as close to the wall under the window as he could. He saw the shadow of Butch loom over him and waited while holding his breath.

"Argh!" Butch cried out in frustration. He punched the side of the fun house. Luis winced. "I'm not done with you, you got that?" Butch shouted, as he moved away. "I'll get you one of these days, you miserable little turd! You can't hide forever!"

Butch's footsteps moved away but never really left. Luis could still hear him searching the playground. One thing to be said about the bully: he may not be very smart, but he was persistent. Most likely, they would be here for a while.

With a heavy sigh, Luis pulled his backpack off and unzipped it. He pulled out the book he'd checked out from the school library, *The Chronicles of Dadria*. He'd been minding his own business—reading all about the tales of knights and shape shifters, princesses and monsters—when Butch came up to him and said today was his turn to be a punching bag. And with the bully still looking for him, he might as well continue where he'd left off. Luis adjusted his glasses, flipped the book open to the last page he was on, and began reading.

Hours passed. The sun steadily fell lower and lower as the sky turned from blue to orange and later to red and finally purple. The inside of the fun house had grown far too dark for Luis to read anymore, and he closed the book. He slipped it back into the backpack, slung the straps over his shoulders, and stepped outside.

"Hello there."

"Aah!" Luis jumped and stumbled back.

A girl stood outside the door. Her hands were clasped behind her back, and her lips turned up in a sweet smile.

She wore blue jeans and a green flannel shirt with a red beanie over her straight auburn hair. "I haven't seen you around here before. What's your name?"

He placed his hand over his heart and gasped for air. "I'm sorry. You startled me. I wasn't expecting to see anyone. Uh, my name is Luis."

"Hi, Luis. I'm Alice." She waved at him. "You've been hiding in that fun house for a while. What were you doing in there for so long?"

"Oh, I was reading."

"For three and a half hours? Must've been a really long book." Alice shifted to her other foot and stuffed her hands in her pockets.

"It is very long." Luis pulled his backpack off and unzipped it. He started to pull the book out. "Dadria is an epic fantasy, in the same league as—" He stopped in the middle of his sentence and eyed the girl suspiciously. "How long did you say I was in the fun house?"

"About three and a half hours. It was after that bully chased you around," Alice said.

Luis quickly zipped the backpack closed again. "Were you watching me this whole time?"

"Well, yes." She scoffed at him. "All of us were."

"All of us?" As Luis looked around the playground, he now saw the kids. Three children were swinging back and forth on the swings, laughing and giggling. Three other kids hung onto the bars of the carousel and spun it around. Two more took turns on the slide, climbing up the metal ladder and sliding back down. One child sat solemnly by himself on a seesaw. "Where did all these kids come from? It's after seven. Where are your parents?"

"Well, where are yours?" Alice asked.

"I'm fifteen. I don't have to have my parents with me all the time," Luis said.

"Well, I was fourteen. So neither did I."

"Wait a minute," Luis said. "You *were* fourteen?"

"Yes, I was," Alice said. "I was fourteen years old when I died."

Luis stared with his mouth wide open. His glasses slid down his nose. Alice looked up at him, her brows scrunched and lips pressed together. She waved one hand in front of his eyes, and when that had no effect, she snapped her fingers. Still nothing. "Hello? Is there anyone in there?"

Slowly, Luis pushed his glasses back up. "Ha ha. I'm sorry. I thought you said you were dead."

"I did. I'm dead. See?" She thrust her arm out and through his chest. Luis let out a surprised yelp, as her arm dissolved and phased right through his torso, sending a chill throughout his body. Luis looked down at the arm that stuck right out of his chest but didn't really touch him. "That's right. I'm a ghost."

Luis grabbed the shoulder strap of his pack and ran. He ran through the girl, her body phased through him. He kept running passed the swing set, the slide, and the carousel, without stopping to look or even glance back. Even after leaving the park, he kept running. He ran until his legs burned and his lungs ached and didn't stop until he reached home and collapsed in bed, exhausted.

Thursday, October 23

An alarm blared in his ear. Luis groaned and slammed his hand down on his alarm clock, silencing it. He rolled back over and tried to fall asleep again. That is until the sunlight filtered in through the window and into his eyes.

"Luis!" His mother shouted from downstairs. "Get up, it's time for breakfast!"

"Okay, Mom." Luis rolled out of bed and pulled on a pair of jeans. After throwing on a shirt and grabbing his backpack, he slowly walked down to the kitchen. His mother stood over the counter, two plates of scrambled egg, toast, and bacon ready-made and steaming. Next to the plates stood two glasses of orange juice. "Morning, Mom." Luis adjusted his glasses and rubbed his eyes.

"You were rather late coming home, didn't even stay up to watch *Clash of the Planets*. I DVR'd it for you." Mom took her plate and orange juice to the dining room.

"I was just tired. Butch tried to beat me up again." Luis grabbed the bottle of ketchup out of the fridge.

"Oh, honey, why didn't you tell me? That boy is nothing but trouble. I should have a word with your principal and get that all sorted out," Mom said.

"Mom, please don't do that." Luis squirted ketchup on his eggs before shoving a spoonful in his mouth. "I already have a target on my back. I don't need a bigger one."

"That's no excuse. You shouldn't let people push you around. Use the system, that's what it's there for." She took a crunchy bite of her toast. "But even so, what does that have to do with you being out so late last night?"

"Well." Luis took a bite of bacon. "He chased me from school all the way to the city park, and I hid in the playground until he left. After that, I started reading my library book again, and I just lost track of—" He paused. The playground. Late at night. The ghost girl. "Just lost track of time."

"Well, you'd better not lose it now. You have to be in school in half an hour." Mom took another bite of her scrambled eggs.

"Yes, Mom." Luis gorged down the rest of his breakfast and headed out the door. He made it to school with plenty of time to spare.

2

With the few extra minutes before the first bell, Luis went to the library. Aside from the computer lab, it was his favorite place on the campus. He walked in and was struck instantly with the smell of dusty old books. It radiated off the shelves and wafted through the air.

"Good morning, Luis," Mrs. Brown, the elderly librarian, said as she looked up from her own book.

"Good morning, Mrs. Brown." Luis wiped his feet off on the outside rug before he stepped inside. "I'm wondering where I can find a book about ghosts."

"Ghosts? You mean like a ghost story or actual information about the supernatural?"

"Information."

"You should know where to look. The section on occult and mythology," Mrs. Brown said. "But need I remind you that you've already checked out all the books you can at one time."

"Yes, I remember." Luis unzipped his backpack and placed his three library books on the front desk. *The Chronicles of Dadria* was among them.

"You finished reading it already? That was pretty fast this time." Mrs. Brown scanned the bar code on the back, and the computer beeped as it logged the book back in.

"I've already read it three times now. I'll be fine." He strolled through the library to the mythology section. Just as he turned to walk down that section, he halted in his track. Someone else was already there.

Serena Ravenwood. She was a junior, one year older than Luis, and the resident Goth chick. She had pasty white skin, along with jet-black hair and purple nail polish. Her eye shadow was also black, along with all her clothes. She wore a long heavy coat and cargo pants with combat boots. The only bit of color at all was her bright red lipstick.

She thumbed through a book, as Luis hesitantly watched from around the corner—a book, he noticed, of medieval torture devices. Her eyes shifted momentarily in his direction. She gave him only a look of indifference or even mild annoyance. "If you're looking for something, you'd better hurry up," she said with a low and scratchy voice. "The bell will ring any minute now."

"Uh, yeah," Luis said hesitantly. "It sure will."

Serena scoffed. "Dweeb," she muttered to herself and walked away.

Once she was gone, Luis stepped over to the shelves and ran his fingers over the spines of the books. He did not know exactly what he was looking for, really. How many academic studies could there be about ghosts? Even then, was he really sure about anything he saw the other day? What if he was just really tired and had imagined things? It was dark after all. Or was it simply a dream he had?

While all these questions ran through his head, the first bell rang. He jumped out of his thoughts. He sighed and started walking to his homeroom class. He would have to find a book later. Luis sat and waited through his first two morning classes. Biology and geometry were usually his best subjects, but now he had a hard time concentrating. Finally, after two hours of learning about cell division and trying to figure out the Pythagorean theorem, the bell for first break rang. He quickly packed up his books, notepads, and pencils before running out the door and back to the library.

No sooner had he walked through the door than he saw her again. Serena. She faced the same wall, the same book rested in her hands. She stood like a sentinel, unmoving and powerful.

Luis stepped over quietly and stood next to her. He hesitantly looked over the books, hoping that he would find something fast. She stood just out of the corner of his eye. He never liked being around other people like this, especially people he did not know, and most especially weird ones like Ravenwood. His palms started to sweat, and his heart pounded.

Serena's eyes shifted and refocused on him, fixing him with a look of simple irritation. "I'm sorry, I'm sorry," Luis stuttered, and he stepped back. "If I'm disturbing you, I'll leave."

She rolled her eyes and groaned. "What are you looking for?"

"Huh?"

"What kind of book do you need? If I can help you find it, you will leave me alone, right?" she said.

"Oh, yeah. Sure," Luis stuttered. "Absolutely. Well, I'm looking for a book about ghosts."

Serena turned back to the shelves. She placed her fingertip on the spine of a book. "And what do you want to know? A scary story? Historical ghosts? Haunted houses?"

"More like ghost behavior. Where do they go, what do they do, things like that," Luis said.

A short half-hearted laugh escaped Serena's lips. "Ha. Good luck finding that at a high school library."

Luis sighed. His shoulders slumped. "Yeah, I figured as much. Well, thanks anyway." He turned to walk away and was halfway to the door when he stopped. "I don't suppose you could tell me anything? Do you know anything about ghosts and the dead?"

"Oh, I get it. Because I dress this way and associate with a particular subculture, you automatically assume I know everything about death and undead. Nice to know profiling is still a thing." She snarked and folded her arms.

Luis held up his hands as if being interrogated. "No, no, that's not what I meant. I just thought maybe...you know what, forget I said anything." He turned away again, but her voice stopped him before he could take another step.

"And you would be right." A sinister smile crept over Serena's face. "I have studied the subject. Sit down." She pointed to a nearby table. "And I'll try telling you what you want to know."

"Um." Luis fiddled with his glasses. Now he was simply confused. At first, this girl did not seem to want anything to do with him. Now she was offering to help. Was this some sort of head game she was playing? Was this her way of getting attention? What was her motivation here? Questions spun through Luis's head. "Okay, if you'd like." He pulled out a chair and sat down.

Serena sat across the table, laced her fingers together, and fixed her gaze on him. They both stared at each other, neither one said a thing. Luis stared intently at the table, a drop of sweat rolled down his face. The wall-mounted clock ticked away, second by second passed.

Tick.

Tock.

Tick.

Tock.

Serena broke the silence. "I know you're supposed to be quiet in a library, but this is just ridiculous. If you won't ask, I'll just talk then." She leaned back in her chair and tilted her head back to look at the ceiling.

Serena began to explain. "A person becomes a ghost upon their death only if the person died suddenly, often violently, or if they have some reason to remain in the living world. We call this 'unfinished business.' It can be anything from as simple as finding a lost baseball to a more vague objective like protecting a loved one.

"Upon completion of their unfinished business, the ghost will normally pass over to the other side. However, more often than not, the ghost doesn't remember much from their mortal life, so they have no idea what their unfinished business is. Now if it was a violent death sort of situation, it gets more complicated. In that case, they may not realize they're dead. Upon realization, psychological breakdown is more common than not. A ghost of this type may develop hateful feelings and a desire for vengeance. If it stays in that frame of mind long enough, the ghost may go poltergeist and start harassing people, sometimes a specific person or just people in general."

"Um," Luis muttered. "Do you know, maybe, how a ghost chooses a place to haunt?"

"Thank you for joining the conversation," she said. "As for that, a ghost doesn't usually choose. Ghosts will normally haunt a place that they had some sort of emotional bond with, like say their old house or school, or they'll stay close to where they died or where their physical bodies are buried. An example like someone who got lost in the woods and died before rescue teams could find them. Their ghost will likely remain in the woods close to their body."

"Can a ghost leave their haunting grounds?" Luis pushed his glasses up.

"Sometimes. A ghost is a spirit no longer attached to a body. They still exist in the physical world because they formed an attachment to another person, or place, or even an object. If that attachment changed to a different person or place, then they would leave the old one and start haunting the new."

Luis adjusted his glasses. "How do you know so much about this sort of thing?"

"I read. It's good for you." Serena leaned forward and rested the chair back on all its legs. "Now I have a question, kid. Why do you want to know so much? Did you meet a ghost or something?"

Luis jumped up from his chair and fumbled, as he pulled his backpack straps over his shoulders. "What? Pfft, no. Of course not! There's no such thing as real ghosts. I mean, this is all just really folklore and stuff to scare kids. I mean who would honestly—"

Serena placed her hands on his shoulders and forced him back down into the chair. She locked eyes with him, and Luis clammed up. Serena narrowed her eyes and furled her brows. "Just silly folklore to scare kids, huh? As soon as I mentioned it, you instantly tried to deny it. That means to me, yes, you have met one."

He gulped and slouched down in the chair. "Yesterday, in the park at the old playground. A girl named Alice, she said she was fourteen."

Serena froze in place. That name, this little kid should not know about that, about her. Alice, fourteen years old, impossible. She grabbed him by the collar, yanked him out of the chair, and slammed him down hard against the table with a loud thud. "Who put you up to this?" she hissed.

Luis, now more terrified than ever, could only wince and stutter. "P-put me up to what?"

She lifted him up again only to throw him back down. "Don't lie to me!" she said, getting louder. "Someone wanted you to make a fool out of me, and you're going to tell me who!"

"I have no idea what you're talking about!" It took all his concentration just to speak coherently. This girl was just going crazy. He had no idea what set her off and did not want to know. All he hoped for now was to get out of this without having his faced pounded in, which at the rate things were going, was not going to happen. "I swear, nobody put me up to anything! Would I lie to you?"

"Not if you want to keep your face in one piece!" She raised a fist over his head.

Luis winced, closed his eyes, and held his arms over his face. This was it. He always figured he would get his ass kicked in high school, he just figured it would be from Butch, not from the Goth chick.

"All right you two, break it up!" Mrs. Brown came charging from behind the counter, book held firmly in hand. She slammed it down on the table next to them, which sent a loud ringing throughout the library. "Young lady, let him go right now before I send you both to the principal's office!"

Serena slowly released her hold on Luis's collar and stepped away, her face still twisted in a look nothing short of loathing. Then she grabbed her book bag and stormed out of the library, slamming the door behind her.

Luis took a minute to catch his breath. He sat up, readjusted his glasses, and brushed himself off. "I don't know what set her off," he said, half laughing. Making light of things always helped him get over the fact that he nearly had his nose broken or worse.

"Are you okay?" Mrs. Brown asked. "Do you need to see the nurse?"

"No," Luis said. As he grabbed his backpack, the bell rang again. First break was over, and it was time for third period.

3

The rest of the day went by rather uneventfully. World history and English literature were neither easy nor hard for Luis. Even PE, which was not his best class, he could do okay since the teacher allowed him to do laps around the football field. If there was one physical activity he was competent in, that would be running. He needed to run a lot, especially when Butch came looking for him after school.

Finally, the last bell of the day rang, and Luis packed up all his books and papers to head back home. As he started to leave the campus, he heard an all too familiar voice. "Hey, pencil neck!" It was Butch. Luis wasted no time. He knew what was coming. He took off like a shot, running as fast as his legs could carry him. "Hey, you twerp! Get back here! I haven't kicked your ass yet!" Butch shouted and took chase after Luis.

Once again, Luis found himself running down the same path as before. He raced off into the park back to the playground. Still the bully gave chase. Luis jumped the same chain link fence and ran to the same tilted fun house.

However, this time, Butch was not far behind. Just as Luis pushed the door open, Butch caught up. The bully yanked him back by the scruff of his shirt and shoved him to the ground. "Thought you could get away like last time, did ya?" Butch stomped his foot on Luis's chest. He slammed his fists together. "I think we need to make up for lost time, don't you think so?" He grinned.

"You'll get in trouble if you do," a female voice said. Butch stopped and turned around. Standing less than ten feet away was a young girl. She wore a green flannel shirt and blue jeans with a red beanie over her straight auburn hair. Luis recognized her instantly. It was Alice, the girl from yesterday.

The ghost girl.

"Where did you come from?" Butch asked.

"I'll tell on you if you don't leave him alone," Alice said in a singsong voice.

"Eh, buzz off, girly. I have things to do," Butch said. He waved his hand, dismissing her.

Alice reached down and picked up a small rock. She tossed it up in the air and caught it as it fell. "You'll be sorry." Again, she talked in a singsong voice.

Butch scoffed. "What are you going to do, brat? Throw rocks at us?"

"Maybe." She smiled coyly.

With a small flick of her wrist, she sent the rock barreling toward Butch and struck him square between the eyes.

He recoiled from the hit, reeling back and clasping his hand over his face. "Ack!" he shouted. Butch looked down and saw droplets of blood gathered in his palm. "Okay, you wanna go? Let's go." He pointed at Luis. "You move from this spot, and I'll gouge your eyes out with your own glasses."

Butch charged. The girl did not move. He swung right at her head, fully prepared to knock a few teeth loose. Just as his fist was about to hit, the girl disappeared. She completely vanished right in front of him. Butch stumbled, fell forward, and landed flat on his face.

What just happened? Butch was sure he was going to knock her lights out, but then she was gone. He jumped back up and spun around in circles, looking all over the playground. The girl was nowhere to be seen. "Where'd you run off to, girly!" he shouted.

"Me?" Alice suddenly appeared on a swing. She kicked her legs back and forth. "I'm right here. Can't you see me?"

"Yeah, I see ya now," Butch sneered. He charged at her, fist at the ready. "And I hope you can see this!" He swung at her and missed the same as before when she vanished again. His legs caught on the swing and face planted on the ground. Butch crawled off the swing, blood dripped from his nose.

"I'll say one thing for you, you are consistent. But not very bright." Alice stood behind him now.

Butch shot up to his feet. "You calling me stupid?"

"Just a little." She pointed at him. "Haven't you figured out you can't touch me? Not unless I want you to." She walked right up to Butch. As she did, Luis looked down at her feet. Not a puff of dust as she walked, no footprints, she was not really touching the ground. "I'm a ghost," she said with a cheerful little smile. "See?" She raised one arm and phased it right through Butch's head.

His jaw slacked, and his eyebrows lifted. He stood dumbfounded for at least thirty seconds before he took off like a rocket. Butch ran away from the playground and down the path out of the park as fast as his legs could go.

Alice watched with a coy smile. "Hm." She placed her hands on her hips. "That was easy. How are you feeling?" she asked him.

Luis slowly pushed himself up so he sat on his knees. He dusted himself off. "Um, fine, thank you," Luis answered automatically. He did not look up to face her yet.

Alice pushed out her lower lip. "You're welcome. You know, you could at least look at someone when they're talking to you. You're pretty rude." She crossed her arms and jutted her hips out to the side.

"And you're pretty dead," Luis said, he swung his pack over his shoulder and faced her at last.

"I know." Her tone was dry. "Why did you come back? After the last time when you ran away screaming like a girl, I thought we'd never see you again."

"Hey," Luis objected. "I did not scream."

"Well, you certainly ran like a girl."

"And you'd know all about how girls run," Luis retorted.

"I am a girl." Alice placed a hand over her chest for emphasis. "Or, at least, I was. Now why did you come back?"

Luis sighed. He pushed his glasses back up and walked over to the swing set. "I was running from that guy. It's kind of a daily thing. After the last class of the day, he chased me home." He sat down on the empty swing. "It's what he does."

"Why do you let him do it?"

"Do you think I enjoy being picked on like that?" Luis became defensive. "If I could stop him, I would. But I can't."

"Why not?" The ghost girl sat herself down on the swing next to him.

"Because I'm not a strong, physical type of person. It's not in my genes."

"Yeah, you are pretty wimpy. Seriously, you just got your butt saved by a girl younger than you," Alice said.

Luis leered over at her. "The ghost of a girl younger than me."

Alice rolled her eyes. "Are you going to keep bringing that up?"

"Yes!" Luis nodded rapidly. "You supposedly are a ghost! That means you have single-handedly changed virtually everything we know about the nature of life and death! You've proved that there is such a thing as an afterlife! That people do indeed have souls! Does that also mean there is a god? And if so, which god?"

Alice stared over at the boy sitting next to her. She leaned forward in the swing and looked him straight in the eye. "You're a dork."

"Thanks," he groaned.

"Anyway, if you're thinking of asking me all those fancy questions, I can sum up an answer in one sentence." She held up her index finger for emphasis. "I don't know. I'm just a spirit hanging out at a playground with a bunch of other spirits and one living kid."

Around the playground, other ghosts started to appear. All of them looked about the same age as Alice. Ten children in total. They ran, jumped, and played together as if they were normal kids.

One of them, a little girl younger than Alice, came running up to them. She held her hands behind her back, as she studied Luis's face closely. Luis pulled back a little she came closer. "Alice? Who is this?"

"This is Luis, a friend," Alice said.

"He's not like us. How can he see us?" the little girl asked.

"I'm not sure. But it's okay. You don't need to worry about anything, Susie. Go and play," Alice said. The girl raced back to the slide to wait her turn.

"How did you all get here?" Luis asked.

Alice shrugged. "We came here over a period of time. We only really become active during these few hours at dusk and then at dawn. At first, it was just me, and I was alone. Later on, some of the others started showing up. Paul over there," Alice gestured to the lone kid on the seesaw, "he's the most recent. He showed up just the other week."

"Just the other week?" Luis asked. "That seems a little strange. You said you were the oldest. How long have you been here?"

"I don't really know. You tend to lose track of time when there's no one to talk to. Years, I think," Alice said. She laughed. "I don't even know what year it is."

"If it's of any help, I could tell you the year," Luis said.

"You could?" Alice chuckled at herself. "Of course, you could. Well, what year is it?"

Luis told her.

Alice's mouth fell agape, and her eyes widened. "Is it really? I've been dead for ten years." She slumped down in the swing. Her hands rested on her knees. "Ten years." She started to fade right before Luis's eyes. Like a dissolve in a movie, she became transparent and then finally invisible.

"Alice?" Luis stood up. The place where she sat was now vacant, only an empty swing. "Hey, are you still here?" He looked around the playground and noticed that all the other kids were gone too. He was all alone. "You could have at least told me your full name!" he shouted. Luis shouldered his pack and just about to leave when he noticed lines being drawn in the dirt. Groves appeared in the earth, and as he watched, they formed letters, then a word, and finally a name. Alice Thomas. Once he had read it, that same invisible hand wiped it away. Luis smiled.

The sun was almost down now. He had to get home. He left the playground and started back down the path out of the park.

"You're late getting home again," his mom called from the kitchen as he walked in.

Luis set his backpack on the floor and took off his shoes. He set them on the shoe rack by the door. "Yes, I know, Mom," he called back. He made his way into the kitchen to greet her.

"That's two nights in a row. Are you spending them with a cute girl?" his mom asked with a hint of teasing fun.

Luis glanced up at the ceiling from the right corner of his eyes. He recognized the irony of that question. *Why, yes, Mom. I have, except she's been dead for a decade now and haunts the town recreational park*, he thought. Yeah, that would get some strange looks from people and make him an even bigger target for bullies. He almost got beat up twice today after all. Don't need a new excuse to be a punching bag. "No, Mom," he said. "I just took the long way home. Through the park. It's more scenic. What's for dinner?"

"Hamburger Helper. Stroganoff. Plus mashed potatoes and green beans. I got back from the office just about half an hour before you walked in, so I didn't have time to prepare anything fancy tonight," she said.

"That's fine with me. I'll be upstairs, call me when you need me." Luis climbed the stairs to his room and closed the door. After booting up his computer and opening a web page, he started a search. Who was Alice Thomas?

It did not take him long to find a file on her. Missing since September ten years ago and suspected to have been kidnapped. Along with her description was a photograph. Luis recognized it instantly; she was even wearing the same clothes.

She had gone to West Point High School same as him, even had some of the same teachers. This was just creepy, and it hit a little too close to home. As he read on, he found a little about Alice's family, her parents and a younger sister who was six at the time. It was here that he found something worse. The younger sister Cynthia witnessed the kidnapping.

"My sissy came and got me from school 'cause Mommy and Daddy were still at work. She took my hand, and we walked a long way. My feet started hurting, so we stopped, and that's when a scary man tried to grab me, but Alice protected me. She fought him, and I ran away really fast. It was scary. I cried and cried until finally someone came and found me. Can you find my big sister? I miss her."

Not long after that, the trail went cold, and no one heard of Alice again.

Luis fell back in his chair, emotionally and mentally drained. She was kidnapped. He now felt terrible, even sick to his stomach. What must she have endured? Since her ghost said she was still the same age, that meant she must have died not long after being abducted. What did that person do to her?

Luis looked back at the report. He fixed his eyes on the picture of the sister Cynthia. This whole thing happened ten years ago when the sister was six. That would make her sixteen now and in high school. Maybe even his. Maybe he could find her.

He found the names of the parents, Luann and Aaron Thomas. One quick Yellow Book search later, and he found them. They still lived in this town. Which meant their daughter would probably be going to his high school.

Luis leaned back in the chair and rested his hand over his chin. He would need a list of the students, but how would he get that? The school does not list sensitive information like that on their website. And teachers don't just hand out rosters. What could he do? The answer popped into his head, and it was so obvious he snapped his fingers. "Last year's yearbook!"

He jumped out of the chair and rushed over to his bookshelf. Among his various role-playing guidebooks and trades of comics sat his freshmen yearbook. He pulled it out and blew the dust off it. It had been a while since he'd last looked at it. Freshman year was not fun. The only reason he even bought the book was because Mom made him. He flipped it open and started going though the list of last year's sophomore class. Each homeroom was listed separately and all in alphabetical order. He finally found her in the third homeroom—Cynthia Thomas.

Luis stared in disbelief at the picture. There was no way this could be true, but it was. The picture above Cynthia Thomas's name belonged to Serena Ravenwood. She was Alice's younger sister.

4

Friday, October 24

Luis's alarm blared at 7:15 a.m. He rubbed his eyes and put on his glasses. After he silenced the alarm clock, he threw on his clothes, tied his shoes, grabbed his backpack, and raced out the door. The sky was still dark, only a hint of sunlight glimmered on the eastern horizon.

Dawn. Alice said she and other spirits at the park were active only for a few hours during sunrise and sunset. Still a little groggy, he made his way to the park and the playground.

He came up to the playground and looked around. All the equipment was empty. The carousel stirred slightly in the early morning breeze, the swings creaked back and forth. Luis looked around puzzled. He cupped his hands over his and shouted, "Hello? Alice? Are you here?"

Silence. Only the falling of leaves and the calls of early birds broke the cold morning air. Maybe it was too early. The sun was still rising. They might come out later. He propped himself up against the fun house and waited. And he waited. And he waited. His eyelids grew heavier the longer he stayed there. His head started to droop before he jolted awake again. Eventually, unable to stay awake, he closed his eyes and dozed off.

Someone grabbed him by the arm and shook him awake. His eyes snapped open. "Huh? What? Who?" He looked down and saw Alice. Her hand rested on his shoulder.

"Good morning. You're here rather early." Alice shoved her hands in her pockets. "What brings you here?"

"I was hoping to see you." He placed his hand on the back of his head. "I wanted to ask you a few things."

"Like what?"

"Well," he paused, "mostly things about your life before you came here. When you were actually alive, I mean."

"Ah, jeez," Alice sighed and stepped away. "I honestly don't know what I can tell you. I don't remember much about my life." She turned and faced him. "What in particular are you interested in?"

"Specifically, do you remember if you had any siblings? Any brothers or sisters?" Luis asked.

Alice placed a finger on her chin. After a second, she closed her eyes and shook her head. "Memories of my past life are all fragments. I hardly even remembered my name."

"Hmm." Luis scratched his head. "Do...do you want to remember?"

"More than you know," Alice said.

A smile formed from the corners of Luis's lips. He nodded. "Now can you leave the playground?" *Hmm*. Alice thought. "You know, I've never tried. Let's find out." She started walking. She walked past the fence and onto the path. She continued to walk, from the dirt path and onto the grass.

As she walked, Luis watched, keeping a careful eye on her. As he watched, he noticed her start to fade. When she started walking, she appeared to be completely solid, but now she was see-through, and she grew more transparent the further she walked. "Alice, stop!" he shouted.

She stopped and turned around. "What is it?"

"Look at your hands!" He cupped his hands over his mouth and called. "You're disappearing!"

She looked, and through her hands, she saw the grass beneath. She sighed and walked back to the playground. Her appearance grew stronger as she came closer until she was whole again. "Looks like I can't leave. My form gets weaker the further I go. I guess I'm stuck here."

"It looks that way," Luis said. He pulled out his phone and checked the time. "I have to be at school soon. If I bring someone back with me, will you still be here waiting?"

"We just established that I'm not going anywhere." She jutted her hips to the side and folded her arms.

"What I mean is will you show yourself if I bring someone to see you?"

Alice snorted, "Maybe. If I want to."

"Good enough." He checked the readout on his phone again. "I have to run. I'll see you later this afternoon!" He took off out of the park and on his way to school. Alice watched him as he ran.

Why did she ever choose to talk to this boy? She could have stayed invisible if she wanted. What drew her to him that day? She shook her head and sat on the nearby swing. She kicked back and forth a little until the sun rose fully, and she dispersed like the early morning fog, leaving only an empty swing.

Luis made it to school just as the bell for first period rang. There was no time to search for her now. He rushed off to class. The teacher was still taking roll when he slipped in and sat down. "You're late, Mr. Chavez," the teacher, Ms. Sterling, said. "I don't suppose you have a tardy slip from the office?"

"I'm sorry, Ms. Sterling. I didn't have time. If you really want, I can go back."

She tapped her pen against her clipboard. "I'll overlook things just this once." As she started to read out the next name, one of the other students lurched out of his chair.

"What the freak, teach!" It was Butch. "When I'm late, you send me straight to the old fart in his office. When the doofus is late, you just say, 'Don't do it again!' What is that all about? You're playing favorites!"

"You are late four times out of the week. This is his first tardy all year. Everyone is allowed three unexcused tardies a semester. It is not my fault if you used yours all in the first week," she said sternly. "Now sit back down before I do send you to the principal for interrupting class."

Butch plopped back down in the chair and slouched. He glared over at Luis from the corner of his eye. Luis could only sigh in exasperation. Surely, he was going to come after him again today, which was not what Luis was hoping for.

After she finished taking roll, Ms. Sterling set the clipboard down on her desk and placed her hand on a stack of paper. "Okay, class. I hope you studied because today is a pop quiz." A collective groan rose up from the students. "I can tell how excited you all are." She handed the papers to each of the kids in the front row; they each took a copy and passed the rest down. Luis looked at the test and rubbed his temples again. He had not studied or even done any homework last night; he'd been too busy looking up Alice's missing person case. Now it had come back to bite him. He sighed, unzipped the front pocket of his pack, took out his pen, and started writing.

Two hours and another class later the first break bell rang, and Luis headed to the library. Mrs. Brown greeted him when he walked in, "Good morning, Luis."

"Morning, Mrs. Brown. I don't suppose Serena came in today?" he asked.

She shrugged and shook her head. "I haven't seen her since yesterday when you and she got in that tussle. Why do you want to know?"

"I need to ask her about something. Oh, well. If she's not here, it's okay." He stepped back through the door. "Thanks, anyways." The door closed behind him, and he sighed. He walked down the hall to his next class.

As he sat in his next class and listened to the teacher, Mr. Harding, drone on and on about every little detail of every other verb in William Shakespeare's *Hamlet*, Luis found himself unable to concentrate. He had not seen Serena all day. Usually, he wouldn't be looking for her, but he wanted to try introducing her to Alice. Would it even work? He was starting to have doubts. Were they really connected at all? Cindy and Thomas weren't that unusual of names. The girl from the report might go to some other school, maybe even a private one. Who was to say?

"Mr. Chavez." The teacher's voice snapped him back to reality.

"Huh? Um. Yes, sir?" Luis said.

"Please stop daydreaming and read aloud act II, scene ii. Starting with, 'What a piece of work.'" Mr. Harding said. Luis stood up, book in hand, and began to read.

What a piece of work is a man! how noble in reason! how infinite in faculty! in form, in moving,

haw express and admirable! in action how like an angel! in apprehension how like a god! the beauty of the world! The paragon of animals! And yet, to me, what is this quintessence of dust? Man delights not me; no, not women neither, though by your smiling, you seem to say.

Luis sat back down. "Good, Mr. Chavez. All right. Now class, what is Hamlet saying in this speech?" Mr. Harding continued.

Luis rested his head on his palm and stared at the wall. While he sat in the classroom, he was not really there. His thoughts were back in the playground with Alice and the other spirit kids. He wanted to talk to them some more, learn a little about them, maybe even help them. And the first step was to help Alice and Serena meet. He would need to find her.

At the end of the day, he found himself walking back through the park. He was on his way to the playground, and he was disappointed. He had not seen Serena at all today, and now he was going to go tell Alice that the meeting he wanted would have to be postponed. It had not been his day.

A twig snapped in the trees to his right. Luis stopped, realizing he'd been followed, and cursed himself for his stupidity. His eyes shifted to the trees, and he started to run. Just then, Butch came charging out from behind a tall oak and smashed into him. The bully's shoulder slammed into Luis's gut and sent him crashing to the ground.

"Well, well, well. Look what we've got here," Butch said. "A little four-eyed freak in need of a good pounding. And I think we have three days of catching up to do."

Butch grabbed Luis by the throat and lifted him off the ground. "Hey!" Luis coughed and gagged. "Come on, stop it!"

Butch cracked his knuckles and smiled. "Sorry, kid. Looks like I finally caught up with you." He slammed his fist right into Luis's stomach.

Luis lurched forward and coughed. "Ack!" He doubled over; tears welled up in his eyes. He felt his legs give out from under him and fell to the ground.

Butch grabbed Luis's face by the chin and lifted his head up. "Not done yet." He punched Luis across the face. Spit and a few drops of blood flew from Luis's lips.

His vision was getting blurry. His head pounded. His legs felt weak and wobbly. Luis could hardly see, as Butch raised another fist to his face—another punch to the jaw. Luis crumbled to the ground, coughing and sputtering. He clutched his stomach and groaned in pain. Just as he started to move, Butch kicked him hard in the ribs. Luis cried out in pain and collapsed back to the ground.

"Sorry, you aren't going anywhere yet." Butch stood over him, a terrifying colossus ready to stomp him into the ground. The bully raised his foot right over Luis's head.

"Hey!" another voice called out. Butch stopped and looked up. Luis readjusted his glasses over his bruised and puffy face so he could see as well. It was Serena. She stood just up the path from them, her brows furled in anger and lips twisted in a sneer. "Leave him alone!" she shouted.

"Yeah? And what are you going to do if I don't? You going to tell on us?" Butch mocked.

"No." Serena started walking forward. "I'll just have to kick your butt and make you leave." She tilted her head to the side and popped the bones in her neck.

"Oh, I'm so scared. Help me, somebody! The emo chick here is going to kick my butt! Aha ha ha ha ha! Like you really can!" Butch laughed.

"Watch me," Serena said in a cold monotone. With a twist of her body, she spun around and slammed the heel of her boot into Butch's back. He pitched forward and crashed right on his face.

Butch groaned as he pushed himself up, his face covered in dirt. Serena grabbed him by the collar and yanked him to his feet. She shoved him against a tree, held him in place with one hand while popping the knuckles in her other. He held up his hands in surrender. "Okay, okay, I give up. I'll just go!" He tried to run, but she held him firm.

"You don't get off that easily." She slugged him across the face. Butch stumbled around and passed out. She released her hold on him, and Butch collapsed.

Luis stared at the unconscious bully and then to Serena. She flipped her hair back. This girl had just taken Butch down as if he were nothing, and she did it without breaking a sweat.

She held out her hand for him. "You okay?" she asked.

"Uh," Luis groaned, struggling to his knees. "Not really." He took her hand, and she helped him stand.

"I can see," she said. "Your face is a wreck."

"I have some ointment and an ice pack at home," Luis said. He took off his glasses and cleaned them before setting them back on his nose. "Thank you for saving me. I thought I was done for."

"I just hate to see people pick on others for no reason," she said.

"I was looking for you all day." Luis winced. It hurt to talk, but he managed to get the words out. "Why weren't you at school?"

She stuffed her hands in her pockets and stared at the ground. "I didn't feel like it," was all she said. "Well, now that you aren't being someone's punching bag, I'll be leaving."

"How did you find me out here? It's rather convenient that you just happened to stumble across me in the nick of time," Luis said.

"Would you rather I left you to get your face bashed in?" She glared at him. "I could have."

Luis slinked away. "Yes, yes, you could have. But you didn't. How did you know I was here? Were you following me?"

Serena rolled her eyes. "Like anyone would want to stalk you. I was already in the park. I needed a break from school, so I stayed out here all day."

"Why?"

She scoffed. "I don't need to explain myself to you."

An idea came to Luis then. "Was it what I said yesterday? Asking about the ghosts and all that?" She turned her back to him and crossed her arms. It appeared he'd hit the nail on the head. Luis pushed his glasses up. "Look, I know why you were upset and why you wanted to deck me yesterday. The fact of the matter is I was looking for you today because I wanted to introduce you to Alice. I think the two of you have something in common."

Serena's face had changed from anger to sadness and now to surprise. She felt a little nervous about the idea and still didn't know if she fully trusted this little twerp. Until yesterday, the two of them never exchanged conversation, and now he was offering something she'd never have expected.

Serena turned back to him, her face hardened in expressionless stillness. "You think we do, huh?"

He nodded sharply. "Yes."

"Okay. Take me to her." She pointed directly at him right between the eyes. "But if this is some sort of trick, I'll finish what Butch started. Got it?"

Luis gulped and nodded. "I got it."

"Good." She slipped her hand back in her pocket. "Lead the way."

The two of them walked together in silence, Luis in the lead and Serena following behind, her eyes on him the whole time. After about five minutes, they came to the playground. The sun had begun to set, and the shadows stretched across the ground. The stepped passed the gate and stopped.

Serena looked around at the old metal carousel and slide. The swings creaked back and forth slowly. A small puff of wind caused the fallen leaves to dance. "What am I looking for?" she asked.

"Just wait for a minute," Luis said. He stepped to the middle of the playground and called out, "Alice! Alice! Are you here? I brought my friend!" The playground was silent except for the metallic creak of the swings. "Hello? Alice?" Luis's heart began to beat faster. Where was she? Didn't they have an agreement? He could almost feel it. He was certain Serena was going to pound his face in now.

But when he turned around to face her, she wasn't staring hatefully or resentfully at him. No, instead she gazed at the ground. Her shoulders slumped, and the corners of the mouth drooped slightly. "I guess it was too much to ask," Serena said in a hushed voice and turned to leave.

But before she could leave, she stopped suddenly. Standing right in front of her was a girl just a couple years younger than her dressed in a green flannel shirt and blue jeans with a red beanie covering straight auburn hair. Serena's mouth fell agape as she looked down at this girl. She was the spitting image of—but that was impossible.

The younger girl looked up at Serena quizzically, her eyes squinted and lips pursed. She tilted her head and scratched her chin. "This is the person you wanted to bring?" she asked.

"Yes, it is," Luis sighed with relief. A weight had just been lifted. "For a minute, I didn't think you were going to show. Alice, meet Serena Ravenwood."

"Wait, so you mean—" Serena said before her words were choked off. A lump formed in her throat, and tears began to form in her eyes. This girl standing in front of her, this ghost person was the real thing. It was really her.

"Okay," Alice said. She stretched forth her hand. "Hi, Serena Ravenwood. My name is Alice Thomas. It's nice to meet—"

Serena threw herself forward and held out her arms. Just as she was about to embrace the younger girl, she phased right through her and stumbled forward. She looked confusingly down at her hands. So this really was a ghost.

Alice stood still, a confused look across her face and eyes wide open. "Well, okay then. I'm afraid you caught me off guard. I'm not used to giving people hugs, but if you want, we can do that." She faced Serena and held both arms out. A cute, sweet smile spread across her face.

Serena could no longer hold back the tears. She practically leaped at the ghost girl and this time embraced her fully. She held Alice tightly, clutching the girl to her chest. Tears streamed down her face, leaving dark trails behind them in her makeup. Serena sobbed freely for the first time in years. "I missed you." She eventually managed to choke out. "I missed you so much."

Alice could only stand dumbfounded. "Um, okay. I'm not sure how to take that."

Serena released her hold and pulled away slowly. "Don't you remember me? It's me, Cindy." Serena paused and then followed with, "Your little sister."

Alice's mouth fell open slightly, and she tilted her head. "Little sister? But you're older than me. And besides, didn't he say your name was Serena?"

Serena let out a halfhearted chuckle. "Does 'Serena Ravenwood' sound like a real name? I started calling myself that after you died." She almost choked on the last word.

Alice stared into Serena's eyes. She placed her hands against the older girl's face, smudging the already running mascara. She pulled their faces together to look deeper.

After at least thirty seconds, Alice started to feel it. She started to remember. Her eyes widened. Her little sister, Cynthia Thomas, six years old. And now she stood in front of her, crying her eyes out. "Cindy?" she uttered. She felt as though she was going to cry too. Her lips quivered, and eyes watered. "Cindy!" Alice jumped into her sister's arms, fully embracing her.

Serena wrapped her arms around Alice as tightly as she could. All the warmth and love she'd been missing for ten long years came rushing back. Her sister. Her older sister who she'd lost so long ago, and now they were finally together again.

Luis sat by himself on a swing. His face was still swollen in some places, his chest and stomach still throbbed, and he was more than sure he had a black eye. But right now, he was happy. As he watched Serena and Alice, he couldn't help but feel just a little bit of the love between them. He felt good, warm inside. He had done this. He had brought these two together again, and it filled him with a sense of satisfaction. Even as they were happy to be together, he was happy to have done it.

5

The sun had set, and darkness fallen over the playground by the time Luis and Serena left. She had stayed to talk with her sister until literally the last minutes she could that day. They walked along the path in relative silence. Finally, Serena spoke up, "Hey, um, I want to just say." She had a hard time verbalizing her thoughts. "Really, just, thank you." She managed to say. "Thank you for that."

Luis smiled. "You're welcome."

"And also," she continued, "sorry I almost beat you up in the library yesterday."

Luis waved dismissively. "It's okay. You don't need to worry about that. People are always trying to beat me up. I mean, you also threatened to do so right after saving me from Butch and his thugs."

"Yeah, sorry." She hunched her shoulders. "I didn't really mean to lash out at you. It was just that, well," she paused, "people can be very cruel."

Luis gave a small chuckle and sigh. "Yeah, I know that feeling."

Serena continued. "After my sister disappeared, I became a target for anyone who wanted to mess with me. I was picked on, bullied, pushed around, and made fun of. Kids would joke that my sister was taken by some child molester and he killed her. I got sick of it. So when you said you saw the ghost of a fourteen-year-old girl named Alice, it brought up a lot of bad memories."

"I can see how it would," Luis said solemnly.

"That's also why I wasn't at school today. All those old feelings came back, and I needed a day to just be alone."

"Is that why you went Goth?" Luis asked.

"Partially. I embraced the dark and macabre aspects of it, the futility of all things. It helped me cope with and accept that my sister was gone," Serena said. "I also took up karate."

"I noticed that." Luis snarked. "Yeah. It was so I could deal with all the teasing. It worked rather well. People usually tease others to get a reaction, but the reaction they want is normally not a broken nose." She smirked.

They laughed together. As they laughed, Luis winced a little. He still hurt from where Butch had kicked him. He groaned and clutched at his side.

"Are you okay?" she asked.

"I'll be fine." His breathing became rougher. "Once I get home, I'm going for a nice hot bath, then I'll be good to go."

"Come on, then." She tilted her head to the side. "I'll walk you home."

"Oh." He suddenly became nervous. He'd never walked home with a girl before, and the idea was both tantalizing and scary. "That's really not necessary. I can make it back, okay."

"I insist. It's the least I can do since you brought Alice back to me." She held out her hand. "Give me your backpack. I'll carry it for you."

Slowly and reluctantly, Luis slipped the straps off his shoulders and handed the backpack to her. She casually slung it onto her back, and they continued walking. They walked in silence together, Luis occasionally glanced over at Serena, until they reached his house.

"Hm." Luis looked at the empty driveway and the dark windows. "Mom isn't home yet. Must be at some kind of big business meeting tonight."

"Where's your dad?" Serena asked.

"Not around," Luis replied. His tone was cold and harsh, perhaps more so than he meant. He did not say anything else on the matter, and she did not press it. "Thanks for walking me back." He held out his arm, and Serena handed him back his pack. "Will you be all right getting home?"

Serena looked up at the purple-black sky. Hundreds of stars twinkled and shimmered on this moonless night. "It's kind of dark out now. Do you have any idea when your mom will be back? I'd hate to leave you at home by yourself."

"I should be fine," Luis said. In the dark, he saw her face tilt slightly down into sadness. "But you were nice enough to walk me home, and I don't want to make you walk the rest of the way back in the dark. How about you come inside and wait until my mom gets back so she can drive you home. Is that okay?"

"Sure." Serena smiled. "That's really nice of you. Thanks."

Luis fished his keys from his pockets and unlocked the door. He stepped in, kicked off his shoes, set his bag down on the couch, and turned on the light. "I'll see if we have some leftovers from yesterday." He headed off to the kitchen. "Make yourself comfortable."

Serena looked around the front room. A television with a cable box was situated on an entertainment stand against the far wall. The DVD player rested on the lower shelf, and a rack of movies stood next to it. A couch and matching loveseat set perpendicular to each other facing the TV with an end table and a lamp between them. A few pictures adorned the walls.

Most of the pictures were of Luis. Mostly they were school pictures. She had to admit, he was a pretty cute kid all the way back in fourth grade, but did he always have such thick-rimmed glasses? He would probably look cuter with wire frames. Serena was taken aback by that thought. Where had that idea come from? She quickly banished it from her mind.

There was one photograph, however, that caught her attention. It was a family photo with Luis as a baby in the arms of his mother and father. All three of them were dressed up with his mom in a formal blue evening dress and his dad in a black tuxedo. His father looked to be tall, over six feet, with slick black hair and a pair of glasses like his son's. His skin was an olive brown, and he had a full mustache. This family looked happy, but as Serena looked up and down the wall of pictures, she noticed that this was the only one with the father. Some others had Luis, some of the mom, and a few of both, but there were no others of the dad.

The single sound of a bell rang from the kitchen as the microwave went off. Luis came back into the living room with two plates of steaming food. "It's ready." He said, handing one of the plates to her. "Tonight, we have day old Hamburger Helper with instant potatoes and canned green beans. Clearly, the dinner of the gods." He smiled.

Serena looked down at the plate in her hands and smiled. He was being so nice to her, even after she threatened him yesterday. It surprised her and made her oddly happy. "Yes, absolutely. Odin would obviously flaunt over this pinnacle of culinary achievement."

"I know, right?" Luis laughed. He sat down on the couch and set his food on the end table. "You don't mind if I watch some TV, do you?" He picked up the remote.

"Not at all. It is your house after all." Serena sat opposite him on the loveseat.

"Good." He turned the TV on. "I've missed three episodes of *Clash of the Planets*, and I need to catch up." He scrolled through the DVR recordings, and once he found his show, he started it up.

Serena watched the show in relative silence. It was an anime, of that she was not surprised, about a motley crew of soldiers on board their spaceship fighting another interplanetary superpower. It also focused a lot on a similar group of characters on one of the enemy ships and giving them well-rounded personalities. All this was with the obvious intent of making the series more realistic and developed. She enjoyed it well enough but couldn't see herself looking it up again after this.

Once the show was over, Luis stood up and stretched. He took his plate and Serena's back to the kitchen and placed them in the sink. "I was going to get washed up. Are you okay being by yourself out here?" he asked.

"Yeah, sure. It's fine," she replied.

"Okay." He headed upstairs to his bathroom for his bath.

As she watched him ascend the stairs, she couldn't help but start thinking. He had been awfully nice to her. He was pretty shy the other day, but that would make sense, he was a social outcast and a target for anyone who wanted to move up the social ladder. Clearly, a fan of science fiction and anime wouldn't make him a popular kid, not in this school. However, he never treated her with disrespect. And for that matter, friends had been a little hard to come by for her as well.

She pulled out her cell phone and started tapping the screen. She typed up a text message: "I'm staying at a friend's house tonight. See you in the morning," and sent it off to her dad. She then replaced her phone and reclined back in the loveseat. Lacing her fingers together over her chest, she closed her eyes and allowed herself to drift off to sleep.

Thirty minutes later, Luis came back downstairs to check on her and see if Mom had come back yet. He found her curled up on the loveseat, her legs brought up to her chest and shoes lying on the floor. Her rhythmic breathing told him she had fallen asleep.

Quietly, he walked over to the hall closet, pulled out a spare blanket, and draped it over her. She twitched a little and then settled down, still sleeping. He smiled, locked the front door, and climbed back up the stairs to his room to rest.

6

Saturday, October 25

Serena woke up groggy. She peeked her eyes open lazily and looked confusingly around. This wasn't her room. This wasn't even her house. Where was she? Why was she sleeping on a couch?

It started coming back to her as she came awake. This was Luis's house. He let her stay the night since it was so dark when they got here. She was going to get a ride back to her place but fell asleep instead.

She sat up and stretched. Looking around, she found her boots sitting on the floor next to the couch. As she was lacing them back up, she could hear Luis and his mom in the other room. She listened in with sly amusement.

"All I'm saying is you could've at least told me you were inviting a friend over. I would've prepared something instead of forcing you to eat leftovers." It was an older woman's voice, obviously the mother.

"I didn't know she was going to stay the night. The plan was to wait for you to get back so you could drive her home," Luis said.

"And what were you two doing out so late at night?" Mom had a sly tone in her voice.

"It wasn't late, we came home around seven. That's not really late at all," Luis protested.

"But really, Luis, I'm a little surprised. I didn't think you'd be into girls like her. I thought that whole Goth style didn't appeal to you."

"Mom! We aren't dating!"

"Oh yes. I know you aren't," she said with a sarcastic tone.

"Seriously, we only really got acquainted yesterday!" Luis said.

"Got acquainted? Is that what you kids are calling it now?" Mom said coyly. Serena stifled a laugh.

"Mom! Stop it! She's right in the next room, she can hear you!"

"She'll definitely hear you if you keep shouting like that. For that matter, why don't you check to see if she's awake yet? I should probably take her back home soon."

Luis sighed and walked into the living room. He found Serena sitting on the couch with her ankles crossed, hands resting on her knees, and an evil smirk across her face. "Good morning," she said.

"Morning," Luis replied. "How long have you been awake?"

"Since about the time your mother mentioned leftovers." Serena stood up off the couch. "So are we having anything for breakfast?"

"Oh, good morning, dear." Luis's mom came in from the kitchen. "Glad to see you're up and about. I was in the process of making French toast. Are you hungry?"

"Quite, actually," Serena replied. "I'd love some."

"Well then, come in to the dining room. It's all prepared." She led the three of them to the dinner table, upon which rested three plates of steaming French toast smothered with melted butter and maple syrup along with three glasses of orange juice. "Make yourself comfortable."

Serena placed herself across the table from Luis. His mom sat at the head of the table. Fork in hand, Serena cut into the French toast with ease. One bite and she was almost in love with it. It was fluffy and delicious, the best breakfast she'd had in a very long time. Serena couldn't help but moan from satisfaction from the first bite.

A satisfied smile appeared on Mrs. Chavez's face. "I can see you like it."

Serena nodded enthusiastically. "Yes," she said, her mouth still full. "It's wonderful, Mrs. Chavez. Thank you."

"You're welcome," Mrs. Chavez said with a sweet smile. "Now tell me a little about yourself. It's not often Luis brings home friends. What are some of your hobbies? What are you taking in school?"

Serena gulped down some of her orange juice. "Well," she wiped an orange drop from her lips, "in school, I'm mostly just taking the general stuff. You know. Things like English, math, and history. Nothing too spectacular there. But I am also taking a creative writing class."

"Oh, creative writing! How fun!" Mrs. Chavez said. "Like poetry and short stories?"

"For the most part, yes." Serena quickly took another bite.

"Do you have any poems with you? Any you'd like to share?" Mrs. Chavez asked.

Now Serena felt like she was on the spot. She didn't feel like she could say no, but she also didn't think Mrs. Chavez would be interested in the things she wrote. It could get pretty morbid at times. "You really wouldn't want to hear it."

"No, no, I insist. Share with us."

Serena sighed, "Okay. This is a haiku I have memorized." She cleared her throat, and after a few moments of hesitation, she began to recite it.

> Killed a man today.
> Shot a bullet through his heart.
> I slept, peacefully.

Mrs. Chavez sat in stunned silence. Luis also stared wide-eyed and confused. A tense quietness fell over the breakfast table. Serena shifted her eyes from Luis to Mrs. Chavez and back again. She quickly stuffed another bite of French toast in her mouth. Finally, Mrs. Chavez broke the silence.

"Well, how, um, creative of you." She also hastily ate her breakfast. The three of them continued to eat in awkward silence. Once they were finished and the dishes were in the sink, Mrs. Chavez said, "I should probably take you home, Serena. Where do you live?"

"With my dad on East California Street. I can give directions on the way," Serena said.

"That would be nice. When would you like to leave?" Mrs. Chavez asked.

"We should probably go soon. I told my dad I would be out last night, but I'm sure he's still anxious for me to get home."

"Okay, then," Mrs. Chavez said. "I'll get ready, and we'll be on our way." She left for her bedroom to freshen up, leaving the two kids alone in the living room.

"I don't think your mom like's me," Serena said once Luis's mother had left.

"That's not true. You just intimidate her," Luis said. "She doesn't think kids should write poetry about death."

"But that's all angsty teenagers write about. That or sex," Serena said. She looked around the living room again. The family pictures all over one wall, an entertainment center next to the other, the shear simplicity of it all. "You have a pretty good thing going on for you here. A nice house, a mom that loves you. Seems like it'd be fun."

"Oh, come on. Are you saying you don't have anything like that?" Luis asked.

"Not really. Alice's kidnapping put a lot of strain on my parents. Eventually, they broke up. Things haven't been very glamorous after that."

"But I saw their names listed together when I looked it up on the online phone book," Luis said.

"That's just because Dad never bothered to change it," Serena said.

"Are you kids ready?" Mrs. Chavez called from down the hall.

"Yeah," Luis shouted back, as he and Serena stood up from the couch.

"Before I leave, I want to get your phone number," Serena said. She pulled out her own phone and pulled up her contacts list.

"Wait, seriously?" Luis asked. He became nervous, and the back of his neck was warm again.

"Sure. You and Alice seem to have formed a bit of a connection, which means that you're likely to be down there semi-often to see her. Chances are I'll run into you there.

We can probably plan some kind of get together and hang out. All three of us."

"Um, sure. Okay." Luis pulled his phone from his pocket. "Okay. My number is 555-7600."

She recorded the number in her contacts and placed it under friends. She then sent a text to him. The text simply read, "You have my number now. Don't hesitate to call."

Luis's mom walked into the living room. "Ready to go?" she asked.

"Yes, Mom," Luis said.

The three of them walked out to Mrs. Chavez's light blue sedan. She got in the driver's side while Luis took the front passenger seat, and Serena climbed in the back seat. She started up the car and backed out of the driveway. They drove through town silently until reaching East California Street. "Okay, Serena. You're going to have to tell me where to go from here."

"It's about two more blocks down and on the left. The house with the red pickup truck," she said.

It was a one-story with paint chipped in some places and grass was a little longer than it should've been. In the front driveway was a '97 red Ford F-150. They pulled to a stop in front, and Serena let herself out.

"Thank you, Mrs. Chavez. And thanks again, Luis. For everything," she said. "I'll see you at school on Monday." She turned and walked into her house.

Luis and his mother waited until she was in her house before driving away. "She seemed like an interesting girl," his mom said.

"You don't have to sugarcoat it, Mom. You thought she was weird," Luis said.

"Well, yes. Her poem glorifying violence was a little disturbing," Mom said.

"I was just as shocked as you. I didn't know she wrote that, although I really shouldn't be surprised at all." Luis shifted in his seat. "She's kind of into that macabre sort of thing."

"I hadn't noticed," Mom said with a hint of sarcasm.

"Oh, please, Mom." Luis's phone buzzed. He saw the message was from Serena and read it to himself.

Serena: *I'm going to visit Alice today. Do you want to come?*

He typed away on his keypad a reply.

Luis: *Yes. What time?*

Serena: *How does 1:30 sound?*

Luis: *It doesn't work that way. She said she only appears at dawn and dusk.*

Serena: *I'm going to try anyways. I'll be there at 1:30 if you want to join me.*

Her phone slipped easily back into her coat pocket. Serena kicked her shoes off at the door and walked through the living room. The TV was on, scenes from some boring crime drama danced across the screen. She paid it little attention.

What she did notice was her father. He sat in his recliner, facing the TV. His feet were propped up, and in his right hand, he held a beer bottle. A TV tray with an empty TV dinner dish stood next to the chair. His head rolled to the side, and he snored loudly.

Serena could only sigh with disappointment. This was not the first time she had found him like this. It was a daily ritual. He'd come home from work, microwave something from the freezer, grab about three beers, and plop down in his chair to watch his stupid shows until he passed out.

She noticed his cell phone on the TV tray. Serena picked it up to inspect it. On the screen, it displayed that her dad had one unread text message. Upon opening it, she was not too surprised to learn it was her message from the night before. She dismissively set it back on the TV tray, saddened.

Her hands found their way back into her pockets. She turned away from her father without waking him. Saturday and Sunday were his days off, no sense in ruining that time to himself by forcing him awake. Instead, she just walked back to her room and closed the door.

She emerged from her room a few minutes later in a different outfit. Now she wore a black short-sleeved T-shirt with a red capital letter *A* in a circle in the upper left corner. Her black pants adorned in chains, buckles, and zippers. On her hands, she wore a pair of black leather fingerless gloves with small plastic spikes on the knuckles. She left out a refreshed breath. No need to spend the whole day in the clothes she slept in.

The digital clock on the stove read 10:23 a.m. Perfect time. She laced her boots back on and stepped out the front door. It clicked behind her as she locked it. So what if Luis didn't want to go, she wanted to spend some time with Alice alone. Or perhaps, she thought she needed to. With the slightest hint of a smile on her lips and a skip in her step, she set off for the park.

7

Luis got to the playground and found Serena sitting by herself on the swing set. He walked over and sat down beside her, saying nothing. She simply stared at the ground dejected.

"She's not here," Serena said. "I've been here since eleven. She never appeared, no matter what I did or how much I called for her." Her hair hung down in front of her eyes.

"I told you it wouldn't work. And why did you send that message to meet me at one thirty when you just came by at eleven?" Luis asked.

"I wanted to spend some time alone with her. It's the first time I've seen Alice in ten years. I wanted to talk and catch up. I don't get it, why isn't she here?"

"I am here." Alice appeared right in front of them. She faded in from invisible to fully formed. "I've been trying to talk to you, but you couldn't hear me."

"Alice!" Serena leapt up from the swing and wrapped her arms around her sister. After a few seconds, she stepped back. "I've been trying to talk to you all day."

"I know. I just said I've been watching you," Alice said. "What are you doing out here anyway? Shouldn't you be in school right now?"

"It's a Saturday. And why couldn't you talk back? Why couldn't I see you?" Serena asked.

"Hold on." Luis jumped to his feet. "I have a better question. You told me you could only appear at dawn and dusk, how can we see you now?"

"I don't know," Alice said. She folded her arms and jutted her hips out to the side. "It isn't the first time, either. Several of us here have tried before talking to other kids when they were here, but they never noticed us. Okay, that's not true. They would notice if we interacted with something or physically touched them, but they couldn't see or hear us. Really, the first person to see us was Luis."

Serena looked over at Luis confused. He could only shrug. "Why only him?" she asked.

"I don't know. In fact, now that I think about it, the only times anyone has seen me was when Luis was here too." Alice motioned to her sister. "You yesterday and the day before with the bully. Each time, Luis was there. I think there might be something special about him."

"Special? Me?" Luis asked.

"Yeah." Alice sat down in front of the swing set and crossed her legs. "I think you have some force about you that lets you and other people around you see spirits. I think you might be some kind of spiritual medium."

"Me?" Luis said, a hint of doubt in his voice. "A spiritual medium? Are you serious? I'm probably one of the least spiritual people I know. I didn't even really believe in an afterlife until you showed up."

"Do you have a better explanation?" Alice leaned her face on the palm of her hand. "No one could see or hear me for ten years until the day you showed up."

"A coincidence," Luis said.

"I doubt it." Alice snarked back.

"Okay, fine. So if I am supposed to be some kind of amazing spirit-talker person, what am I supposed to do with it?" he asked.

"I think I know," Serena spoke up. Alice and Luis both turned to her. "Just think. Almost as soon as you met her, you tried to figure out who Alice was and what happened to her. And once you found who her family was, you decided to bring us back together. Your gift allows you to give wayward spirits closure. You can help them pass on. Help them to finish that unfinished business I told you about."

Luis fixed his eyes on the ground and rested his hands on his lap. This was more than he wanted to get into. A medium for spirits to commune with? Helping them get closure? Was he really supposed to be some kind of savior to wandering souls? "This seems like a lot to take in all at once. I'll need some time to think on it."

"Yes, it is," Alice said. "But I do thank you, Luis. If not for you, I might've never remembered who my sister was or any of my family. I want to see them again. I want to see Mom and Dad."

Serena turned her gaze away. "That can't happen."

"Why not?" Alice asked.

Serena inhaled, taking several deep breaths. After a long time, she spoke again, "Because Mom's dead."

Luis's and Alice's mouths fell agape, and their eyes widened. "What?" Alice stood up. "Mom's dead? You didn't tell me this." She rushed over and grabbed Serena's shirt with both hands. She shook her sister, screaming, "Why didn't you tell me this earlier?"

"I didn't want to bring it up," Serena said. She didn't meet Alice's gaze, and her eyes began to tear. "I was just so happy to finally see you again, I didn't want to mess it all up."

Alice released her hold on Serena's shirt. "When did it happen?"

"Less than a year after you disappeared. When you went missing, it put a lot of stain on Mom and Dad. They fought a lot, screamed and yelled at each other. Eventually, Mom decided she couldn't stay in the house anymore. It was too full of memories. She packed up a bag and left. It was raining that night, the roads were wet, the other driver couldn't see." Serena rubbed her eyes on her sleeve. "It was a head-on collision. Mom didn't survive the ambulance ride."

Alice, Luis, and Serena remained in stunned and horrified silence. Luis could hardly believe what he was hearing. Two days ago, he had pretty much no idea who Serena Ravenwood was, but now she'd opened up so much. Perhaps not to him directly, but she wasn't holding anything back around him. She's had to endure so much pain. First, the loss of her sister, and then less than a year later, the death of her mother. And she was only six at the time. What kind of mental and emotional burden does that place on a child that young? Luis placed his hand on her shoulder, only to have her push it away. "I don't need sympathy." Her voice was stern.

"Maybe not," Luis said. "But I'm giving it anyway."

"Well, don't!" she shouted. "Too many people have said they were sorry. Too many people tried to say something to make it better, all of it fake. I don't need or want anyone's fake compassion! And certainly not yours!"

"What's wrong with my support?" Luis jumped straight up out of the swing. "Why can't I be sympathetic? Is there something wrong with caring about you? Why are you so against it?"

"Because no one cares for caring's sake." Serena lurched upright. "No one ever just wants to make sure you're all right! Everyone is in it for themselves! The world and every-thing in it is rotten!" Tears flowed down her cheeks, and her voice cracked. "Some monster stole my sister from me right before my eyes! I watched it happen! Grabbed her right off the street! Then someone else killed my mother! My whole life people have been trying to comfort me and tell me how sorry they were for me, but they never really were."

She sobbed, held her face in her hands and wept. All these emotions had come bubbling up to the surface, and she couldn't keep them held back anymore. It was all too much for her now. She thought she had gotten over all this already, but here she was crying like a small child and una-ble to control herself. Why was she so weak? Why wasn't she good for anything?

Serena gasped when Alice and Luis suddenly embraced her. They held her close until the worst of her weep-ing ceased. "Cindy," Alice said. "I'm so sorry you had to go through all that. If I had only been there, none of it would've happened."

"I wish I had gotten to know you sooner. So that you didn't have to go through it alone," Luis said.

Slowly, a small smile spread over Serena's face. She reached out and grabbed hold of both of them. She held them close, feeling their warmth flow through her. They all stood together, unmoving for a long time, none of them wanting to let the others go. After what seemed like an eternity, they stepped back. "Thank you," Serena said. "Both of you."

From a distance, another kid watched. It was another one of the ghost children, Paul. He sat on the seesaw by himself, his arms rested over the handlebars and a scowl on his face. He stared at them intently, his brows pointed angrily down. He'd been here only two and a half weeks, and his memory hadn't started to fade as it had for the other kids. He still remembered everything—everything that man and woman did to him. If Alice could remember what those monsters did to her, she wouldn't be so happy. And he was not going to let it go. Paul clenched his fists. He would get his revenge. His murderer was going to pay.

He noticed a small movement next to him and turned to see. A few small stones had what looked like trail marks behind them, like they'd moved across the dirt. Had he done that? He stared at the tiny rock, focused all his attention on it. But nothing happened.

Late that night, the waxing crescent moon showed brightly in the sky, casting rays of silver light across the playground. Alone among the old rusted equipment stood Paul. He focused on a small rock lying before him, stared at it with all the intensity he could muster. Then it moved, only a little, less than an inch, but it moved nonetheless. He grinned.

"Paul?" Alice appeared behind him. "Don't you want to rest a little? It's pretty late."

"I don't need to rest. I'm dead already. Rest is only for the living," he said. He focused on the pebble again and this time started to lift it off the ground. He only held it up for a few seconds before he was forced to let it go. "I need to practice more."

Alice watched the pebble rise and fall. Her brows furled. "How did you learn to do that?"

"I'm not entirely sure. I first noticed earlier today when you and the two living people were still here. I was just thinking about who I was and what I'm going to do when I saw a small rock moving," Paul said, his eyes still fixed on the rock. It started to roll across the ground, and a wicked grin slipped over his face. "I can do it. I can move objects at will."

Alice placed a hand on his shoulder. "Paul, I think this might be a bad thing. Maybe you should stop for a little bit."

"No!" he shouted, throwing her hand off. "This is my gift! My power! You want me to stop because you're jealous!"

Alice stepped back, her hands held in the air. "That's not it at all. I'm just concerned for you. Maybe you should rest and pick it back up tomorrow. I mean, look at yourself, you're pastier than usual." She reasoned.

Paul looked down at his hands. Even in the dark light of the moon, he could see he was paler than before. "Maybe you're right." He closed his eyes and allowed himself to fade out of sight.

Alice looked suspiciously down at the pebble. She'd never been able to move things with mere thoughts. What was going on with Paul? She decided to rest too. She closed her eyes, exhaled, and vanished.

8

Monday, October 27

Monday morning rolled back around again, and Luis found himself on the path through the city park on his way to school. As he passed by the playground, he saw Alice leaning on the fence waving at him. "Morning, Luis!" she called.

"Good morning!" He waved back.

"Did you come by to visit again today?" she asked.

"Sorry, I'm already later than I'd like to be. I'll see you this afternoon, if you'd like," he said.

"Aw, come on!"

"Sorry, it's all I can do. I'll talk to you then." He kept walking passed the playground and out of the park.

Alice leaned forward on the fence and propped her head up on her arms. She had been so eager to see him today, but now she would have to wait another eight hours. That was just totally stupid. If only she could follow him, it wouldn't be a problem. She stood upright as a thought came to her.

Why not follow him? She used to think she was only active during dawn and dusk, but now she knew that wasn't true. She used to think that she was bound to the playground, but what if she wasn't true either? They'd already established that Luis was whom let people see her. Besides, this might be fun too.

She walked through the chain link fence and floated down the path after him. Today, she was going back to school.

Attendance had just been taken in homeroom, and Ms. Sterling placed her clipboard down. "All right class, today, I have some tests to hand back. And there is good news and bad news." The class muttered in fear. "Good news, several of you scored hundreds on last week's pop quiz. The bad news, more of you scored F's than I would like." She walked down the rows of desk, handing back the test papers as she did.

Luis took his when Ms. Sterling came by his desk. He quickly glanced at the score on the top of the page. 75 percent. Not as good as he had hoped. He rolled his eyes and set the test down. "What are you so upset about?" a voice said. His eyes snapped open wide. They moved back and forth across the room, looking for the source. He recognized that voice, but it shouldn't be possible. "I'm up here, if you're wondering."

Slowly, Luis tilted back his head and looked up toward the ceiling. Floating right above his head was Alice. Her big blue eyes and smiling face beaming down at him. "Hi," she said.

He just looked at her for several seconds. His mouth hung open, and eyebrows climbed his forehead. "Mr. Chavez, is something wrong?" the teacher called to him.

"Huh?" He came back to his thoughts and faced the front of the class. "No, nothing is wrong."

"Good, then take out your notes and pay attention." She turned back to the whiteboard and continued her lecture.

Luis did indeed take out his notebook but not to take study notes. He quickly scribbled across the page.

What are you doing here?

"Is that any way to greet me?" Alice folded her arms and pushed out her lower lip. "I wanted to visit you while you were in school. See how the place has changed. Is that such a bad thing?"

Luis wrote again.

I thought you couldn't leave the playground.

"Turns out, I can. I just lose my visibility when I'm not around you. Remember? You're special that way."

So can anyone see you now?

"No. I've made myself visible only to you and to my little sister if I see her today." Alice floated through the air and hovered next to the teacher's head. "I'm sure you'll get a kick out of this." She phased her arm through Ms. Sterling's head. "In one ear, out the other." She grinned. "And look at this." Alice floated so that her face was right behind Ms. Sterling's hair. She then closed her eyes and made herself turn invisible. When she opened her eyes, they were the only thing Luis could see of her. "The teacher's got eyes on the back of her head."

Luis couldn't help but smile. That was kind of silly, he had to admit. He scribbled something else down, and Alice flew back over to read it.

You'd better cut it out. I could get in trouble.

"Oh, get in trouble for what? Laughing in class? The way I see it, this classroom could use a little extra fun. It's just so boring in here." Alice floated up in the air. She held out her arms, motioning to the whole class. "I mean, just look at these kids, they all look bored out of their skulls."

Luis glanced around the room. She was right, they did all appear bored, but that wasn't out of the ordinary. This was a biology class after all, what was she expecting? Luis stopped when he noticed Butch. Butch's eyes were fixed at the ceiling, and his mouth hung open stupidly. Luis followed his gaze. He was staring at Alice. Luis became nervous. Could Butch see her too? How was that possible?

It then hit him like a ton of bricks. That day in the playground when he tried to escape Butch, they'd caught him and were going to beat him up when Alice intervened. At the end, they ran away screaming. Butch had seen her then. Did that mean she was visible to him now?

Luis glanced back to the teacher and saw she was still facing the whiteboard. As quietly as possible, he wrote another note.

I think someone else can see you.

Alice read the note and looked over the room. She saw Butch staring at her. Slowly, she pulled her arms back and descended. Butch's eyes followed her. "That's the kid who tried to beat you up the other day, isn't it?"

Yes.

"Hey, punk!" she shouted. Luis had to wince since she was standing right next to his ear. "You can see me, can't you?"

Butch nodded his head slowly.

"You can probably hear me too, right?"

Another slow nod.

A sneaky grin came over Alice face. "I think I can have some fun with this." She floated over to Butch's desk, phasing through the other kids on the way. He watched her the whole time, his eyes never moving.

"I bet you think you're kinda a tough guy, don't ya? Think you're so bad." She picked up the pencil off his desk and fiddled with it between her fingers. He could only watch in shock. She set his pencil down and picked up his graded test instead. The score at the top was only 15 percent. "Well, guess what? You're not very smart. And you aren't so tough." To anyone else in the class, it would've looked like the paper was floating by itself, but to Luis and Butch, there was a girl holding it and waving it around in his face. She crumpled it up into a paper ball and tossed it over her shoulder.

The paper ball bounced off the whiteboard before it dropped to the floor. Instantly, the teacher's dry-erase marker stopped; her lecture ceased. A hushed silence fell over the class. Slowly, each movement deliberate, she capped the pen, set it down on the pen rack. And then the teacher reached down, picked up the paper ball, and still moving at a deliberate slow speed, uncrumpled it, and read the name. "Butch." Her voice was low but harsh.

Alice stepped out to the side so Butch could see the teacher clearly. Sweat almost poured down his face. He swallowed hard. "Yes, Ms. Sterling?"

"What is your crumpled test doing up here?" the teacher asked sternly.

"Um, well, I." He stumbled for a competent response. "I was trying to throw it away, but I missed the trash can."

"You mean the trash can at the back of the classroom?" Ms. Sterling said with a cold voice. She was right. There were no garbage cans near the whiteboard, only by the door.

Butch's shoulders slumped. He knew he had no way out of this now. Alice stood right next to him the whole time with an evil smile. Luis could only watch as it all unfolded before his eyes, his heart pounding in his chest.

Ms. Sterling forcefully pushed the test paper to her desk. "Take all you things, and go to the principal's office. Immediately."

Butch opened his mouth to protest but closed it instantly. There was nothing he could say that would make anything better. Sour, defeated, he picked up his backpack and walked out of the classroom.

"Aha ha ha ha ha! That was great!" Alice rolled over in the air, laughing.

Luis watched with a mixture of happiness and a hint of regret. On the one hand, he was happy to see Butch get some comeuppance. But he also felt that the whole incident was more than a little harsh.

You know, that was a very mean thing to do.

"Oh, come on. Now you're going to start defending the guy who's tried to beat you up on a daily basis? It's not like he didn't deserve it." Alice crossed her arms and legs. She hovered in the air. "Don't try to hide it. You're happy to see him get in trouble." Luis placed pen to paper again.

Did it occur to you that maybe he'll try to get back at me for it? He saw you, he might think-

Luis stopped writing. A thought had occurred to him. Butch saw Alice, when no one else in the class could. Why was that? Was there something special about him too? Was he just endowed with an ability to see spirits?

Alice tapped Luis's shoulder. "You're off in a daze, man."

After school, we should have a talk with Butch.

"Oh, really?" Alice hung upside down in front of his face. Her brows pushed down, and her lips pressed together. "The guy you were just scared would beat the crap out of you today for something I did? You now want to talk to him?"

He was able to see you when no one else could.

"And you want to find out why." She crossed her arms. "Getting a little curious. Are you afraid you won't be as special if someone else has your gift?"

I still don't really believe I have any gift.

"If you say so." Alice shrugged.

First break came as it usually does. Luis quickly texted Serena and asked to meet her in the library. They sat across from each other at one of the tables while Alice floated overhead. "So you decided to follow him around today?" Serena rolled her eyes.

"Eh, I got bored. You can only sit around at the playground for so long before it gets tiring," Alice said.

"Actually," Luis interjected, "I'm interested in finding out more about Butch."

"Why?" Serena said. No pretense, she made her feelings on the matter known with her harsh tone.

"Because earlier in class today, while she was buzzing around my head," he gestured his thumb at Alice above him, "Butch could see her. I think that's a little strange, and I want to find out how he could."

"And what does this have to do with me?" Serena asked. "I'm not a big fan of his myself."

"I just thought that if the three of us confront him together, then he wouldn't try anything," Luis said.

"Confront? Do you ever listen to yourself? Confront him? You sound like you want to attack him or something," Serena said with a snide tone. "And besides, after what you said she decided to do, I doubt he wants to talk to you at all."

"That's why I want the both of you to be there," Luis said. "Will you help me?"

Serena sighed and rested her head on her hand. She pursed her lips. "Fine. Only because you asked."

"Thank you. After school then." Luis stood up from the table.

"Yes, after school." Serena stood up as well. She stuffed her hands in her pockets and walked out of the library.

"Okay, then. Alice, I'm off to world history, are you coming?" He looked up at where she used to be, but now the air was empty. He scanned around the library, but she was nowhere to be seen. "Alice?"

Serena strolled down the hall grumbling to herself. "Talk to him? I don't even like the guy. He's an obnoxious, irritating jerk who needs a good comeuppance."

"That's what I said." Alice appeared in the air next to Serena. She hovered next to her younger sister.

Serena raised an eyebrow. "And now you're following me?"

"You seemed a little jealous that I was hanging around with Luis this morning. I figured I could spend the rest of my day with my little baby sister." Alice patted the top of Serena's head and pinched her on the cheek.

Serena smacked her hand away. "I'm older than you now," she said in monotone.

"I know, and that's a little weird. But aging stops when you're dead." Alice floated above her sister. "So are you and Luis planning anything for Halloween? Did you get invited to a party? You seem like you would be really exciting at one." Serena walked on silently. She didn't answer and didn't turn around. "I'm going to take that as a *no*." Alice grinned.

"I wouldn't want to be invited to any of those stupid jock parties. They wouldn't know how to throw a Halloween bash if I bashed them over the head with one," Serena said.

"Well, why not?" Alice floated on behind her.

"I have no idea," Serena lied.

"Sure you don't," Alice said sarcastically. "I think it has to do with your attitude. People are afraid of you."

"Good. I want them to be."

Alice leaned in close to Serena's face. "Do you want Luis to be afraid of you?"

"What?" The question caught Serena off guard. "No, he's not afraid of me. We're friends."

"And is that all?"

"Yes, that's all." Serena's pace quickened. "Geez. We've only known each other for less than a week."

Alice folded her arms and smiled. "Baby sister, do you have a boyfriend I don't know about?"

"No."

"Have you ever had a boyfriend?"

"No." Serena scrunched her shoulders up.

"Mm-hmm." Alice placed a finger to her chin, her devious smile still plastered across her face. "And do you want one?"

"Not particularly. I'm just fine the way I am." She stepped past her ghost sister. "Boyfriends are for people who give a crap about them."

Back at the playground, Paul continued to fiddle with the rocks. He could now make two or three float in the air at once for close to ten seconds at a time. All he needed was practice. Soon he would be able to move larger objects and for longer. Once that happened, he would go after the man who killed him.

"Paul?" a tiny voice called to him. It was Susie, one of the younger ghosts of the playground. She was only seven when she died, the youngest here. "Where did Alice go?"

Paul scoffed. "She's gone off to stay with her sister and that four-eyed doofus. She's left us."

"She left us? Why?" Susie tilted her head to the side.

"Because she found her family. She doesn't care about the rest of us anymore." Paul knelt down to Susie's level. "Remember how she used to play with you on the slide? Or push you on the swing?" Susie nodded. "I don't think she's going to do that anymore. She doesn't want to spend time with us now that she has living friends."

"That's not true!" Susie shouted. She stomped her feet. "Alice wouldn't leave us like that!"

"You might not think so, but she did." Paul placed his arms around Susie. "It's okay. It's not her fault. It's that boy, Luis. He took her away from us. And we need to get her back."

"How do we do that?" Susie asked.

"Oh, that's simple. We will just have to kill Luis," Paul said.

At the end of the school day, Butch packed his bags. He had gotten another Saturday school from the principal. Not just for throwing the paper in class, which he didn't even do this time, but also for his low class scores. He was failing every class. Math: 17 percent. English: 12 percent. Biology: 9 percent. He was lucky that any of his courses had grades in the double digits. It wasn't his fault; he just couldn't read the books. The tests, the homework, all the words looked mixed up and jumbled to him.

That plus the fact that he was not sleeping well the past few days. The images of ghosts keep coming back in his dreams. Frequently, a monstrous white face would appear from a black void in his dreams with a cold hand grasping his throat and shutting off his breath. He would struggle in his sleep—fighting this invisible force holding him down, strangling him—then he'd wake up in a cold sweat, finding he'd wet the bed again. Inevitably, his old man would ridicule him.

"What are you, some weak little baby? Are you three? Can't you sleep without wetting your bed like a child? I can't believe you." Pop would say. "I can't believe this."

He was on his way home when he saw that dweeb Luis standing where he would usually meet his friends. He was looking up at him, one hand holding his backpack strap and the other stuffed in his pocket. Next to him floated the ghost girl. Butch stopped in his tracks. He didn't want to face them again. He turned to walk away and came face-to-face with the pale white face and creepy black mascara eyes of that freaky Goth chick. He remembered her too well. She was the bitch who kicked his butt. She pointed over to the dweeb and ghost girl. "That way." Her voice scratched.

"What if I don't want to?"

"Then I'll punch you in the face and drag you over there anyway," she said.

Dejected, defeated, he turned back around and walked to Luis and the ghost girl. Goth chick followed three steps behind him. They stopped in front of Luis. "Yeah, what do you want?" Butch asked.

"Nothing much. Just wanted to ask a question," Luis said.

"Yeah, what?"

"Why can you see her?" Luis motioned to Alice.

"What do you mean *why*? She's right there. I see her because I can. I thought I was seeing things the other day. I tried to forget that stuff in the park, but then she showed up in class," Butch said. "What are you trying to do anyway? Are you trying to get back at me? Is this your idea of a joke?"

"What joke?"

"Bringing her with you today!" Butch pointed accusingly at Alice. "You did it just to mess with me, didn't you? A little bit of payback, but you can't face me yourself, so you have your dead girlfriend and the girl who wishes she was dead do it for you, is that it?"

Serena grabbed him by the back of his collar and turned him around. "Be careful what you say, or you might have to breathe through a straw for the next three months."

"See? That's exactly what I mean! This is your idea of payback!" Butch shouted.

Luis slapped his hand against his forehead. "I don't want revenge for anything. I just wanted to know how long you've been seeing ghosts."

"I never had that problem before I ran into that dead bitch!" Butch pointed at Alice. "Since then, her ugly face has been haunting my nightmares. And if she weren't here, I'd pound your teeth in!"

Serena, still with her fist clenching his shirt, shook him vigorously. "And what did I just say?"

Luis raised his hand. "Serena, stop. He answered my questions, we can let him go."

Her eyes shifted to Luis and then back to Butch. She shoved him away. "Fine."

Butch stumbled to catch his balance. Once he had it, he straightened out his shirt as he power walked out of sight. The three of them watched silently as he left. "So does that help with anything?" Alice asked.

"Maybe." Luis scratched his head. "He said this didn't start happening until after the playground. Maybe it's just people who've been there can see spirits."

"I still like my theory better," Alice said. "After all, he was beating you up the first time he saw me. I still think you are the catalyst that set this off."

"If you say so," Luis said.

9

Butch walked down the park path toward the playground. Nothing deliberate, this was just his usual way home. As he came upon the chain link fence, he paused and looked over the old rusted slide and seesaw, realizing where he was. The swings slowly moved back and forth with a low creak.

He scowled. He took a deep breath and spit at the playground before he started walking again. But he stopped in his tracks as he heard a voice. "Is that any way to treat a burial site?" Slowly, Butch turned around. A young kid, probably about twelve years old, stood with his hands in coat pockets and a devilish smile on his face. "Not very couth, I'd say."

"And who are you?" Butch growled.

"My name is Paul. I recognize you. Yes, you were the person attacking Luis the other day. Before Alice got involved," Paul said.

"And how do you know anything about that?" Butch took a step back.

"Because I was here. I was watching the whole time. It looked like it was a lot of fun, actually. Why do you target Luis, anyway?" Paul asked.

"He annoys me, that's why. His face offends me," Butch spat. "And I didn't see you here that day. Where were you hiding, brat?"

"I wasn't hiding. I was just invisible at the time. I'm like Alice." He pulled one hand from its pocket and held it in the air. "You see," he made his hand dissipate, "I am also a ghost." Butch's face turned white. He wanted to run, but his legs wouldn't move, almost like he was stuck in this spot. He tried to talk, but no words came. "You don't have to be afraid." Paul slipped his hand back to the pocket. "I'm not after you. But I do think we have a common enemy, if you could call him that. I find Luis to be an annoyance to me as well. What do you say we work to get rid of him?"

"Get rid of? How do you mean?"

Paul shrugged his shoulders. "How it's usually meant. Take care of him. Use any kind of fake mob speak you want, it all just comes down to killing him."

"Hey, man! I don't do that." Butch pointed forcefully back at Paul. "I may give the kid a beating or two, but I'm not a murderer."

Paul sighed and rolled his eyes. "Okay, if you don't want to, I guess I can find someone else." He walked through the chain link fence before turning to look at Butch again. "Just keep my offer in mind."

Butch started to leave then stopped. He managed to find his voice. "What did you mean by 'burial site?'"

"What it usually means. A place where people are buried. My body is buried here. So are the bodies of Alice and at least seven other children." His wicked grin came back. "We were murdered, and I know the murderer will be looking for his next victim soon." His form then disappeared completely.

Butch felt his heart pounding. His breathing came hard and fast, almost like he was hyperventilating. This was all a hallucination; it had to be. There was no way this was real. He took off like a shot, running as fast as he could out of the park.

It was not ten minutes later that Paul saw Luis and Serena coming toward the playground, Alice walking alongside them. They were talking, even laughing with one another. Paul watched with disgust. Why did she like them so much? What was so special about these walking meat bags?

They stopped at the fence around the playground. They said their good-byes, and the two living humans walked away, leaving Alice behind. Paul stepped up next her. "Did we have fun today?"

"Yes, actually, I did," Alice said, a joyful smile on her face.

"Good." Paul nodded. Suddenly, the other ghost children in the park rushed out and grabbed Alice. They took her arms and pulled them behind her back, forcing her to her knees. One of them grabbed her by the hair and yanked her head back. "Because it's the last time you will."

"Ack!" She squirmed. She pulled as hard as she could, but the other kids held strong. "What's going on? Paul, tell them to let me go!"

"You've been rather lazy, Alice. Didn't you ever experiment with what you could do as a ghost? All the abilities you have?" Paul raised his hand, and a circle of small rocks floated around it. "I did. I can control objects with a thought now. And I want revenge."

"Revenge? Revenge for what? What have I ever done to you?" Alice fought but couldn't escape.

"Not against you. You've been like a mother to us, taking care of each of us when we came here, isn't that right, kids?" All the other children answered affirmatively. "We have nothing against you. It's that *human* friend of yours we want revenge against."

The way he said *human*, as if it were some sort of slime-covered vermin to be killed, sent a shiver through Alice. "Luis? What has he ever done?"

Paul crouched down to look Alice in the eye. "He stole you from us. All we have is each other, isn't that right? There's no room for a human among us."

"Paul, listen to yourself! Don't you remember that you were once human too?" Alice shouted.

"I do, and I remember how much I hated that worthless existence. My parents hardly recognized that I existed, my brother tormented me every chance he got. And to top it off, I was kidnapped, abused, and later murdered. Or did you forget that we're all here because that sick monster buried us here?" He scooped up a handful of dirt and let it slowly fall back to the ground. "This is our grave site. And I intend to also make it his grave. As well as Luis's."

"No!" She lunged at him, but still the other ghost children held her back. As much as she fought, she couldn't break free. "I won't let you hurt him!"

"Don't worry too much. I don't intend to go after him just yet. I have a few other people on my list first." Paul stood up. He shifted focus from Alice to the children. "Make sure she doesn't go anywhere. I will be back after I've taken care of a few things." His form then disappeared right before her eyes.

Alice watched as he disappeared, unable to stop him. She tugged and pulled as hard as she could against her captors, but they held firm. "Why are you listening to him? I never abandoned you! Don't you know I'm your friend?

Susie, don't you remember the times I pushed you on the swings? Or played with you on the slide?"

Susie, who held Alice by her right arm, nodded. "Yes, but Paul said you weren't going to do that again. He said now that you'd found your family, you didn't care about us."

"That's not true!" Alice shouted.

"No?" One of the older ghosts, Jason, said. He held Alice by her hair. "Then how come the first chance you got, you ran off to be with them?"

"I hadn't seen my sister in ten years!"

"So that Luis kid helps you to find your sister but not the rest of us? We had parents, brothers, and sisters too! Why are you the special one!" Jason screeched.

"I'm not special! There's nothing different about me from you! Let me go, guys!" Alice struggled. Still they held her firm.

"We aren't letting go!" Jason shouted. "Not until Paul gets back, so you might as well stop trying. We know the truth! You've been keeping us here this whole time because you didn't want to be alone. Paul said we were your prisoners. And now that you have Luis and your sister, you don't need us anymore. Well, guess what? We don't need you now. Paul will help us now. He'll help us all get revenge."

Alice fell silent. Her heart was broken. She started sobbing. She'd lost the will to fight anymore. Only now, slowly, did the other children loosen their hold on her. She collapsed to the ground and buried her face in her arms. She wept; the ground beneath her eyes would be soaked if only she had tears to cry.

An apartment building on the far side of town, the sign out front read Pleasant Hill apartments. Paul hovered in the air right above it. He glared down at the mass of steel, glass, and concrete. This used to be his home, back when he was alive. His mother, father, and brother still lived here in apartment number 316. They would be the first on his list.

He descended to the third floor and walked up to number 316. The sounds of a TV emanated from behind that door. He phased through it and stepped into the living room. His family sat on the couch and stared at the flickering images, which danced across the TV screen. Even if they could see him, they would not have noticed his entrance. It was so typical of them.

Paul moved around the apartment freely. He let himself into his brother Damian's room and looked around a bit. A messy floor covered in a layer of dirty clothes was the first thing that caught his eye, followed closely by the posters of nude women across the walls. Neither of those interested Paul, his main priority was the cell phone that rested on the nightstand next to his brother's bed.

A devious, sadistic grin slithered its way across Paul's lips. He took the cell phone and made his way back to the kitchen. The blender rested on the counter, its cord was plugged into the wall outlet. Good. Just what he wanted. He dropped the phone into the blender, making sure it fell between the blades, and then set the blender on its highest setting, but he didn't turn it on. Not yet.

Paul moved over to the house phone mounted on the kitchen wall, dialed Damian's cell number, and then set the house phone on the counter. In the blender, the cell phone started to buzz. Its stupid rap song ringtone blared throughout the house. In the other room, Paul heard his brother jump off the couch and run into the kitchen. Paul stood right next to the ringing cell phone, knowing full well he was invisible.

"What is this thing doing in the blender?" Damian walked right over to his phone and reached in to grab it, as Paul knew he would. Just as his fingers touched the buzzing phone, Paul hit the power button.

The sharp stainless-steel blades spun blindingly fast. They shredded the plastic and silicone phone almost instantly. At the same time, the spinning blades slashed into his elder brother's fingertips. They tore chunks of flesh away, blood splattered all over the clear plastic pitcher. Damian screamed out in agonizing pain. He tried to pull his hand away, but Paul grabbed him by the arm and forced it back in as hard as he could.

Damian's screams alerted the parents still in the living room. They raced into the kitchen and found their son fighting with a blender and losing. The machine ground and stalled as it tried to cut through bone. The father grabbed the power cord and ripped it from the wall. The blender lost power, and the blades stopped spinning. Paul released his hold on Damian, allowing his parents to pull the blood soaked kitchen appliance from his brother's stump.

Bright red spurts of blood erupted from the mess of shredded flesh and bone that used to be his older brother's hand. Damian screamed soundlessly, he was in too much pain to utter any noise. The same sadistic grin came to Paul's face, along with eyes wide with excitement. He was enjoying himself. So much red now covered the floor, coated the countertops and walls. The sight of his older brother in such horrific pain excited him.

His father ran to the wall-mounted phone and tried to call for an ambulance. Before he could touch the first number, Paul tore the cord from the wall. He pulled it with such force that the phone jack ripped out of place along with chunks of drywall. Paul loved seeing his father's terrified face as he stared at the dangling phone jack in silence. From his point of view, it had just been ripped out by nothing.

Paul lifted his hands before him, like a priest about to address a congregation, and all the cabinet and cupboard doors swung open. One cupboard slammed so hard it snapped off its hinges and sailed though the air before imbedding in the far wall.

One small flick of his finger and Paul caused a plate to spin like a Frisbee off the shelf to shatter against a wall. His mother screamed when it did. More plates, bowls, and dishes shook in the cabinets before being launched around the small kitchen. His family ducked and covered their heads as much as they could to avoid the flying dining ware. China and porcelain shattered against the walls and floor, turning into piles of jagged shrapnel. Paul gained control of this and sent it through the air as well. Chunks of it dug into his family's skin and drew blood.

This was fun and everything, but Paul felt he needed to up his game. The silverware drawer slid open with forks and knives floating in the air. Paul sent them careening around the kitchen, flying in random patters through the air. The steak knives tore into his father's flesh, eliciting screams of agony before Paul took direct control of one and stabbed it in the man's back.

His mother and brother watched as the knife plunged into his father's back over and over, splashes of blood sprayed up with each thrust. Once Paul felt satisfied with this, he released the knife and let the old man fall to the ground, blood staining the floor.

Paul looked at the horrified faces of his mother and Damian, the shock and terror in their eyes sent a gleeful tingle through him. He noticed they lay crouched on the floor beside the refrigerator, and his twisted mind came to an easy conclusion. He dropped his control of the dishes, which all suddenly fell to the floor. Instead, Paul focused all his power on the fridge. Even as his mother and Damian began to notice how everything stopped, the refrigerator started to tilt. By the time they noticed, it was too late.

Damian, despite the blood loss, was still fast enough to get out of the way. His mother, however, was not so lucky. She got most of the way when the fridge came crashing down on her legs. The sickening sound of snapping bone split the air followed closely by a bloodcurdling scream of agony. To Paul, this was getting better by the second.

Out of the corner of his eye, he noticed something in the living room. Placed on top of the television was an open water bottle. Either his mother or father must have placed it there when they heard Damian scream, and now Paul knew how he could finish with a bang. He left his bleeding and dying family in the kitchen and went to the living room. Paul grabbed the water bottle and poured everything it had over the electrical socket behind the TV. Sparks flew from the outlet. The curtains behind it quickly caught fire.

It was not long before the fire spread across the drapes all the way to the furniture. From there it caught on the carpet. Red and orange flames filled the living room. Soon, it would spread, not just to the rest of the apartment but also to the whole building. As the air became clouded with smoke, the smoke alarms sounded throughout the apartment. Paul felt it was his time to leave. He phased through the door but not before latching the dead bolt.

Paul watched from the far side of the street. Smoke had begun to seep out of the building. It wasn't long before the other tenants came out to investigate. Upon seeing the fire, some ran back into their homes and called the fire department. Others grabbed some of their valuables and fled. It was close to forty-five minutes before the fire trucks showed up. By then the entire third floor was bellowing smoke. A portion of the roof collapsed, and flames erupted up to the sky. Paul watched in silence, the same excited, sadistic, evil grin across his face.

10

L uis lay asleep in bed. His face twitched slightly as he
dreamed. Normally, his dreams were quick snippets
he never remembered after he woke up, but this one
was different. He tossed and turned in his sleep, droplets
of sweat appeared on his forehead. In his dream, he saw
smoke. A building ablaze, smashing plates, the grinding of
a blender. What was the meaning of this?

In the blackness of smoke and dancing flames, Luis saw
a face. Lit by the orange fire, he saw the eyes and the smile.
Red-and-orange light danced across the exposed teeth. The
teeth opened, and a wicked laugh escaped, along with the
terrible screams of people dying.

Luis jolted straight up. His eyes were wide, sweat poured
down his face. His heart hammered in his chest; he gasped
and panted for air. It felt like someone had been trying to
smother him. He placed a hand over his chest and steadied
his breathing. It was all a dream, just a dream.

He turned on the lamp by his bed. With the room illuminated, he put on his glasses, pushed the blankets off, and

stepped out of bed onto the cold floor. Being jolted awake like that made him need to use the bathroom.

As he walked out of his room, he looked out a nearby window. His eyes widened with horror. The horizon glowed red but not with the sunrise. In the distance, he saw a column of smoke, which rose up to the black night sky from a burning building, conceal the stars. Red, orange, and yellow flames shot up into the air. Luis raced to the window and threw it open.

He could smell the smoke now as it burned his nostrils. Sirens blared from the fire trucks and ambulances, and he realized the truth. This was in his dream. But how? It had to be a coincidence, but standing in the hallway and staring at the fire in reality made him doubt that. Somehow, he had envisioned this. That face, hidden in shadows, lit only by flame—was that the reason for this? Was that the person who caused the fire?

Luis felt his legs give out beneath him as slumped down against the wall. He had to tell Serena about this. Jumping to his feet, he raced back his room, grabbed his phone off the charger, and started to dial through the contacts only to stop himself. What time was it? He checked the clock on the phone. It was 2:30 in the morning. Would she even be awake? If not, would she bother to pick up the phone?

He decided to call anyway. Placing the phone to his ear, he heard the dial tone hum three times and then a click on the other line. "Hello?" a groggy voice answered. He was relieved. She answered.

"Serena," Luis said frantically. "It's Luis. Look outside the window."

She groaned on the other line as she sat up. "And what am I looking for?"

"You should see it," Luis said. He heard her floor creak as she stood up. It groaned with each step she took. Her walking stopped, and Luis heard her gasp on the other line. "I told you you'd know."

"Oh, my god! What's on fire?" Serena asked.

"It looks like an apartment building. But that's not the strange part. I was dreaming about it just before I woke up," Luis said. "In my dream, I saw fire and smoke and a creepy person smiling and laughing in the middle of it."

The line was silent for over a minute. Luis almost thought the phone had gone dead until Serena finally answered. "What do you think it means?"

"I think it means you and Alice were right. I think that was some kind of vision. I think somebody set that fire intentionally to kill people," Luis said. "Someone with a grudge."

"Who?" Serena asked.

"I don't know, but we need to find out. If I saw it in a dream and I am some kind of spiritual medium, then I think it was a vengeful spirit that set the fire. And that the spirit wanted someone dead."

"I'll help you figure this out. And we can get Alice to help too. For right now, we need to get some sleep. I'll see you in the morning in the park, okay?"

"Okay." Luis hung up the phone and placed it back on the charger.

A vengeful spirit. Someone with a grudge. Who? He did not know very many ghosts, and even then, he couldn't be sure it was or was not any of them. But he wouldn't be able to figure out anything if he was sleep deprived.

After remembering he had to use the bathroom, Luis relieved himself and went back to his bed. He took off his glasses and turned the light off, flooding the room in darkness.

Tuesday, October 28

Luis waited at the entrance to the park; the eastern sky was burned orange with the rising sun. The smoke in the air from last night's fire only added to the creepiness. Frost covered the ground and the fallen leaves. With each breath, a small steam cloud formed before his face; the cold chill of October had finally arrived. He checked the time readout on his phone again—7:25 a.m.—then slipped it back into the pocket of his jacket. He tugged on the strap of his backpack as it dug uncomfortably into his shoulder; he held a folded newspaper under his left arm. He'd been standing out here for at least twenty minutes, waiting for Serena to show up. He said he'd meet her in the morning at the park, so where was she?

Off in the distant fog, a pair of lights grew bright as they approached. Luis cleaned off his glasses and squinted into the mist. As the lights neared, a car drifted out from the mist and parked in the small dirt parking lot. It was an old car, a drab-gray two-door Honda with a hatchback and flip-up headlights. As the car came to a stop, the engine shut off, the lights folded down, and the driver's door opened. Luis found himself smiling as the person stepped out. It was Serena. She wore a large black coat over her normal attire. She emerged from the fog and yawned, waving halfheartedly. "Morning."

"Good morning. Took you a little while to get here." Luis waved back. He eyed the Honda curiously. "You have a car?" Luis asked.

"Dad bought it second hand so I could practice with it. He doesn't really like me driving it to school and such, but I figured today I needed to save time getting here," she said. An eyebrow arched as she registered what he'd said. "Took a while? It's 7:30 in the morning. I normally don't get up this early, even on a school day. Besides that, you woke me up in the middle of the night." Serena rubbed the sleep from her eyes.

"I remember." Luis handed her the newspaper. "It made the front page already. Only happened last night, but I guess news travels fast."

Serena took the paper and started to read.

Devastating Fire: Three Confirmed Dead

At approximately 12:30 last night, tragedy struck at the Pleasant Hill apartment complex. This complex, which consisted of almost fifty families of low-income households, caught fire and burned until nearly three o'clock this morning. Fortunately, most of the tenants were able to escape the burning building. The fire apparently started in apartment 316 and is thought to have been caused by a faulty electrical socket. The family living in apartment 316, sadly, did not escape the fire. Nathan Jameson, his wife Madeline, and eldest son Damian all perished.

The article went on. Serena folded the paper and handed it back to Luis. "Yes, it's sad. Is there anything else that you've been able to bring up? Otherwise, I might as well have stayed home."

"It has to do with that family," Luis said. "I thought their names sounded familiar, and that's because they did. I remember hearing a news story a few months back in July about a kid who went missing. A ten-year-old kid named Paul Jameson. I looked up the old newspaper article and found that he was indeed their child."

"Huh." Serena's brows scrunched together. She stood quietly in thought. "So first, the youngest child disappears, and then the family dies in a fire a few months later. Seems too strange to be coincidence," she said. "And then that dream you said you had."

"Yes, the dream." Luis tucked the newspaper back under his arm. "In the dream, I saw fire and smoke. Something was burning. And I also saw a face appear from the blackness. A face lit by the fire. I just saw the outlines of a smile and the eyes. It looked evil. Like the devil himself was coming out of hell. Then I heard him laughing." Luis shuttered in the cold. "That's when I woke up, saw the fire outside, and called you."

Serena's face again turned to a look of one deep in thought. He placed her finger against her chin. "Do you think this is some sort of warning?"

"Warning of what?" Luis asked.

"We did put forward the idea that you had a gift. You can see spirits naturally. I only could after exposure to you, the same thing with Butch. I think you are a medium of sorts. I don't think your dream happening on the same night, at nearly the same time as the real life fire, is by accident," Serena said.

"But what kind of connection could they have? Was the dream supposed to warn me against it? But why would that matter? I was nowhere close to it. I was in no real danger."

"You said you saw a face," Serena said. "A face in the darkness that laughed."

"Yes?"

"Maybe the fire was started by someone or something. Did the cops ever figure out what happened to Paul, the youngest son?" Serena asked.

Luis shook his head. "No, he's still considered a missing person."

"I think that would be a good place to start." A thought occurred to Serena. "Maybe," she said, "if we can get to the burned building, and if you really can see spirits naturally, then we might be able to find the ghosts of this family."

"The place is probably blocked off by police while they're investigating, though," Luis said.

"Then we should bring Alice along. She can get in past the police lines and see if she can find anyone." Serena started to walk into the park. "Come on then. Let's get her."

"You mean right now? We have to be at school soon," Luis said.

"Oh, come on. Haven't you ever played hooky? You can afford to miss one day, this is much more interesting." Serena called over her shoulder and kept walking.

Luis sighed. He'd never skipped a day of school in his life. He never wanted too. He always got good grades, never dropped below a B minus. He'd always been the good student and the teacher's pet in class. A first time for everything, he guessed. Luis jogged down the road after Serena.

A low white fog crept through the playground. The mist clung to every surface. The swings slowly swayed back and forth in a motionless wind. Alice sat upon one of them; her head hung low, arms draped over her knees. She sat motionless except for the steady rhythm back and forth of the swing.

The sound of footsteps walking along the path, dirt and pebbles crunched beneath them, reached her. Her head jolted up in surprise. She saw the figures in the mist, a pair of shadows slowly growing larger and darker as they moved closer. As they emerged, they revealed themselves Serena and Luis. Alice felt a surge of happiness. Never before had she been so glad to see any two people.

But just as she did, she heard Paul's voice behind her. "Remember what I said," he whispered. "I won't kill them, but I can make them wish they were dead. And bring them close enough to it that it won't matter." He then faded away into the mist. She watched him with fear as he disappeared over her shoulder. She could never remember a time when she was more afraid of a single person.

"Alice!" Luis called out.

His voice snapped Alice back to reality. She walked out of the playground and met them on the path. "Good morning, guys." She smiled sweetly. "You both look cold, all bundled up as you are in those coats."

"It is the middle of October. Fall is finally starting to show itself," Serena said. She smiled and stretched her arms out. "My favorite time of the year."

"Really? You never told me that," Alice said. "So you guys off to school again? I liked it so much yesterday, I think I'll go with you again today." She began to float down the path toward the school but stopped when she noticed they weren't following. "What are you guys waiting for?"

"Actually, Alice," Luis steered the conversation back, "we weren't going to school today. We need your help with something else."

"Okay then. Let's go." She started floating back down the path in the direction Luis and Serena had come from.

Serena and Luis looked at each other in confusion. "Hey," Serena called after her sister, "don't you even want to know what it is?"

"It's okay. You can tell me on the way." Alice spun around in the air to face them before turning back and floating away.

Serena jogged after her sister until they walked side by side. Luis followed shortly after, the newspaper still folded under his right arm. The three of them walked together out of the park. The sun continued to rise, burning away the mist. The air became warmer. Once they were out of the park and back in the parking lot, Alice spoke up, "So what's the adventure today?"

Luis took out the newspaper. He held it up in front of her. "This happened last night." Alice quickly skimmed over the article, and her face turned paler than the usual. "At the same time, I had this dream last night. I think we should go there and see if we can talk to the people who died there."

"And what if they don't want to talk?" Alice said. She surprised herself with how fast she spoke. The confused looks on Luis's and Serena's faces showed they had also been caught off guard. "I mean," she slowed down, "since they died just yesterday, their spirits might not even be active yet."

Serena crossed her arms. "I sincerely doubt it. So soon after such a violent death, they would likely be up and about wondering what the hell happened."

"Hey! Who is the ghost here?" Alice said forcefully. "I'm the ghost, not you! I know about this sort of thing!"

Serena stood dumbfounded, her eyes wide with surprise. "Alice?" Serena's tone was worried. "Is something wrong?"

Alice looked away in sadness, her arms wrapped around her center. Her eyes fixed on the ground. "I'm sorry, Cindy," she said. "Yes, something is wrong, but I can't tell you about it now. It's too soon."

"Too soon?" Serena leaned down and looked Alice in the eye. "Alice, please don't keep secrets from me. I'm your sister. I've been without you for years. I don't want to lose you again."

A sad smile came over Alice's face. "I won't leave you." She embraced Serena with both arms and held her close. "I'm not going to abandon you, and I don't want to lose you ever again." Her voice cracked as she spoke. "And I will tell you what's going on, just not yet."

They separated, and Serena nodded. "Okay. I trust you."

"Thanks, sissy." Alice wiped a tear from her eye. "Okay then. Where is this place we're going?"

Luis glanced over the paper again. "The Pleasant Hill apartments. I know where that is."

11

Luis and Serena stood outside the charred black remains of the burnt-out apartment complex; Alice hovered in the air next to them. The top floor and a half had caved in. A police barrier had been placed around the building, along with three squad cars and a fire truck. The three of them weren't the only people here this morning; a small crowd of onlookers had arrived to gape at the devastation. A few had taken out their phones and snapped pictures.

They stood at the back of the crowd. Alice hovered in the air, her legs cross and hands grasping her ankles. "Well, guys and gals, I don't know what you expect to do here. There's no way you can get through to the building," she said.

"I know," Luis said. "But you can."

"Huh?"

"No one else here can see you. You can just float over everyone, go inside, and scope the place out for lost spirits," Luis explained.

Alice stared at Luis and tilted her head in confusion. "Is this why you wanted to bring me along?"

"I also like spending time with you." Luis folded his arms over his chest. "There are just some things you can do that we can't." He held his hand out to the burnt building. "So if you could, please?"

Alice sighed with exasperation, "Fine." She ascended in the air above the crowd. She held her arms out to the side as if flying.

As a little girl, she always wished she could fly, to spread her arms like a bird's wings and take off to the sky. Even now, without a physical body, she still felt the exhilaration of flight. She flew in circles through the air, giggling all the while. Nothing was quite as fun as just flying.

She floated down to the top of the crumbling structure. The roof had collapsed and caved in though the floor, most of the walls had toppled over and only a few burnt support beams still stood. Everything was charred black, covered in soot and ash, whatever wasn't already ash. Alice moved around the top floor. She scanned back and forth, trying to catch any movement if it came. "Hello?" she called out. "Is anyone up here?"

No reply came.

"This used to be your home, didn't it?" Alice kept calling out. "Are you still here? Is this still your home?" She looked around and still found nothing—no sound, no movement. Alice sighed, "Maybe they passed on." She shrugged.

"Hello?" a teenage boy's voice replied. Alice stopped in her tracks. She shifted her eyes to her left and saw the boy standing behind a fallen charred beam. He remained hidden as best, his legs curled up and chin resting on his knees.

Alice stepped around the beam. She gazed down at the boy. He was older than she was, about seventeen or eighteen. His hair was a dirty blond, and his clothes looked singed. He looked up at her with hopeful eyes. "Hi." Alice held out her hand to him. "My name's Alice. And you are?"

Slowly, hesitantly, he shook her hand. "Damian. Thank God, you're here. You're the first person to find me. I've seen firefighters and cops come up here, but none of them saw me. They all just walked by."

"Anything's okay now. I'm here to help." She took a deep breath. "Let's start at the top. How long have you been up here?"

"You mean like how long have I lived here? A few years," Damian said.

"Not quite what I meant." Alice sat down next to him and crossed her legs. "What do you last remember?"

"Well, let's see." Damian's eyes focused on the floor. "Last night, I was watching TV with my folks. I heard my phone ring in the kitchen, and I went to get it. For some reason, it was sitting in the blender. I tried to get it out and then—" He stopped, and a confused look came over his face. He held up both hands in front of his face. "My hand," he said. "The blender turned on, and my hand got caught in it. So why does it look okay now?"

"I can explain in a minute, just tell me what happened after that," Alice said.

"Well, my parents came in, turned the thing off. I was bleeding a lot, and I started getting faint. I think the plates started flying everywhere and the fridge fell over. Then the place caught fire, and I passed out. After that, I woke up here. I've been trying to get someone's attention so they could come save me, but no one found me until you," Damian explained.

Alice nodded. She knew what she had to do now, and she wasn't looking forward to it. It was never fun breaking the bad news to someone. "Okay, Damian, I have to tell you something."

"What?"

"In that fire last night, you didn't just pass out." She paused for a second to get her words right. "Truth be told, you didn't survive. You died in the fire."

Damian stared at her, his eyes wide in shock. All his strength flowed away. "I, what?" He managed to force the words out. "I'm dead?"

"To put it bluntly, yes," Alice said.

"How can I be dead?" His voice shuttered.

"I know it's a lot to take in all at once, but you'll see in time."

"How do you know?" Damian shouted suddenly. He jolted to his feet. "How do you know I'm dead? What would that make me then? A ghost or something?" he chuckled. "I don't think so."

Alice rolled her eyes. She stood up and crossed her arms. "Then tell me, how did you get your hand sliced up in a blender last night and have it perfectly whole this morning?"

Damian scoffed. "Yeah, and what are you? Some kind of experts on ghosts?" Damian swung his arms around in over dramatic arcs. Alice had seen this kind of behavior before. Most newly dead spirits go through a stage of denial.

"I do have some experience. I've been one for ten years," she said in a matter-of-fact tone.

"Wait, what?"

"I'm a ghost too."

A moment of confusion passed before Damian laughed. He threw back his head and howled into the air with laughter. After nearly a minute, he managed to calm down. "Oh, that's a good one, girl. I haven't had a good laugh in weeks."

Alice pursed her lips and looked out the upper corner of her eye. "Fine, you want me to prove it? I will." She walked over to the burnt but still standing support beam and phased through it. She stepped back and forth through it several more times from multiple directions before facing

Damian again. She once again crossed her arms and jutted her hips. "See?"

Several tense seconds passed where Damian looked shocked and afraid at her while she simply waited. He took a couple steps back and held his arms out in front. "Okay, creepy ghost chick. I'll just leave you to yourself. You don't have to haunt me or anything. I'll just be going now."

"Oh, just accept it. You're dead too. You are a ghost, the same as me. Get used to it because it's not going to change anytime soon." She picked up a chunk of blackened wood. "And if you don't believe me, then just stand there." She threw it at his head, and he instinctively tried to block. But instead of bouncing off his arms as he expected, the burnt wood sailed through him as if he were air.

Visibly shaken, Damian started to hyperventilate. He folded back into the fetal position. "It's true. I really am dead."

"Yes, you are." Alice crouched down next to him and placed her hand on his shoulder. "It's not as terrible as it seems, you'll get used to it."

"I don't want to get used to it! I want to be alive!" he cried.

"That's not something you can do. But I do know some-one who can help. He's down on the sidewalk, and he wants to speak with you, if you'll just come with me." She offered her hand out to him. Once again, with hesitation, he took her outstretched hand. "Okay." Alice smiled reassuringly.

"Just trust me." She lifted off the floor and started to pull him along.

"Wow! Hey, you're flying!" Damian said, amazed.

"I am floating, yes. We're spirits. Normal laws of physics don't really apply to us anymore," she said. "One of the upsides of being dead."

A smile came to Damian's face. He lifted his feet off the ground and found himself floating in midair. "You know, I think I could get used to this."

"I thought this would help," Alice said. "Now let's go meet my friend." The two of them floated, hand in hand together away from the scorched structure and over the crowd of onlookers. Alice saw Luis and Serena watching from below and descended to them. "Hey, guys. I'm back." She motioned to Damian. "This guy's name is Damian. Damian, meet my friend Luis and my little sister Cindy. She goes by Serena now."

"Little sister?" Damian asked. "She looks a little older to me."

"That's what happens when you've been dead for a decade. You don't age, everyone else does," Alice said. "Luis was the one who found me and reunited us after so long. If anyone can help you, it's him."

"Yeah, thanks for the vote of confidence. No pressure or anything," Luis said dryly. "Well, Damian, it's nice to meet you."

"Likewise," Damian replied.

"Firstly, I would like to know what happened here last night. What do you remember before the fire?" Luis asked.

Damian proceeded to retell his story. About his phone, the blender, the flying dishes, the refrigerator, and finally, the apartment filling with smoke before he blacked out. Luis pulled his homework notebook from his backpack and wrote down as much as he could. "It was that time that Alice found me." Damian finished.

"I see," Luis said. "Serena, what do you make of it?"

She shook her head. "Almost a textbook example of an angry spirit. I think you were right, Luis."

Luis nodded. "A vengeful ghost. I'm going to take a wild guess and say nothing like this ever happened before, right?"

"No, nothing like this," Damian replied. *Hmm.* Luis thought. He placed the notebook under his arm with the newspaper. "But what kind of ghost was it? For a ghost to target someone, there's usually a reason. Either some kind of vendetta against the people or a claim on the location. Did this apartment have any sort of history to it? Any bad tenets that you know of?"

Damian shrugged. "Not that I know of. And I don't think I offended any spirits out there."

"There is something else," Serena said. "You had a little brother named Paul, right?"

Damian's face turned sour. He shifted his eyes away and stuffed his hands in his pockets. "Yes."

"And he disappeared some months ago, right?" Serena continued.

"Not disappeared. He was kidnapped. On our way home from a friend's house late at night, some guy in an SUV pulled up and snatched him right off the street. Then drove away like a bat out of hell."

A concerned look came over both Serena's and Luis's faces. Alice was also just as stunned and horrified. "How do you know?" Luis asked.

"Because I was there," Damian said. "I watched him get dragged away right before my eyes." He tensed up; he clenched his fists to his fingers dug into his palms. "I ran after them as fast as I could, but they got away, and I never saw my brother again. It's something I'll never forget."

Serena exchanged looks with Luis. She was stunned, eyes wide with shock and grim realization. "That's what happened to me," she said. "Damian, that happened to me and Alice!"

"What?" His face shot up to meet her eyes. "Are you serious?"

"Yes. I was six when Alice was kidnapped on our way home from school. I never forgot the look of terror on her face as she was dragged away. Sometimes, I still see it in my dreams," Serena said. "I never really got closure for it until after Luis reintroduced us."

Luis ran his index finger over his chin. "I think there's a darker aspect to this. Serena, you and Damian both experienced almost the exact same thing. That seems like too big a coincidence."

Serena, Alice, and Damian all exchanged looks. Each one had a face that reflected a growing suspicion and horror. "Luis, you don't think—"

"Yes. The MO was almost exact. I think the same person kidnapped both Alice and Paul," Luis said.

"But they happened nearly ten years apart," Serena reasoned. "That's a pretty big gap in time for anyone to sit around and wait."

"Who said he waited?" Luis said. He adjusted his glasses. "What if there wasn't a ten year gap between incidents? So far, we only know about Alice and Damian's brother. But what if there were more? What if there's some sort of child serial killer living right here in town? Someone who grabs kids right of the street and does horrible things to them before killing them and disposing the bodies?"

Damian shook his head. "If there is and it has been going on for ten years at least, then how come this person was never caught? Why have no bodies been found? No bones, no clothes—nothing. Ten years is a long time to go around preying on kids and never get found out," he said.

"This is our grave site," Alice whispered the word Paul had told her. She started to draw the connections in her mind. Paul said he was going to get revenge for something. Then a vengeful spirit burns down this apartment complex that very night. The victims of the fire lost a son months earlier, son named Paul. The son they lost and the ghost that killed them were one and the same.

And if they were the same, that would mean she and Paul were killed by the same person. And if they were, then all the other ghost children from the playground are victims of the same killer.

"Alice?" Luis waved his hand in front of her face. She jolted back to attention. "You okay over there? You zoned out for a minute."

She glanced over at Damian and was about to tell him, but she stopped. Now was not the time. "I was just thinking. I'll tell you later." The last thing she wanted to do right now was tell the person she just met that the one who killed him was the younger brother he failed to rescue.

"I think I should do some research," Luis said. "I'll go home and start looking up missing children from this area from the past ten years, see if there's a pattern."

"Um, Luis," Serena said. "Won't your mom be a little concerned about you being home so early from school?"

"She's off at work by now," Luis said. "It won't be a problem."

"And what am I supposed to do now?" Damian asked. "Am I just supposed to float around here forever?"

"That's a good question," Luis said. He turned to Serena. "You said a ghost only stays around if they have some unfinished business, right?"

"Generally," she replied. "But it could also be from a violent death, a strong connection to something, or not realizing they're dead."

"I think we can rule out that last one," Luis said. "I was just thinking that we should help Damian figure out what his unfinished business is to help him to pass on."

"Well, that's very nice of you, but how do you plan to do that?" Damian asked. "I don't even know if I have any 'unfinished business.'" He made quotation marks in the air with his hands. "So how do you expect to help me finish it?"

"We'll figure something out," Luis said.

"That's always a great plan," Serena said dryly.

"If you have a better one, feel free to speak up," Luis remarked. No one else said anything. "Okay then. I'll get started looking that up now."

"I'll go with you. Need to do something while I'm out of the house. Dad would be pretty worked up if I came home early and all," Serena said.

Alice put on her best fake smile. She was still preoccupied with her thoughts. "Damian, I think you should stay here for a while. Your spirit is still attached to this place. Until we can work on changing that, you can't go far from here."

Damian looked back at the charred skeleton of the apartment that used to be his home. "Do I really have to? I'd rather go back with you guys. At least then, I won't be alone."

"Alice is right," Luis said. "She's had the most experience, and Serena is the one here with the most knowledge about the supernatural. The first time Alice tried to leave the playground where her spirit haunts, she started fading away like a washed out picture. I still don't know exactly how she can move around so easily now. The point being, I don't think you can move around much farther than this anyways."

Damian sighed, "Will you at least come back?"

"Of course, we will," Serena chimed in. "We'll be back as soon as we know more or even just to visit."

Damian smiled a sad but still hopeful smile. With Alice's guidance, he floated back to the charred remains of his old apartment. As soon as Alice returned, Luis put his notebook back into his pack and slung it over his shoulders. "Okay, are we ready to go?"

Serena nodded. "Ready when you are."

"Hey, guys," Alice spoke up. "If it's okay with you, I'd like to go with the two of you instead of back to the playground."

Luis and Serena exchanged brief glances of confusion. "Any particular reason?" Luis asked, as he turned to face Alice again.

"Well," she shrugged. "This whole thing is kinda about my murder, right? I think I should be there when any new information pops up. It is relevant to my interests."

"She's right," Serena said. "She needs to be there."

Luis thought about it for a second, and it made sense. "Okay, sure. You can come back with us."

12

A short drive later and the trio arrived at the front door of Luis's house. He unlocked the door and let them inside, closing the door behind them. "If you don't mind," he said, "could the two of you wait down here for a minute? My computer is upstairs in my room, and I want to straighten it up a little before I let you in."

"Why don't you just bring the computer down here?" Serena asked.

"Because it's a desktop," Luis said, his tone dry and plain. He responded as if it was the dumbest question in the world.

"What is this, the nineties? Who still buys desktops? Seriously?" Serena scoffed.

Luis was halfway up the stairs when he shouted back, "People who use their computer for gaming, that's who!" His bedroom door opened and shut, leaving Serena and Alice down in the living room.

Serena could still hear Luis moving around in his room. The floor squeaked with each step he took. Serena tilted her head over at her sister, giving her a sly grin. But Alice didn't return Serena's glance. Instead, the ghost girl stared the floor with her hand held over her lips. She looked nervous, but more than that, she was afraid. This did not escape Serena's attention. "Alice," she asked, "are you okay?"

Alice did not move to face her sister. Instead, she only shook her head slowly from side to side. "What's going on? You've been acting strange all morning. Do you need to tell me something?"

"Once we get in Luis's room, I'll tell you," Alice said, swift and to the point.

It was about this time Luis came back down the stairs. "Okay, you can come up now," he said, motioning up the stairs with his thumb.

"What were you doing up there? Hiding dirty magazines?" Serena said. She gave another sly grin.

"I was not!" Luis shouted, louder than he'd expected to. "I was just straightening things up. I didn't want you to see the mess I live in. Would you like it if I just walked into your room without giving you a chance to put things away?"

The ever-present smile beamed from Serena's face. "What kind of things?"

"The kind you don't want other people to see!" Luis's face turned bright red. "Dirty clothes, old food wrappers, character sheets, any other things like that." He adjusted his glasses. "And besides, why would I need dirty magazines when I can get everything I need off the internet?"

Serena glanced up to the ceiling and nodded in agreement. "This is true." She then followed him up to his room, Alice floating right behind her.

Once inside Luis's room, Serena scanned over the still light amounts of clutter. The wastebasket in the corner was overflowing with clear plastic wrappers and empty Hot Pockets boxes. In another corner sat a dirty clothes hamper with a pants' leg spilling out. As she looked over the floor, she quickly noticed that even if he picked up all the large trash, the carpet was still in serious need of a vacuum. "A typical boy's room."

Luis waved his hand dismissively. "Yeah, yeah, I know. I still need to work on it." He pulled the chair out from in front of his computer desk and sat down. "Now we can get to work on the more important things right now."

Alice couldn't hold herself back anymore. "I know how many kids were killed!" she shouted louder than she intended. It startled Luis and Serena so much they jumped a foot back.

They stared at her, shocked, confused, and more than a little startled. After taking a minute to collect himself, Luis cleared his throat. "Okay, Alice, let's start at the top. You know how many kids were killed?" Alice reined herself in after that. She closed her eyes and took a deep breath to calm her nerves. "The kids at the playground, all the other spirit children. I never understood why all of us were there, but now I know. I and every other ghost there were the victims of this child murderer."

"How do you know?" Luis asked.

"Because of something else that's happened," Alice said. She held her hand clasped together at her waist. Her eyes fixed on the floor, with a look of sadness and fear. "Luis, you were right about me and Paul. We were both taken by the same person."

"You were?" Luis leapt up from his chair. "Why didn't you tell us earlier? When we were still with Damian?"

"Because—" There was a pause in her statement. She took several deep breaths to try to focus herself. She needed to get this out. "I think Paul is the reason Damian is a ghost now. I think Paul killed him and their parents."

Luis and Serena stood in shock. Their mouths fell open. "You think Paul was the vengeful spirit?" Serena asked.

"Yes," Alice said. "Paul showed up at the playground two weeks ago. He was always more distant from the rest of the group up until just the other day. I've caught him doing things—trying to lift rocks with just his thoughts, move stuff around."

"And why do you think he did this?" Luis asked.

"The other day, the day I went to school with you, I came back to the park, and he'd somehow turned the other kids against me." Alice had trouble controlling herself. Her voice cracked a little as she spoke. She pulled her legs up so that her chin rested on her knees and her arms wrapped around her shins. "They grabbed me, held my arms back, and forced me to the ground. He said he was going to get revenge on someone. He mentioned his parents and a brother. Then today, you showed up with the newspaper about the fire, and Damian said he used to have a brother named Paul who was kidnapped just as I was. The similarities are too close."

Luis heard everything she said. Steadily, it all began to seep in. He slumped over in his chair, his arms rested over his knees. He let out a deep sigh. "Alice, this is...this is some serious stuff."

"And there's more," Alice said. Tears would have streamed down her face if she could still cry. "He threatened you guys too."

Both Luis and Serena froze. Aside from the hum of the computer, the room was filled with dead silence. Serena was the first to talk. "Alice, what did he say? Did he want to kill us?"

"He just said," Alice buried her face in her knees, "he'd make you wish for death before he was done." Her face twisted into a look of pure terror and sadness. "He convinced the other kids that you two stole me from them and that the best way to get me back was to get rid of you. I don't want to see either of you get hurt!" She all but sobbed. Her voice cracked and strained.

With breakneck speed, Serena grabbed hold of her sister and embraced her. They held each other as tightly as possible. Even knowing Alice would become intangible at any moment didn't dissuade Serena from it. They shared no words, just emotions. Eventually, they pulled away from each other. As they did, Serena planted a small kiss on Alice's forehead.

Alice let out a small laugh. "Funny, I remember doing that to you," she said as she rubbed her eye.

"Yes, you did." Serena smiled.

Luis spoke up again, "This is very bad. I never expected to get on a ghost's hit list. What can we do about this? Is there any way to make him see we aren't a threat?"

"I don't think so." Alice floated over to the bed and crossed her legs. Serena sat down next to her. "He seems to be reveling in his new abilities. And I don't know how far he'll go."

"I think we do know how far," Serena said. "If he's willing to kill his own family—rather graphically, I might add—then we know he has no problem with violently trying to kill us. What we need is some way to keep him away from us."

Luis crossed his legs and readjusted his glasses. "Did you have something in mind?"

The bedsprings creaked as Serena stood up. "Not so much something as someone. There is this lady in town I know.

She's supposed to be a psychic and a spiritual medium." Serena tilted her head to the side and glanced up at the ceiling. An ironic smile formed over her lips. "I never put much thought into those claims, but I bought some of my room decor from her. We can probably talk to her and see if she has anything that can ward off evil spirits or the like."

Luis and Alice exchanged looks. He shrugged and placed his hands over his knees to stand up. "Makes about as much sense as anything else we've done. Can we see her today?"

"She does take walk-ins," Serena said. She chuckled a little as she walked to the door. "Actually, she only takes walk-ins. She says 'I was expecting you' every time someone walks through her door."

"I guess that's just part of her shtick." Luis followed her out the door, Alice floating behind them. "So where is this place?"

13

Feeling his glasses slip down his nose, Luis pushed them back up with a gesture so automatic he hardly recognized doing it. "This is the place, huh?"

"Yup." Serena stuffed her hands in her coat pockets, and she leaned casually to one side, all her weight supported on her right foot. "Madam Morgana's Psychic Readings and Predictions. Just rolls off the tongue, don't it?"

Luis scrapped his foot on the sidewalk and scratched the back of his head. "If you say so." They stood silently on the sidewalk staring at the sign hanging over the door. Luis had to admit to himself, this was more than a little awkward for him. Seriously, going to see a psychic? He doesn't do that sort of thing. He's a rational human being, preferring logic and truth to such ludicrous things as psychics and the supernatural.

Except, of course, for the fact that he was now friends with a ghost and her Goth sister. He sighed, mustered up his courage, and marched up to the door. Raising his fist to the door, he was about to knock before he paused.

"Do we really have to do this?" he asked, looking over his shoulder.

Serena's arms folded across her chest. "No, we don't. You can just go back home, never mind that there is an angry poltergeist that has you on the top of his to kill list."

"Good point," Luis replied. Still his hand hovered inches away from the door, unwilling to knock.

"Oh, for crying out loud." Serena rolled her eyes with frustration. She came up behind Luis, grabbed him by the shoulder, and pushed him aside. "It's not this difficult." She grabbed the doorknob and twisted. "You just turn the knob and walk in." She shoved the door open in a huff.

The smell of incense wafted. Inside, the only light came from dozens of small burning candles, which cast dancing shadows upon the walls. Rolls of different colored lace and cloth hung from the ceiling, and many ornaments and trinkets adorned the shelves and tables, small statues of skulls, dragons, and fairies. A small round table with a purple tablecloth draped over it stood in the center of the room with a small glass sphere resting in the center.

"Yeah," Luis said with a strong sarcastic tone. "This certainly looks promising." He winced when Serena jabbed her elbow into his ribs.

A rustling of beads alerted them to a woman entering the room. She was an older woman, skinny and frail looking, wearing a long dress of green and purple fabrics layered over top each other. A scarf was wrapped around her fore-head and tied in the back, a small metal coin hung down from the middle between her eyebrows. Large looped ear-rings hung from each earlobe, and a jewel-encrusted ring adorned the third finger of each hand. "I was wondering when you'd come in. You're lucky patience is one of my best virtues. Please close the door behind you."

Serena slowly latched the door back as soon as she and Luis stepped inside. Alice phased through the wall behind them. Luis could already feel the heat rising on the nape of his neck. He wasn't very comfortable here. "Hello, Madam Morgana," Serena said. "I brought a friend with me today."

"I can see that. It's been a little while. I'm glad to see you again, Serena. And what is your friend's name?" Madam Morgana asked.

Serena placed her hand roughly on Luis's shoulder, almost knocking his glasses off. "This is Luis."

"Yes, I see," the psychic responded. Her gaze shifted to the wall behind Serena and Luis; she tilted her head quiz-zically. "And your other friend?"

Serena and Luis paused, confused and more than a little shocked. They exchanged glanced, looked over their shoul-ders at an equally surprised Alice, and turned back to the fortune-teller.

"Are you telling me you didn't notice she was there?" Madam Morgana asked.

After a few moments of silence, Serena finally spoke, "No, we know. We just didn't think anyone else could see her right now."

The corners of her lips perked up a little. "I see. You didn't believe I could see anything related to the supernatural, did you? It's not uncommon. Many people don't take me very seriously."

"How can you expect them to?" Luis muttered under his breath. "This place looks like something straight out of some B-rated horror movie. Ack!" He winced again when Serena elbowed him more roughly in the ribs.

"This," Morgana moved her hands over the room in great sweeping arcs, "is mostly to set the mood. People expect a certain kind of atmosphere. But make no mistake—my gifts are real. As real as yours are, boy." Morgana pulled a chair up to her small center table and sat down, her legs crossed and hands folded over her knees.

Luis stepped forward. "Then maybe you can answer a few things for me."

"Such as?" the psychic asked.

"When we first met, Alice could only appear at dawn and dusk and eve then only for a few hours at a time. Now she can appear at any time of day or night. Why?"

Madam Morgana placed the tip of her long boney finger to her chin. "I think I know where you're going with this question, and I'm sure any others you have will be in the same vein. You're probably also wondering how she was able to leave her haunting grounds instead of being bound to them, am I right?"

Luis's eyebrow arched. "Yes, how did you?"

"I am psychic," Madam Morgana said. "The answers are twofold. The first if your influence on her, and hers on you."

"What do you mean?" Luis asked.

"The contact between you two has given her more freedom. The old limitations of a spirit bound to the material world have weakened, and she can now move more freely," Morgana explained. "This is part of how she can now appear in the middle of the day and follow you around instead of being trapped to a time and place."

"Part of?" Luis asked, adjusting his glasses again. "You said it was twofold. What is the other reason?"

"I'd think it was rather obvious. The time of year. We're in the third week of October. Halloween is almost here."

"Hm?" Serena spoke up, "I like Halloween as much as the next person, but what does that have to do with it? I thought it was just some holiday."

"Now, Serena, I'm sure you know about the origins of Halloween. The ancient Celts believed that the last day of October was the night when the dead would return from the grave as ghosts. This night is about halfway between the fall equinox and the winter solstice, as such it has a strong connection to dying and death.

"The Celtic people weren't wrong. The worlds do overlap more strongly on that night then on any other, so ghosts are more powerful during Halloween then at any other time of year. And the closer we get to it, the stronger their presence becomes.

"But I'm guessing the real reason you're here doesn't have to do with a history lesson." She rested her chin on the heel of her palm. "Now what is it I can help you with?"

"Well, the thing is"—Serena took a chair herself, straddling it backward and resting her arms on the back—"since you can already see Alice, there's no need for pretense. We have an angry ghost after us."

"You don't mean this sweet thing, do you?" Madam Morgana motioned to Alice, who hovered over their heads. "I can sense her from here. This lonely soul wouldn't harm a fly."

Luis pulled up a chair to the table now, seating himself on it appropriately. "No, she's fine. It's one of her. Let's just call him an acquaintance of hers."

"It's kind of a long story. We just need something that can help ward off evil spirits. Do you have anything like that?" Serena asked.

Madam Morgana sighed. She stood up, stretching out her legs a little, her bones popped as she did. "Most of the time, when people come to me asking for wards of charms, there is nothing spiritual or supernatural ailing them. I have a small number of items on hand to sell those kinds of people, which do nothing except in the psychological sense. A placebo effect, so to speak." She walked through her beaded curtains, which clinked and clattered against themselves as she did, and stepped into the next room. "That being said, I do in fact have a few real charms and talismans." She came back holding two necklaces, one in each hand. They each had a large stone dangling from them, dark green in color covered in rust-colored spots. "These are bloodstone pendants, which have special properties to ward off dangerous spirits. They are the strongest charms I have in my store, and they also aren't cheap."

Luis rolled his eyes. Of course, she was just going to drag them in and convince them they needed to buy some of her useless junk. Well, he wasn't going to fall for it. He was on his feet and almost to the door when Morgana called him back. "I am willing to give you them for free, but you have to answer a few questions I have."

With a heavy sigh, Luis sauntered back across the room and sat back down at the table. He propped his head up on his right hand.

Madam Morgana placed the necklaces down in front of her and laced her fingers together. "Now you said your name was Luis, correct?"

Luis nodded.

"I have a little curiosity. One medium to another—when did your gifts first manifest?" Morgana asked.

"Well, the first time I experience anything of a supernatural nature was when I met her." He tilted his head over to Alice. "I saw her at the playground about a week ago."

"Hm," Madam Morgana said. "Only a week? That's interesting. And what was the incident that gave you these gifts?"

"Huh? What do you mean?" Luis asked.

"You know. The incident. Very few people are born with the ability to see ghosts and spirits. Usually, it's because of something that happened to them, such as a close brush with death or having witnessed a death.

"For example, when I was a little girl, I took my four-year-old brother down to the river to go swimming. We were splashing around and having a good time, up until the moment when he jumped head first into a shallow area and hit his head."

She paused, her eyes fixed on the table in front of her. Nearly a minute passed in silence. "I'm sorry. Bringing this up always gets to me a little." She cleared her throat. "Anyways, he hit his head and was knocked out instantly. By the time I brought him back up, it was already too late. My little brother died in my arms that day. I was only seven years old."

Luis and Serena sat together in stunned silence. Neither one knew what, if anything, they could say in response. For her sake, Alice continued to hover in the air, looking down at this woman with a heavy heart and sorrowful eyes. Finally, Madam Morgana dried her eyes. "It was afterward I started to notice things, spirits, and things of that nature. In fact, the first ghost I ever saw and talked to was my little brother. I helped him cross over and also received some closure." She leaned forward on her arms. "So now that I've told you how it happened for me, it is your turn to do the same."

Luis gave an exasperated sigh. He ran his fingers through his hair. "I still don't know what to tell you. I can't remember any sort of traumatic or near death experience that could have done this."

The psychic rested her head on the heel of her left palm; her right arm fell to the table, which she started tapping with her long-painted fingernails. She shrugged with disappointment. "Well, I suppose there is another way." She placed her free hand on the crystal ball resting in the middle of the table.

A look of annoyance came over Luis's face. His lips pressed together, and he raised a single eyebrow. "You can't be serious."

"It is the condition if you want these necklaces for free. If not, then they cost $50 a piece." Madam Morgana smiled.

"Fifty bucks for a necklace? That's highway robbery!" Luis's voice rose a little higher than he wanted it to.

"No need to raise your voice." Both of Morgana's hands lifted up in a defensive posture. "Just let me do a little psychic reading, and you can have the necklaces for free. What do you have to lose?"

"My dignity," Luis said with a dry tone. Serena quickly jabbed Luis in the shoulder, causing him to wince. "Ouch!" He rubbed the sour spot on his arm and looked over at her angrily. "What was that for?"

"Stop acting like a bratty little twerp," Serena said, picking up one of the necklaces. "She offered to give these to us for free, and all you have to do is let her read your fortune. Suck it up, and just do it already." She placed the pendant back on the table.

With his lips pressed out and brows scrunched, Luis scooted his chair in closer and rested his elbows on the table. "All right, fine. Let's just get this over with."

"Good." Madam Morgana brought an incense burner and a few small candles to the table and lit them. The whiffs of smoke drifted through the air, filling the room. The psychic held her hands over the crystal ball. Her slender boney fingers moved with elegant grace back and forth over it. Inside the ball, a cloud of purple smoke began to form. It swirled and twisted, folding on over itself again and again. "Ah, the first step has been taken. The image is forming. Now let us watch to see what happens."

14

A car drove late at night. The windshield wipers slid back and forth, wiping the water away only for more to take its place. Rain plummeted from the black clouds overhead and collected in puddles on the road here on this late September night. The car, an older model red Ford Focus, moved slowly and deliberately down this road. Inside sat a young boy playing with his new hand-held games and his father in the driver's seat next to him.

"Did you have a fun time at your party?" the father asked.

"Yeah." The boy barely turned any attention from his game. The screen danced with lights and graphics, as his thumbs move across the D-pad and buttons. The game chirped when he gets a power-up.

"Luis," his father said, "how about you turn that off and wait 'til we get home?"

"But, Dad," Luis whined, "I need to finish this level and get to the checkpoint so I can get my score bonus before I can save the game and achieve my new high score and—"

"Luis, don't talk back right now." Dad cut him off. "I know you're excited, but I need to see where I'm going. I can't see very well with that light in my eyes."

"I can turn the brightness down." Luis proceed to do just that, and the screen dimmed.

His father gave in. "All right then. Just don't turn it any brighter, okay?"

"Okay, Daddy." The young boy's attention fixated once again on the game.

"What are you going to tell your mom when we get home?" Dad asked.

"Um"—the little boy adjusted his glasses—"thank you."

"Thank you for?"

"For getting the video game that I wanted for my birthday?"

"Good. Yes, you need to tell her that." The father took his eyes off the road for only a brief moment and ruffled the hair on his son's head.

Just as he looked back, another car came around a blind corner, barreling down the wet road toward him—its headlights were bright and blinding in his eyes. He freaked out, foot slammed on the brake pedal, and arms braced against the steering wheel.

The two cars collided with a terrible crash, the metal twisting, grinding, and bending as if it were made of cardboard. The boy jolted forward in his seat, his head hit the dashboard with a dense thud before the seat belt pulled him back into his chair. The father was thrown about the cabin; his chest slammed against the steering wheel, his ribs crack and break.

The father looked out the windshield, now covered with spider web cracks and watched as smoke billows up from the destroyed engines. A woman's body dangled out of the shattered driver's window of the other car, blood slowly dripped down the car door and mixed with the rain. He sees his son on the seat next to him, the boy's glasses were shattered, and blood covered his face.

With great care and also great pain, the father pulled his cell phone from his jeans pocket. He dialed the number and placed the speaker to his ear.

"911, please state your emergency."

"I've just been in an accident." His voice was low and scratchy; he could barely get the words out. "My son and the other driver are really badly hurt."

"Okay, sir. Just stay calm, breathe slowly. Where are you currently?" the operator asked.

"I don't know exactly."

"Don't worry, sir. We can get your position, and the ambulance is already on its way. Just stay on the line."

"I will try." His eyes grew heavy, and his breathing slowed. His chest hurt so bad, he could hardly bring himself to breathe. The phone slipped from his hand and clattered to the floor, his arm hung limp from his shoulder.

The operator called out for him. "Sir, sir, are you still there?"

◇◇◇◇◇◇◇◇◇◇

An olive-skinned woman with long wavy black hair stepped through the sliding doors of the hospital. Her purse was slung over her shoulder, which she gasped tightly with both hands. She stepped up to the front counter. "Excuse me," she said to the receptionist. "Can you tell me which room my son and husband are in?"

"Yes, ma'am." The receptionist pulled up a list of patients. "Can I have their names?"

"Oscar and Luis Chavez."

The receptionist flipped through the pages and scanned the list of names. "I'm sorry, ma'am, but I can't tell you. They are still listed as critical. If you would, please take a seat. I will let you know as soon as their situation changes."

The woman, Maria Chavez, nodded slowly and stepped back to the lobby. She found a chair and sat down, her gaze fixed on the floor and hands wrung the strap of her purse. Her worry was visually evident.

On the wall hung a clock, the red second hand moved around its face. The ticktock echoed through the room, aside from that it was silent. The seconds passed like minutes, the minutes like hours, the hours like days.

After what seemed like an eternity, a doctor came to the lobby. Maria Chavez immediately jumped to her feet. The receptionist stood up and addressed the doctor. "Sir," she said. "Mrs. Chavez is here."

The doctor's eyes met hers. He nodded to the receptionist then approached with a solemn look on his face. "Mrs. Chavez, I am Dr. Wilson."

"My husband and my son—are they all right?" she said without a moment's hesitation.

He motioned back to the chair. "If you would please sit down."

"I don't want to sit down, just tell me if my family is all right!" Her voice trembled.

Dr. Wilson breathed a heavy sigh. "I'm sorry to have to tell you this, ma'am. You husband didn't make it."

Maria gasped, her hands clasped over her mouth. Tears welled up in her eyes and streamed down her face. She collapsed back in her chair, her face held in her hands and wept. After she sobbed, she pulled a tissue from her purse and wiped the tears away. "My son?"

Dr. Wilson sat down next to her, his elbows rested on his knees and hands clasped together. "Mrs. Chavez," he said. "The good news is your son is alive and in stable condition. He's unconscious right now, and I can't let you see him yet. But I promise to do everything I can to help him."

"Dr. Wilson!" A voice rang out as a nurse came bursting through the doors. "The boy has regained consciousness!"

Both Dr. Wilson and Mrs. Chavez jumped to their feet and rushed though the swinging doors. They ran through the hospital until they came to room 315, where the young Luis lay in bed. He wore a neck brace and had plastic tubes going up his nose. A clear plastic bag hung from a metal stand by the bed, dripping a clear fluid into his bloodstream. His eyelids hung slightly open, but open nonetheless.

Luis smiled as his mother walked in the room. "Hi, Mom." His voice was low and raspy. "Dad asked me to say thank you for the present."

His mother darted across the room and clasped his free hand in hers; two dark lines of tears flowed down her cheeks and splashed to the bed. Now, however, her tears were happy. Her son was alive and was going to be all right.

The purple cloud of smoke in the crystal ball shrank and finally dissipated. Madam Morgana pulled her hands away as the vision concluded. "I see," she said solemnly. "That explains the depths of your gifts. As I promised, you can take the bloodstone pendants for free."

Luis stared at the now empty crystal ball. His father and he had been in a car accident? Why didn't he remember it? Granted, he was only five when it happened, but that should be a major part of his life. How come he couldn't remember any of it? Why didn't his mother tell him? Did he honestly never ask? The more the thought about it, he started to remember. "I always thought my dad just walked out on me," he finally said. Slowly, he grabbed the pendants. "Well, Serena," he chuckled, "I guess now we know why."

Serena slammed her hands on the table hard enough to knock the crystal ball off its stand. She stood up so fast, and with enough force, her chair fell over backward and hit the floor with a splintering crack. "You disgusting bastard, how could you?"

Luis, Alice, and Morgana were all taken back by this, recoiling in surprise. "Serena," Luis said tentatively, "what's going on?"

"You dare ask me that?" Her lips pulled into a sneer, mascara bleed down her face from the tears in her eyes. "I trusted you, why didn't you tell me?" She stormed to the door. As she stood in the doorway, just about to leave, she turned back to face Luis once more. "I hate you." Her voice was cracking, as if she was full of pain. She walked out and slammed the door hard enough to shake the room.

Dumbstruck and in shock, Luis could only stare at the door where Serena used to stand. The engine of her car rumbled from outside just before it drove away. "Um," he finally managed to say after several seconds. "What the hell just happened?"

"I've never seen my sister this angry before," Alice said. "What's wrong with her?"

"I'm sorry." Madam Morgana held the crystal ball in her hands. She looked down at it in solemn silence. "I didn't realize it before, but now I do." Slowly, she placed it back on its stand in the middle of the table. "Luis, you and Serena have more history that you think. That car accident didn't just claim your father. The woman in the other car was Luann Thomas, Serena and Alice's mother."

15

The bell for third period rang and echoed throughout the halls of West Point High School. Butch dug through his locker for his history textbook. He recognized it by the picture of a large marble statue on the cover, who the statue was of and why this dude was so important didn't really matter to him. Moreover, if that information was in the book somewhere, he couldn't get it anyways. Words just appeared jumbled to him.

Grabbing his history book, he slammed the locker door shut and began walking to class. His eyes looked down at the floor, and his lips pushed out in a frown. The last couple of days had not been fun for him, what with that ghost girl causing him problems and the creepy chick giving him a pounding, he'd been thoroughly humiliated.

"You don't look so happy today."

Butch's eyes shot open, and he looked around frantically. Other students walked casually around the hallway as if they didn't hear anything. That voice seemed familiar and also threatening. He couldn't quite remember where he's heard it, but he didn't like it.

"Up here, genius," the voice said.

He looked up toward the ceiling and found the source. It was that young kid from the day before, the one at the playground—Paul. Butch turned around as fast he could and was about to run, but the ghost kid floated down right in front of him, his arms crossed.

"Now is that anyway to greet a friend?" Paul said.

"You ain't no friend of mine!" Butch tried to push past him but just phased through the kid and stumbled over his own feet.

"Hm," the ghost muttered. "I'm heartbroken. I just came by to give you my offer again and see if you'd take me up on it this time."

Butch pushed himself off the floor and dusted himself off. "I already said no! I'm not going to off some kid just because I don't like him. Beat him up, sure. But not kill him."

Paul turned to face Butch. "That's just because you haven't felt what it's like to kill someone yet. Would you like to know what it's like?" A twisted grin came over the specter's face, his eyes grew wide and brows furled. He held out his hands in front of his face and looked at them. "It's exhilarating. When you watch something that is alive and see them struggle and fight with all their might, but it's just not enough." He clenched his fists. "Do you want to know the first thing I killed? I was only six."

Butch stared in frozen terror. He shook his head.

"I think I'll tell you anyways," Paul said. "My mom came home from the hospital with my baby sister. Sonia was her name. She was this tiny little thing, so small and fragile. But she could make a screaming noise like nothing else. I hated it. It drove me mad. So one night, when everyone was asleep, I snuck into the Sonia's room, and I placed a pillow over her face.

"Oh, she woke up, of course, and struggled against me. But I just pressed that pillow down harder. She couldn't scream, couldn't cry, nothing. Even after she stopped fighting, I still held her down just to make sure.

"And then that life was snuffed out, vanished forever. And I was the one to do it," the ghost giggled with child-like excitement. "Nothing can compare."

Butch stepped away. "You are one messed up dude. Now just leave me alone." He started to walk away when he was suddenly pulled back and thrown against the wall of lockers hard enough to dent the metal doors. He slumped to the floor in pain.

"I don't think you're going anywhere yet, bitch," Paul said. He knelt down and held out one hand. "If you won't help me kill Luis, then you can help me to find him. Because if you don't—" His hand phased through Butch's chest. Butch convulsed and gasped as he felt the ghost's cold fingers wrap themselves around his heart. They lightly grasped around the pulsating organ, which proceeded to beat faster and faster. "I've been thinking about killing a person this way for a while now. Just reach into their chest and grab their heart then squeeze it so tight it stops beating. Now tell me, where is Luis right now? Which class is he in?"

Butch gasped for breath. He felt the cold seeping through his body as his heart struggled to beat with Paul's hand slowly closing tighter and tighter around it. "He would be in my class." The words had to be forced out. "But he didn't show up for class today. I don't know where he is."

Paul tilted his head in mock compassion. "That's too bad. Because now I have nothing to get from you." He tightened his grip, feeling the muscular organ in Butch's chest struggle to beat under this new pressure. Just a little more and it would cease. The joy in Paul's mind was almost palatable as he saw Butch's life start to slip away.

"Butch, what are you doing down there?" A teacher came walking past—Butch's third period history teacher, Mrs. Anderson. She was an older woman in her late fifties with graying hair and a pair of spectacles over her eyes with a gold chain attached to the edges that looped around her neck. "You're going to be late if you don't get up off your lazy bum and get to class." She didn't see Paul and just continued on her way.

Paul released his hold over the bully's heart upon seeing the teacher. He could hardly believe his eyes, but it was her. Her! He recognized her instantly. His shoulders hunched, fists clenched, and if he had any, his blood would be boiling. He hardly even registered that Butch was now gasping for breath, his hand clasped over his chest as his heart rate returned to normal.

"You almost killed me!" Butch sputtered.

"That was the point!" Paul shouted. A powerful gust of wind blew through the hall when he did. He restrained himself and crossed his arms. Can't let his powers get out of control, not yet anyways. "I could kill you now, but I want you to do something for me instead."

Paul reached his arm through a locker door and pulled out a small booklet of matches. He tossed them down to Butch, who was still sitting on the floor. "I want you to start a fire. I don't care where, just start one and pull the alarm after you have."

Butch looked at the matchbook. "Why?"

"Just do it!" Paul yelled. "Do it, or I'll kill you! Got it?"

Butch jumped up to his feet. "Yeah, yeah, I got it!" he said in a terrified hurry. He ran down the hall, the worn out soles of his shoes slipped on the laminate floors as he did, and rushed into the men's bathroom. Inside, he turned on the sink and slashed water on his face.

This wasn't real, it couldn't be! There was just no way this could be happening to him! Yet he held the matchbook in his hands. Was he really going to do this? Arson was something he'd never considered doing and never wanted to do, but his life was at stake.

In the corner, he saw a round plastic trashcan, the top overflowed with used paper towels. With fumbling fingers, Butch flipped open the matchbook and tore one out. He stuck it against the black strip on the back, and on the third strike, the red tip burst into flames. Holding it against the tip of a dry paper towel, the fire quickly spread and engulfed the ugly brown paper. Before it could reach his fingers, he dropped the burning paper into the trashcan where the fire spread.

The black plastic bag that lines the can was burning and melting, black smoke rose into the air. Butch threw the rest of the matchbook into the fire, ran out the bathroom door, and grabbed hold of the fire alarm on the wall. The alarm blared so loud he had to hold his hands over his ears, wincing.

Every classroom, which had just settled down to begin, was now in confusion. As soon as she heard the alarm, Mrs. Anderson stopped her lesson, set down the dry-erase pen, and addressed the class.

"Is today a fire drill?" one of her students asked.

"No, there wasn't one scheduled for today. Okay, children, stay calm. Now just like we've practiced." She raised her hands up. "Please, calmly stand up, and form a single file line next to the door."

The class, with a lot a hustling and running into each other, managed after several agonizing minutes to form a single line next to the door. Some of the kids were fidgeting, others almost hyperventilated, and a few even appeared to be bored. Mrs. Anderson scanned over the room to make sure everyone was up before opening the door and letting the kids out. Rows of other high school students walked down the halls toward the exits, Mrs. Anderson's class followed suit. She held the door open, watching as the classroom emptied and making sure no one remained.

As the last of her student walked out, Mrs. Anderson suddenly felt someone grab her by her blouse and pull her back into the classroom. Her shoulder slammed against the ground with a bone shattering crash. She winced and gritted her teeth in pain. She started to stand up but stopped when the door slammed shut right before her eyes.

Her purse lifted from her desk and floated through the air, carried by unseen hands. The top zipper opened, and her keys floated out. She could only watch in stunned terror as the keys levitated over to the door, slid into the lock, and bolted the door shut.

The key snapped off in the lock and fell to the floor with a clink. Mrs. Anderson found herself lying on the ground with a sprained shoulder, speechless and terrified.

A figure began to appear by the door. At first, it was just a wisp of vapor, but soon, it took form. Appearing out of thin air, Paul stood silent and glaring at the woman before him. "Hello, again," he said. His tone cold and hate filled.

Mrs. Anderson almost jumped out of her skin in fright. She recognized this boy, but that was impossible! There was no way it could be him!

"Yes," Paul said. "It's me. You know who I am. Maybe not my name, but you know me all the same." In a split second, he closed the distance between himself and the frightened old teacher and wrapped his fingers around her throat. "You killed me!" His grip tightened as the woman gasped for air. She clutched at his hands but couldn't touch him. It was as if she was being strangled by nothing. "And now I will return the favor."

Paul released his hold on her throat, and she gasped for air. Her relief was short lived, as the ghost thrust his arm into her chest and grabbed hold of her heart. His fist clenched around the pulsating organ, squeezing tighter and tighter with all his might. The woman convulsed before him, her body thrashing as she tried to get away but to no avail.

The cold fingers of death clenched so tightly around her heart that it became impossible to beat. Her blood stopped flowing, every fiber of her being screamed out in agony, but she could do nothing. Seconds passed like minutes, minutes like hours. Eventually, her brain shut down, and her eyes rolled back as she breathed her last breath. Her body slumped against the floor, dead.

With an exhilarated grin and eyes wide with excitement, Paul withdrew his arm from the old woman's chest. He gazed at his hand, almost contemplating it. He tightened his fingers into a fist and stood up. This would be his means of killing from now on, and he was right about one thing. It was exhilarating, the greatest high he could ever imagine. And it wouldn't stop with this woman. He would also find the man who murdered him, plus Luis and Serena, and he would inflict the same torturous death upon them.

16

Alice sat next to Luis as he waited at the corner bus stop for his ride home. Serena was long gone by now, having left Luis without a way to get home or any understanding of the bus schedules. He stared at the sidewalk beneath his sneakers and fiddled his thumbs.

Alice rested her hand on his shoulder. "Are you feeling all right?"

Luis shook his head. "Not really," he sighed and ran his fingers through his hair. "I didn't even know what happened to my dad, or that it was the same accident. When she told us what happened to your mom, I never drew any connections."

"She doesn't really hate you, she's just upset," Alice said. "Give her some time, and she'll come back around."

"Yeah, that doesn't help me all that much right now," Luis responded. "I just don't know what to do. How am I supposed to feel about this?"

After a pause, "I don't know," was all Alice could say.

A bus pulled up and stopped, its doors opened with a hiss. Luis stood up and fished the necessary change out of his pockets. "I'm going home. I have homework I need to do, and I need to think of a way to work things out with Serena." He stepped on the bus but stopped when Alice didn't follow him. "Are you coming?"

"I think I need some time alone too," she said. "Just to think this all over."

"Where will you go?" Luis asked.

Alice shrugged. Her hands fell into her pockets. "I don't know right now. I'm not going back to the playground yet, not with Paul doing what he's doing."

"Well, just try to be safe at least," Luis said. The doors closed, and the bus rumbled as it pulled away from the curb, continuing on its route.

"I'll try to be." With a small push, Alice lifted up into the air. She soared through the sky, watching as all the houses and buildings blurred below her. Ever since she learned she could fly, it had been her favorite thing, leaving the limitations of the ground behind and taking to the air.

Not far off in the distance, she saw the burnt skeletal remains of the Pleasant Hill apartment complex. Upon seeing it, an idea came to her. Why not spend the day with Damian? They'd only gotten to talk for a little bit earlier and mostly just on a superficial level. There could be so much to talk about with him. She adjusted her course and flew over to the apartment building.

A few fire trucks and police cars still surrounded the burnt-out husk of a building. The perimeter was marked off by yellow caution tape. Several news vans were parked around the building, most had their camera equipment and reporters already set up and filming. Alice bypassed all this, simply floating up to what was left of the third floor. She landed softly. "Damian?" she called out, her hands cupped around her mouth. "Damian, I came back!"

"Alice?" Damian reappeared, becoming visible from out of thin air. "Hey, I didn't expect to see you so soon. It hasn't even been a full day yet. Are the other two here too? The glasses kid and the Goth chick?"

"Well, actually, no." Alice hunched her shoulders a little. "There was a little incident, and they each went home. I just got bored and decided to visit for a bit."

"What kind of incident?" Damian asked.

"Oh." She reached her hand to and scratched the back of her head. "They just had a little fight, but we shouldn't talk about that right now."

Damian smirked. "A little lover's quarrel?"

"They're just friends, not dating. And don't say things like that, she's my sister!" Alice said.

"That still seems weird to me. She is your little sister, but she's older than you. I know how, but it's just strange." Damian pressed the heel of his palm against his forehead.

Alice shrugged. "These things happen." She and Damian both laughed at the absurdity of what she'd said. "Yeah," she said after catching her breath. "Things like this just happen."

"They sure do." Damian sat down on the edge of what used to be the balcony and hung his legs over the side. "I'm glad you came to see me. It's been rather boring the past few hours up here by myself."

Alice sat down next to him, swinger her legs back and forth. "If you think a few hours are boring, just imagine what a few years feel like," she retorted. "After I died, I woke up at the playground in the park. I had no idea what I was doing or how I got there, but I was all alone."

"For years?" Damian asked.

"I don't know exactly how long, but the leaves were falling by the time I met someone else. She was another ghost named Susie, and we quickly grew close," Alice said. "She even came to see me as her big sister figure."

"That's nice," Damian said. He slouched over, his head propped up in his hands and elbows resting on his knees. "What about your real sister, Serena?"

"It's kinda strange. I forgot I even had a sister for a while," Alice said. "Years went by, and I steadily forgot things about my life. By the time Luis found me, about the only thing I still remembered was my name. But he used that to track down Serena and reunite us." She placed her arms behind her and leaned back. "He's really a great guy, a little shy at times but kind."

"Glad to know you approve of him," Damian replied. "And what were to happen if he started dating your sister?"

"I haven't given it much thought." Alice stared out at the clear blue sky, a few white clouds floated past. The fog that once filled the air had long since burnt away in the sunlight. "I think he'd be good to her, but their lifestyles might be too different. I don't think she would be interested in a nerdy guy like him."

"Are you serious? Goths are just nerds with a little more fashion and makeup," Damian retorted.

"Oh, really," Alice said. The two of them sat together, looking out over the rooftops of this small town. Some cars drove along the black top roads, bicyclists rode alongside them. A faint breeze rustled the changing leaves, and more fell to the earth below. "I always liked fall. The air is cool, the leaves change color. I remember now that Cindy and I would rake up big piles of leaves and then jump into them. We'd play around like that for hours at a time."

"Cindy?" Damian asked.

"Oh"—Alice remembered—"Serena. Her real name is Cynthia, but I used to call her Cindy. I guess when she chose her lifestyle, she changed her name to Serena Ravenwood."

"So her Goth name is Serena Ravenwood?"

"Yeah, sounds like a name someone would pick for themselves, doesn't it?" Alice giggled. "I personally think it's kind of adorable."

"And what about your ghost sister, Susie? How has she taken you reuniting with your real sister?" Damian asked.

Alice sighed, "Not terribly well." Alice remembered vividly how Paul had turned the other ghost children against her and made them hold her down. It sent a shiver up her metaphorical spine. "But it's fine. I just need to talk to her about it a little bit about it, that's all. You seem to be a little preoccupied with the concept of sisters, though."

"Well, the thing is"—Damian locked his fingers together—"I had a sister once."

"Really?" Alice asked, surprised. "You only mentioned the little brother before. Who was your sister?"

Damian didn't answer right away. He stared out at the scenery, his hands clasped together and a pained expression on his face. After what seemed like an hour, he finally spoke, "Her name was Sonia, and she was just a baby."

It didn't take Alice long to figure out where this was going. She pulled her legs up to her chest and wrapped her arms around them, resting her head on her knees. "I'm sorry. I didn't mean to bring it up."

"It's okay. It was no one's fault really," Damian said. "It was a few years ago, I was twelve, and Paul was only about six when Mom came home from the hospital with her. It was a busy couple of weeks adjusting to a new baby in the house, but we were getting used to it. Then one morning, we didn't hear her crying. Mom and Dad went to investigate and found her cold and stiff. The whole family was heartbroken. Mom and Dad had been trying for a girl for a while, so when this happened, they were so distraught."

"That's horrible." Alice placed her hand on his shoulder. "Did anyone figure out what happened?"

Damian shrugged. "SIDS."

"SIDS?"

"Sudden infant death syndrome. No one knows why, it just happens," Damian explained.

"I can't imagine what that must've felt like." An idea came to Alice then, an idea that sounded sickening but incredibly likely considering the circumstances. "How did Paul take it?"

"He stayed locked up in his room for a while after," Damian said. "He didn't really come out to talk to anyone unless Mom made him."

Alice turned her gaze away from Damian. She didn't want to think about it, but the thoughts would not leave her mind. What if Paul had been dangerous even from a younger age? She knew for a fact he'd killed his parents and older brother. What if he'd also killed his baby sister?

Off in the distance, another set of sirens began to scream. Alice and Damian saw a fire truck speed down the road; its lights flashing. A faint pillar of black smoke reached up to the sky from further in town. Alice watched the smoke and followed its trail back to its base. She was shocked when she saw its source.

"That's coming from the high school!" she shouted, jumping to her feet.

"Someone's trying to burn the school down?" Damian stood up next to her.

"It looks like it." Alice lifted her feet up and began levitating. "I'm sorry I can't stay, but I need to warn Luis and Serena about this. I doubt two fires in two days is a coincidence."

17

An old one-story house rested on the corner of a street block with the paint chipping in places and the lawn a little too long. Despite this, Alice recognized it all too well as the home she used to live in. She descended from the air and stood on the doorstep, facing the rusted address numbers on the door. It didn't used to look like this. Once, long ago, the paint was bright, the grass was neatly trimmed, and the house was full of life. Now, however, it seemed dull and decrepit, like an old car at a junkyard just waiting for the day of reckoning.

This was the first time Alice had seen her old house since the day she went missing, and she was both happy and sad to gaze upon it again. Happy because of all the memories it brought back, all the things she had forgotten, like the day Mom came home from the hospital with little Cynthia in her arms. Or the time she scraped her knee learning to ride a bike and Dad put a Band-Aid on it and took her for ice cream to cheer her up afterward.

But these memories also brought despair. Those good times were long since over, and nothing could bring them back. With a heavy sigh and an even heavier heart, she phased through the front door and stepped into the living room.

It looked even worse in here. Where once the carpet was vacuumed, now it lay cluttered with dirt and old food wrappers. Dirty dishes were stacked on a TV tray, which stood next to a recliner. And scattered all around this recliner were empty bottles of beer. Alice breathed a heavy sigh of sadness. Was this really how far they had fallen? How much pain was caused to her family because of her death?

She left the living room in its messy state and floated down the hall to her sister's room. A large poster of a rock band was plastered over the door, an all-woman group called "The Daughters of Darkness." Alice worked up her courage and floated straight through and into Serena's room.

The lights were off, and the curtains drawn closed. Every wall was painted black; a few had purple designs painted over them. A bookshelf stood in one corner with several rows of books as well as small ceramic figures adorning them, mostly figurines of skulls and skeletons, a few large dragons as well. Next to the adjacent wall was the bed, and in that bed laid Serena, sobbing into her pillow.

N. J. HANSON

Serena lay flat on her stomach, her arms wrapped around the pillow and pressed against her face. Her shoulders quivered with each breath as she wept, her tears soaked the soft fabric beneath her eyes.

Alice levitated across the room until she hovered next to the bed. She crossed her legs and sat down on the bed, placing her hand on her sister's shoulder. "Don't!" Serena pushed her away. "Just leave me alone!"

"You don't really want that," Alice said.

"Yes, I do," Serena cried.

"No, you don't. You've been alone for too long."

Serena pushed up from the bed, wiping her nose on her sleeve. "Yeah, and now I know why."

"You mean because of Mom? Because of Luis?"

"Yes!" Serena shouted, perhaps louder than she had wanted. "How could he keep this from me? Why didn't he tell me? I trusted him."

"Cindy, it was just a car accident. What happened that night was no one's fault," Alice said.

Serena continued to brush tears away from her eyes. "If you hadn't gotten taken, then Mom wouldn't have driven off that night."

"Are you now saying it's my fault?" Alice lifted away from the bed, her arms folded. "Am I to blame for Mom's death? Well, guess what, I already know whose fault it is that Mom died. No one's. And you can't keep projecting blame on people."

"I need someone to blame!" Serena's voice was cracking. "If I can't blame someone, then it was just senseless death, and I can't accept that Mom died senselessly." She pulled a tissue from a box on her nightstand. "You don't understand. I lost my big sister, and less than a month later, I lost my mom. And even though he hasn't died, I lost Dad too. All he does is drink. I've had to watch him spiral into depression ever since you died. And just when I find someone I like and who brings you back to me, I learn he was in the same accident that took Mom from us. How am I supposed to deal with that?"

Alice sat back on the bed and embraced her sister. "I don't know how you're supposed to. But you cannot blame him or anyone else for Mom's death. And you don't really hate Luis for it."

Serena welcomed her sister's embrace. "No, I don't."

Alice pulled away, a smile on her face. "And did I hear that right? Did you just say you liked him?"

"Well"—Serena averted her gaze—"I just meant as a friend. He's a good friend, that's all."

Alice nodded. "That he is. So you aren't mad at him anymore?"

"Not really." Serena shook her head.

"Good." Alice lifted back into the air. "Then I think it would be a good time to give him a call and let him know." As Serena fished her phone out of her pocket, Alice spoke up again. "Also, after you stormed off home and Luis left, I visited Damian and have some disconcerting news."

Serena held her phone in her hands, not having dialed Luis's number yet. "And what's that?"

"First, I'll just tell you what I know. I saw smoke coming from your high school," Alice said.

"Smoke? Someone started a fire?" Serena asked, jumping from the bed. "Well"—she attempted to laugh it off—"I guess it's a good thing we didn't go today."

"Don't you find it a little suspicious? Last night, an apartment complex burns down, and today, the school catches fire. Two fires two days in a row is too much of a coincidence," Alice said.

Serena tossed her phone up in the air and caught it as it fell back into her hand. "Do you think it's Paul looking for us?"

"I would not be surprised. Also"—she paused for a few seconds—"Damian told me something disturbing."

"There seems to be no shortage of those today." Serena snarked.

"I know what you mean," Alice said. "He said he used to have a baby sister, but she died about six years ago. One morning, they found her in her crib not moving."

Serena quickly put the pieces together in her mind. "Do you really think Paul had something to do with that?"

Alice nodded. "He's already killed the rest of his family and threatened to kill you and Luis. I wouldn't put it past him now."

Touching the screen of her phone, Serena scrolled through her contacts to bring up Luis's number. "I'll let him know the situation now." But before she could dial, another call came through. Her ringtone came blaring out the speaker, startling her and making her jump. Hitting the pickup button, she placed the phone to her ear. "Hello?"

"Hello, Serena. It's me," the voice on the other line said. It was Madam Morgana. "Did I catch you at a bad time? You left in a hurry. I just wanted to make sure you were okay."

Serena sighed, "Yeah, I'm fine. Thanks for checking up on me."

"You're welcome, dear," the older woman said. "I'm sorry you had to see that today. I wouldn't have guessed Luis was in any way connected to that incident."

"Yeah, I wouldn't have either," Serena said.

"Anyways, I thought I should tell you this. After the three of you left, I looked back in the crystal ball and saw your future. I mean the future for you and Luis."

There was a pause on the other line. After waiting for several seconds, Serena asked, "Is it bad?"

Madam Morgana sighed on the other line, "I don't know if I should tell you over the phone."

"You're just going to make me anxious and worked up if you don't." Serena started to pace around her room. "What is it?"

"If you insist, then I think you should sit down first," Morgana said.

Serena sat back down on the bed and crossed her legs at the knees. She folded one arm under the other, still holding the phone to her ear. Alice hovered in the air, anxiously listening and waiting. "Okay, I'm sitting. What it is?" Serena asked.

"Okay, since you insisted," Morgana said and took a deep breath to ready herself. "Luis is going to die. Very soon."

The phone slipped from Serena's hand and fell to the bed. Her eyes were fixed open in shock, and her body ridged. Had she really just heard that? It must be some kind of mistake. Alice floated right in front of her, waving a hand over her eyes. "Hello?" the ghost girl asked. "What's going on? What did she say?"

Serena scooped back up the phone. "Did you just say what I thought you said? You're telling me Luis is going to die soon?"

"Luis is going to what?" Alice shouted.

"Yes," Madam Morgana confirmed. "And before you start to argue with me, just remember that you also saw that my crystal ball does in fact work to channel my psychic abilities. After all, that's how you saw the way he acquired his gifts."

Serena stood up with lightning speed. "Yes, but that was different. That was looking into his past, seeing old events. How can you be so sure about something in the future?"

"I am psychic," the fortuneteller said. "And I don't think this is really about whether I can see the future. You're concerned about Luis, aren't you?"

"Of course, I am. He's my friend. I don't want to see him get hurt," Serena stammered.

"Serena," Madam Morgana said in a hushed tone, "I don't need to be psychic to see you have feelings for him."

"Wh-what? Pfft, that's ridiculous," Serena stuttered, her face turning visibly redder. "He's just a good friend, nothing more."

"I just told you he's not going to live long. Don't you think you should admit how you feel? Not just to yourself, but to him also? Make his last few days a little nicer?"

"Last few days?" she shouted into her phone. "You're saying he's going to die in a few days? How?"

"I don't really know," Morgana said.

"Oh, so you can just see enough to know that he dies, just not how! That's really helpful!" she exclaimed, hanging up the phone and throwing it on the bed. She crossed her arms and scoffed.

Alice watched with a mixture of apprehension and fear. Aside from earlier today, she'd never seen her sister freak out so much. "Do you really think any of it is true?"

Serena didn't respond at first, just stood in the middle of her room with her arms folded and eyes fixed on a small patch of carpet before her. Her cheeks were still slightly pink, and her face felt warm. "I don't want to think about it."

Alice floated over to her sister and hovered right next to her. "So do you like him? I mean, *like* him like him?"

She spun around on her heels and threw her arms up in the air. "You're really going to ask me that? Out of everything she said, that's the big question on your mind?"

Alice smiled innocently and shrugged. "I guess I can take that as a yes. You wouldn't flip out so much if you didn't."

"Oh, shut up. I don't need any sass from you." The older girl placed her hand against her forehead. She paced around her room while Alice hung lazily in the air. "I still don't want to believe it."

"Believe that you like Luis?"

"No," Serena said with an exasperated sigh. "I don't want to believe what Madam Morgana said. I don't want Luis to die. And of course, she was less than specific about how he's supposed to expire, wasn't she?"

"I don't know. You didn't let me listen," Alice retorted.

Serena rolled her eyes. "Well, what am I supposed to do?"

Picking up the phone, Alice held it out to her little sister. "Give him a call. Apologize for blowing up at him, and ask if you can do anything to make it up."

Annoyed and still blushing, Serena snatched the phone away from Alice. "Fine. But not now. After what I just heard, I don't know if I can talk to him right now."

"Really? I'd think now would be best," Alice said.

"Well, I just don't feel now is good," Serena replied. "And if you don't mind, I'd like to be alone for a bit. I need to sort this out."

Alice rolled her eyes and sighed, "Fine. I guess I'll be leaving. But promise me you'll call and talk to him soon, okay?"

"Okay," Serena said, exasperated.

"Good." Alice lifted back up and floated out of the house, leaving Serena with her thoughts.

As she flew away from the house, she glanced back at it over her shoulder. It was still a sad sight, and it pained her to look at it. This was her old home once, but now it was in ruins.

"Quite interesting, isn't it?" a voice behind her said. With shock and horror, she turned around and came face-to-face with Paul. He wore a wicked grin and looked with evil eyes.

"How long have you been here?" Her voice trembled.

"You can't even tell, can you?" Paul's words dripped with a vile tone that made Alice's metaphorical stomach turn.

"In actuality, I've only got here in time to watch you leave. I wanted to find you sooner, but I had some things to do."

"So that was you. The smoke I saw coming from the high school, you caused it." She accused.

"Hm. Yes and no," he said with a shrug. "It was that idiot who likes to use Luis as a punching bag. Butch—I think his name is. He's the one who set the fire, but I made him do it." He moved in close, his face inches away from Alice's scared eyes. "So I could get close to the woman."

Alice trembled in the air. "What woman?"

"Think for a minute, will you?" His tone harsh and angry. "The woman that helped kidnap and kill us. She worked there. I was just as shocked then as you are now to see her again. But don't worry, I took care of her." He held up his hand, palm open. "I crushed her heart in my hands until it stopped beating." He clenched his fist for emphasis. "No one will be able to tell the difference. They'll just think it was a simple heart attack."

Alice was horrified. This boy was only twelve when he died, but already he was thinking of things like this—to so casually talk about killing and murder. "Paul, you are a monster."

"I know what I am," he said. "You don't need to remind me." With terrible speed, he stretched out his hand and clasped it around her neck. She gasped in surprise, feeling the cold seep through her form. "I'm sure you didn't know just how far a ghost can go in harming another ghost. Almost as far as a human can hurt another, the only exception being you can't die again. But that just means you will be forced to endure much more pain."

She gasped, clawing at his fingers, but to no avail. "Why are you doing this?" She wheezed.

"Didn't I warn you not to tell them about me?" Paul tightened his grip. "But you did anyways, why else would they have skipped school today."

"To investigate the fire from last night." Alice choked. "I didn't tell them anything about you."

Paul smirked. "And why would they have gone and done that if you hadn't told them?" He tightened his hold, and Alice gagged. "Do you think I'm stupid? You tried to warn them about me, and it will cost them their lives."

"No, Paul." Alice struggled. "I swear, I didn't tell them about you."

"I can tell you're lying. Monsters are very good at telling lies from truth." He grabbed her arms and twisted, holding it behind her back. "And as for you, you're going back to the playground with me, and you aren't leaving ever again."

18

Luis stared at his computer screen, nothing on it in particular, just the screen itself. His copy of William Shakespeare's *Hamlet* sat on the desk next to his keyboard, and he knew he needed to read it for his English assignment, but he just was not into it right now. Not with Serena as mad at him as she was.

What was he supposed to say to her anyways? Was he supposed to apologize? That would probably be the best thing to do right now, but he just couldn't bring himself to do it. He couldn't face her right now.

He found himself racked with self guilt. In watching that vision in the crystal ball, he saw his father look away from the road to address him, and that's when the accident happened. He didn't want to think about it, but the idea kept coming to mind. Was he really responsible? Did he cause the deaths of Serena's mom and his own father?

Pulling his glasses off, his eyes clamped tightly shut, and he shook his head trying in vain to banish that thought, but it didn't work. He rubbed his fingers across his forehead as if he had a headache, but nothing could alleviate his worried mind.

The worst of it was Serena and what she had shouted when she stormed out of the fortuneteller's place. Hearing her say that she hated him made Luis feel like he had been stabbed through the heart. He'd never had a girl say that to him, and it made him feel like something to be scraped off her shoe. He hated himself now, not just for being the possible cause of the accident but also because of what it did to Serena.

A sudden blaring ring made him jump up from the chair. The screen on his phone was lit up. He picked it up and brought it to his ear. "Hello?"

His mother's worried voice came from the other line. "Luis, are you all right?" she asked.

"Yeah, Mom, I'm fine," he said, confused. "What's going on?"

"I got a call from your school. Is everything okay? Did you make it home all right?" Mrs. Chavez said. "I was afraid something might've happened to you."

"Um, yeah. I'm okay, Mom," Luis said with confusion.

"Oh, good," she said with relief in her voice. "I'm coming home now, and you can fill me in on everything then. I love you."

"I love you too, Mom," Luis said automatically. The line fell dead as his mother hung up. He set his phone back on the desk and leaned back in his chair, questions ran through his head.

What was she talking about? Why would the school call her? How did she know he was home? For that matter, why did she expect him to be home in the first place?

Luis stood up and moved to the window. He looked out in the direction of the school, and as soon as he did, he found his answer. A faint, thin draggle of smoke curled up in the sky away from the high school. It was nothing like the fire from last night, but it was still evident.

Someone must've set a fire and evacuated the school. The fact that this was the second fire in two days was not lost on him. He fell back on his bed with his fingers laced together behind his head. Outside, the blaring of sirens could be heard, but he paid them little attention. His head was swarming with thoughts.

A thought kept coming to him, and it had to do with that ghost Alice warned them about. She said his name was Paul, and that he was also Damian's younger brother.

Could Paul have gone to the school to find him or Serena? The possibility was too good for him to brush the idea aside. Luis reached for his phone again to call Serena, but then he stopped. She might still be mad at him, and if she was, then it wouldn't be a good idea to try talking to her just yet.

Instead, he jumped on his computer and started browsing. He knew some of the handles, his classmates used, and needed to find out what happened at class today. He looked down their feeds and soon found the truth. Someone had set a fire in the bathroom and then pulled the fire alarm. Then everyone evacuated just as they'd practiced since he was in first grade, and the fire was quickly extinguished.

"Okay, that's all good. But they wouldn't close the school for the day if that was all," Luis said to himself.

The computer beeped as a new post appeared. He read it and was shocked. His third period teacher, Mrs. Anderson, was dead.

He stepped away from the computer and fell back on his bed again. His teacher was dead. Mrs. Anderson was never his favorite teacher, but the news still strongly affected him. He didn't know what to feel anymore. So much had happened already today—from learning the truth of his father, to discovering that he might have also caused the accident that took Serena's mom, and now the fire at the school and his teacher's death. It was getting to be too much for Luis to handle.

It wasn't too much later that he heard his mother's car pull into the driveway, and he went downstairs to meet her. Once she set her shoes on the rack by the door, his mother took him in both arms and clutched him close, tears ran down her face. "I'm glad you're safe," she said between sobs.

He hugged her back. "Me too," was all he could reply.

"I don't know what I would have done if I'd lost you," she said, as she ran her hands over his hair.

"It wasn't that bad, Mom," Luis said. His face grew warm with embarrassment. It had been a long time since his mom hugged him like this, and it made him uneasy. "Just some small fire in the bathroom, and they put it out fast enough."

"I know. But when I was told, I was afraid I might've lost you."

"You mean like Dad?" Luis asked without thinking. Almost as soon as he had, he regretted it.

His mother stepped back. "How do you?" Luis read the look of surprise and fear on her face. "Honey, why would you bring up your father now? He left us years ago, remember? I told you never to ask about that."

"Mom, I know the truth." Luis couldn't bring himself to meet her gaze. "You don't need to lie to me anymore."

"I've never lied to you." His mother's voice was growing harsher, even if she didn't intend it to. "And I don't need to explain things to you, not after—"

"Stop lying!" Luis shouted.

His mother fell silent with shock. Luis was just as stunned at himself as she was. He had never raised his voice like that to her in his life. "Dad didn't leave us, at least not the way you always told me he did," he said before he could stop himself. "I know the truth, Mom. Dad died driving me home when I was very little. And it was—" The tears began to flow. A lump formed in his throat. "It was my fault."

"Oh, Luis." His mother grabbed hold of him again. "Don't think that. It was just an accident."

"Then why did you lie to me?" he asked between sobs.

"It was for your own good."

"My own good? Why would it be good for me to think my father walked out on me? On us?" He was fully sobbing now, the first time since he was a toddler, but he didn't care. "Why would you say something like that unless you didn't want me to know the truth?" He looked up at her with tears streaming down his cheeks. "It was my fault, wasn't it? Dad died because of me, and you kept the truth from me so I wouldn't blame myself."

His mother took the tissue from her purse and wiped his tears away. "Yes. I lied to you about your father because I knew you would blame yourself for it, but that doesn't make it your fault." She placed a small kiss on his forehead. "It was an accident, that's all. No one blames you for it except yourself."

"No," Luis said quietly. "Someone else does too."

"Who?" his mother asked.

Luis took a deep breath to steady himself. "Serena," he said after a minute. "I learned the truth today when she told me about how she lost her mom. Her mother was the woman driving the other car that night."

A hand moved in front of his mother's mouth, and she let out a gasp. "Oh my god. Luis, I had no idea."

"Now she hates me. I'm sure of it." He choked back his tears and scoffed. "And she has good reason to. Not only did I kill my own father, I also killed her mom. I took one of the few people she had left in her life from her just when she needed them the most." He found himself unable to speak; the lump in his throat was too strong now. He pulled his glasses off and rubbed his eyes with his sleeves.

He felt his mother's arms embrace him again. "I'm sorry I never told you the truth. I was afraid of what it would do to you if you knew, but I see that it only hurt you more in the long run." She held him close. "I've been a horrible mother. I hope you can forgive me."

Luis placed his arms around her as well. "Mom, you've done nothing wrong," he said between breaths.

"Well"—she dabbed the tissue against his cheek to clear away his tears—"if I did nothing wrong, then neither did you. So how about this? If I can't blame myself, then you can't blame yourself either. Deal?"

Luis couldn't help up smile. He recognized what his mom had done, playing the guilt card to help him get over himself. "Deal," he said.

"And don't worry about your girlfriend. I'm sure she doesn't hate you," his mother said with a hint of good-natured teasing.

"She's not my girlfriend," Luis said with annoyance.

His mother just smirked. "Of course."

19

A young girl, about or close to the age of ten, stood on a sidewalk. She wore a red-and-white baseball cap over her short curly black hair. A heavyset backpack was slung over her shoulders, and her hands were stuffed in her denim coat pockets. A pair of black ear buds rested in her ears, they pumped music deep into her brain.

It had been three songs now, and her mother had yet to show up. She tapped her foot against the concrete with irritation. School got out fifteen minutes ago, why wasn't she here yet? The girl pulled out her cell phone and dialed her mother's number. She got her mom's voice mail and left a short message.

"Hey, Mom, it's Tamika. I'm waiting for you at the usual spot. Are you on your way? Call me back." She hung up and slipped the phone back in her pocket.

The sun was already beginning to set in on the horizon. It was that time of year—the sun sets earlier and rises later. Golden beams of light cast down through the tree boughs and caught the dust, like light through the windows of a cathedral.

Just down the road and around the corner sat a forest-green SUV. A man stepped out from the driver's side. He wore gloves and a large black coat with the collar turned up to obscure part of his face. He stepped behind the little girl, her music played so loud she didn't hear him even as he came up right behind her.

The man pulled a small rag from his pocket. Quickly, he grabbed the girl and slapped the rag over her mouth and nose. She jumped with surprise and tried to scream, but the towel was already stopping her. She struggled, kicked, and hit as much as she could, but the chemicals on the rag took effect too quickly, and she passed out.

He lifted her up in his arm and carried her bridle style back to the SUV. She lay so peacefully still in his arms, asleep like a little angel. She was so beautiful to him, and he would make her his new queen. Oh, the things he would do for her and with her, it brought a smile to his face.

As he slid her into the back seat, her cell phone fell out of her pocket. It landed on the street with a clunk on the pavement next to the car tires. He noticed this, and with a small kick, he knocked the phone down a storm drain. With the girl unconscious in the back of his car, he climbed back into the driver's seat, and drove away with her. There were no witnesses.

Five minutes later, Tamika's mother drove up to the street corner looking for her daughter. She couldn't believe she lost track of time at the meeting and almost forgot to pick Tamika up from school. If only the girl's father would help, but of course, he wouldn't. Deadbeat bum.

She pulled up to the curb and sat in the car with the engine running for several minutes. When Tamika didn't show, the woman became irritated. That girl calls about her being late and then decides to run off somewhere doing who knows what? She scoffed at the idea, shut the car off, stepped outside, and called her daughter's phone.

A familiar ringtone started to play. She recognized it instantly as that annoying song her daughter spent $1.99 on for her phone. But it sounded so close. A concerned look came over her face. She followed the sound to the storm drain and looked inside. The screen shone brightly inside against the mud, grime, and decaying leaves around it.

The mother almost dropped her phone in horror. No ten-year-old girl would so casually drop her cell phone in a storm drain like that. Someone else must've thrown it down there.

Someone else.

That realization was itself enough to send shivers down the woman's spine. Someone else had taken Tamika, and without her phone, there was no way to find her. Where was Tamika? Where was her little girl?

Wednesday, October 29

Luis tossed and turned in his sleep. Beads of sweat appeared on his forehead. He grimaced and groaned. His eyes snapped open as he suddenly awoke. Another dream, this one stronger than before. Not just a face or some shadows, but a person. Two people actually.

One was a child, a little girl with dark skin and short curly black hair. The other was a man. But while he could see the girl clearly, the man was a blur. Everything about him was obscured, like trying to look at something while underwater.

Luis rubbed his eyes and put on his glasses. He climbed out of bed and made his way to the bathroom for some water. This was only his second dream vision like this, after the one about the fire. What could this one mean?

Luis was too tired to think about it now. He drank his water and then crawled back into bed to try to catch some sleep.

The next morning, his alarm sounded again. He slapped the snooze button and rolled over. His strange dreams had left him sleep deprived, and it was annoying. Why was this still happening? His mother called up to him, "Luis! Wake up! Breakfast time!"

He groaned, "All right, Mom." He pulled himself from the warm blankets and rested his feet on the cold hardwood floor. He got himself dressed, brushed his teeth, grabbed his backpack, and went down stairs. His mother had the TV on for background noise, the weatherman talked on about an upcoming low-pressure system that would bring possible thunderstorms near Halloween. Luis didn't pay it much attention.

"I made scrambled eggs," his mom said. She scooped a spoonful onto a plate and handed it to him. "Do you have any plans for Halloween?"

Luis took the plate that was offered him. He shrugged. "Not really. I was just going to watch a few old scary movies."

"You did that last year. Don't you want to do anything different?" Mom prepared her own plate. "Go to a party? Spend time with some friends? What about the one Goth girl? What was her name again?"

"Serena." Luis stuffed a forkful of eggs into his mouth.

"Yeah, her," Mom said. "She seems like she'd be a lot of fun on Halloween."

Luis rolled his eyes. How many parents actually wanted their teenage kids to go out to parties on Halloween? This just went against all the laws of nature. He looked back at the TV and saw the news anchor begin on a new topic. The school photo of a little black girl appeared in the corner of the screen.

> Ten-year-old Tamika Little disappeared on her way home from school yesterday. Her cell phone was recovered from a storm drain near the corner of 8th St. and Fulsome Ave. Police are asking anyone with any information to call the number below.

Luis stopped mid bite, his eyes fixed on the screen in stunned surprise. That was her! The same little girl from his dream! There was no mistaking it, that was the girl listening to her headphones on the corner waiting for her mom and who got taken by the man in the green SUV.

So it wasn't just a dream. It was another vision! She wasn't just some little girl; she was being kidnapped! That was the kidnapper! The same one who took Alice and all the other kids at the playground, it had to be!

He jumped to his feet and ran out of the room, leaving his mother confused. Luis charged back up the stairs in such a hurry that the knob of his bedroom door slammed against the wall behind it hard enough to leave a small dent when he threw it open. Rummaging through his messy room, he quickly found what he was looking for. Holding them up before his eyes, light fell through the window and glimmered off the stone pendant necklaces.

They were the bloodstone pendants Madam Morgana gave him yesterday. He hung one of them around his neck and stuffed the other in his left pants pocket. In his mind, he knew they were only rocks—heliotropes with a little bit of iron oxide in them—and how much faith he put in them was still debatable, but better to be safe than sorry.

He threw his backpack over his shoulder and was out the door before his mother had time to stop him or even question what just happened.

Running down the street with his backpack bouncing up and down against him with every step, he dug his phone from his right pocket and, with fumbling fingers, dialed Serena. The phone rang three times before someone picked it up. Her voice was still groggy when she spoke. "Hello?"

"Serena," Luis said, still running and gasping for air. "We have a new problem."

"Luis? Is that you?" she groaned on the other line as she slowly crawled out of bed. "Can't it wait until I've woken up some more?"

Luis wasted no time in getting to the point. "Another little girl was kidnapped yesterday!" he shouted.

The line was quiet for a brief pause, and then he heard the rustling of her jumping out of bed. "Okay, that's serious." It continued while she got dressed. "Want to meet me at the school library?"

"I'm already on my way." He clicked his phone off and put it way. With his hands free, he concentrated solely on running. The muscles in his legs burned; his chest heaved. He couldn't remember ever running this hard in his life, even from all those times Butch tried to beat him up.

Speak of the devil, as Luis came up to the school grounds, he saw Butch at one of the outside tables. He was hunched over, his arms resting on the tabletop and head hung low. Luis slowed to a jog upon seeing his old enemy before coming to a stop. With him slouched over the lunch table like that, Luis couldn't help but think how Butch looked so sad, almost depressing.

Butch slowly lifted his head up. His eyes were encircled with deep black grooves, and his black hair was an absolute mess. When he saw Luis, the bully's eyes shot wide open. He tried to jump up from the table, but his foot caught on the supports, and he fell hard to the ground, crying out in surprise and pain.

"Hey," Luis called to him, walking over to help him up. "Are you okay?"

"Stay the hell away from me, you freak!" Butch screamed. Frantically, he twisted and kicked his leg until it got loose. "It's you he wants! Just leave me alone!" Terrified, Butch clambered back to his feet and started to run. "It's you he wants!"

Confused and more than a little disturbed, Luis shouted back, "Who?"

"That ghost kid! Paul!" Butch shouted. "He wants you dead!" He ran off, leaving a deeply worried Luis behind.

So his suspicions were right, Paul was here yesterday. This only placed more apprehension on Luis's shoulders. A biting wind picked up, causing Luis to shiver. A low mist hung in the air and drifted around the school. The sweat he'd accumulated from running sapped the heat from his body in the cold October morning. He quickly made his way to the school library and once inside was greeted by the warm familiar smell of the books.

The librarian Mrs. Brown was seated at the check-out station with a book in hand. She waved to Luis as he walked in, but it was obvious how unhappy she was. "Good morning, Luis."

"Good morning, Mrs. Brown," he responded, placing his backpack next to one of the reading tables. "What's wrong?"

"I don't suppose you heard what happened yesterday, have you?" she said, placing her book down.

"I wasn't here, but I heard of it afterward," he said.

Her eyes shifted back to the desk in front of her. "Yes, it's true. Mrs. Anderson died yesterday. There's going to be a moment of silence held for her in your homeroom class this morning."

"Yeah," Luis said, pushing up his glasses. "I can understand that. I heard them say it was a heart attack, is that true?"

"I don't remember her having any issues with her heart or a family history of it," Mrs. Brown said. "Then again, she was old."

"Last time I checked, fifty-eight wasn't terribly old." Luis remarked. It seemed a little weird to him. A fire that was most likely caused by Paul, and yet the only death this time was a result of a heart attack. Why? What was the connection, if there was one at all?

The creaking hinge alerted him to the library door opening. Serena stepped inside; her heavy boots thudded against the red carpet as she did. Seeing her again, even in the midst of all the weirdness going on, made Luis flustered. It was only yesterday that she cursed him out and said she hated him, and they still hadn't talked about it since then.

"Luis," Serena said, hardly looking at him. She seemed almost as uncomfortable as he was. "You had something important to talk to me about, right?"

"Yes," he said, adjusting his glasses.

They sat down across from each other; Serena leaned forward with her hands folded together on the reading table. "So tell me what happened."

"Okay," Luis said. "Last night, I had another dream. Like, remember how I had that vision the night of the fire that killed Damian? Same sort of thing, except it was much clearer this time," he told her about his dream—the girl on the sidewalk and the man in the SUV. How the man grabbed her, drugged her, and threw her in the back of his car before driving away. "And then this morning on the news, they were talking about a kidnapping, and they had her picture. It's not just a coincidence. I think it's the same person who took Alice."

Serena's hands clenched tightly into fists. She stared down at the table with eyes filled with rage and hate. Her teeth gritted together behind sneering lips. "That bastard," she snarled. "He's still out there. Still doing this to kids." She looked up at Luis, her face twisted into such a look of anger it disturbed him. "Luis, we have to stop him."

He placed his hand over hers, relaxing her a bit. "I know, but I don't know how to yet. In my dream, I didn't see his face."

"Why not?" she shouted, louder than she meant. "You could see her but not him?" She quieted down a little after getting a look from the librarian.

"I can't control my dream visions. I don't know why it didn't let me see them both more clearly, but I can't do anything about it." He held her hand tightly.

"I know," she said, her voice became wobbly. "But this is the same monster that took my sister from me. He destroyed my family and countless others too. He has to be stopped."

"I know he does," Luis replied. "We just need to use what we know." Just as he said that, the school bell rang for first period. They both got up and headed for the door. "We can work on it more at first break, okay?"

"Yeah, okay," Serena said, heading for her first class.

20

His first class was biology with Ms. Sterling. He took his seat, with Butch two rows to his left. The other students also filed in and sat down; the teacher stood at the head of the classroom to address them. "All right, class," Ms. Sterling said. "I have some sad news this morning. Mrs. Anderson, a teacher many of you probably had, passed away yesterday during the fire evacuation."

A low murmur floated around the classroom. For many of the students, this was the first they had heard of it. Luis and Butch, however, merely sat in silence looking down at the desks before them. Ms. Sterling lifted up her hands to the class. "Please, be quiet everyone," she said. "The principal has asked that we have a minute of silence in respect for all the long years she's been with us." The teacher gazed up at the clock as the second hand ticked toward the twelve. "So if everyone can please sit down and remain quiet starting now."

The room fell dead silent except for the steady ticking of the clock. Most of the students had their heads bowed;

others leaned over their desks. Some even leaned back in an almost relaxing pose. In all this, Luis stole a glance over at Butch. The bully had drops of sweat on his face, which slowly rolled down and fell to his table. His eyes were wide with fear and hands clasped tightly together.

Luis could tell Butch was scared out of his mind. He must've seen Paul yesterday and been confronted by him. That was the best explanation Luis could think of. The minute passed, and the class resumed like normal. Still out of the corner of his eye, Luis could see Butch, as well as just what kind of impact Paul was having on the people here.

As soon as class ended, Butch hurried for the door. He was halfway down the hall when Luis called out to him, "Butch, wait a minute!"

"Go away, dweeb!" he shouted back, pulling his coat up around him more.

"Hold on for just one minute!" Luis grabbed him by the shoulder, but as soon as he did, Butch shoved him away into the lockers.

"I don't want anything to do with you anymore. Isn't that what you want?" Butch said angrily. "So just go away."

Luis stood back up and brushed himself off. "I want to stop him too. But to do that, I need your help. You were here yesterday. He talked to you. Can't you tell me what happened?"

"Yeah," Butch said. "I can tell ya. He just about ripped my heart out Temple of Doom style, that's what happened! He reached into my chest and was trying to kill me!"

"But he didn't, why is that?"

"I don't give a crap! I just know I don't want it to happen again." Butch turned away and was just about to leave when he stopped. His eyes flashed wide like a lightbulb had just gone off in his brain. "It was Mrs. Anderson."

Luis snapped to attention. "What?"

"He stopped trying to kill me when he saw her. It was just like"—he struggled to find the right words—"like he'd seen her somewhere before and he got real mad. After that, he let me go and told me to set the fire."

"That was you?"

"It was either that or he'd rip out my heart and feed it to me!" Butch got defensive. "What else was I supposed to do?"

Luis didn't have an answer. But now he did have information. "Okay. That's all I needed to know. Thanks."

As he turned to leave, Butch called out to him, "What are you going to do? That kid's messed up in the head! He told me he killed his own baby sister when he was six. What do you possibly think you can do about him?"

Luis froze in his tracks; a cold shiver ran down his spine. If what Butch was saying was true and Paul really had murdered his own baby sister when he was only six years old himself, then that kid was already on his way to being a serial killer before he died. Luis soon found himself realizing that Paul was someone with sociopathic tendencies, no inhibitions, and the powers and abilities of a ghost. Nothing could stop him, and Luis was now his target.

He left Butch alone and headed to his geometry class.

All through geometry, Luis could hardly concentrate on the lesson. He was too busy thinking about what Butch had said, but he just couldn't figure it out. What was the connection? Why did Paul target Mrs. Anderson? He tapped the eraser end of his pencil against his desk; today's work assignment lay empty before him. He was deep in thought.

Soon, the bell rang for first break. He packed up his bag and headed off to the library. Serena was already waiting for him. She waved as he walked in. "Hey," she said. She was sitting at the reading and study table.

Luis placed his backpack on the floor and sat across from her. "Okay." He started. "I asked Butch about yesterday. He said Paul was here, and that he was responsible for the fire. And also, that Paul killed Mrs. Anderson."

Serena nodded. "I figured as much. But what does that have to do with the kidnapper?"

Luis sighed, "I don't know yet. Butch just said that Paul freaked out and got really mad when he saw her. I don't know why, but I'm certain there was some connection between them. Otherwise, why would he kill her?"

Serena only shrugged. "I have no clue, but why are you worrying about that? Don't we still have a kidnapper and serial killer to find and a girl to save?"

Luis nodded. "Yeah, you're right." He folded his hands on the table. "Okay, what do we know for sure?"

Serena leaned back in her chair. "That he abducts kids and later murders them. That their spirits haunt the playground in the town park. That he's been doing it for at least ten years and hasn't been caught."

"We need to know how many victims he'd had. How many ghosts are at that playground?" Luis asked.

"I think the last time I was there I counted ten," Serena answered.

Luis folded his arms and placed a hand to his chin. "Ten children in ten years, evens out to a victim a year with Paul being that last from just this past September." His eyes fixed intently on the table before him but looked passed it. "And now this anomaly, a second victim this year less than a month later. The pattern changed. Why?"

Serena threw her arms up in the air. "What's with the why? Why do we need to know why it changed?"

"From what we know, he's stayed true to the pattern of only one kidnapping a year. But now after ten years of staying the same, it changed. Something must've set him off." Luis thought long and hard, deep grooves appeared on his forehead. But still nothing came to mind. "Argh," he groaned. "We need more information."

Serena propped her head up with the heel of her palm. "You should become a detective after high school. With all this reasoning stuff you're doing now, you would give Sherlock Holmes a run for his money."

Luis half smirked and let out a small laugh. "Holmes would have figured this out by now," he sighed and shook his head. "If only we could just ask Alice about it, then this would be so much easier."

Serena slapped her hand against her forehead. "Why didn't we stop at the playground before coming to school and get her?"

"Because Paul is still at the playground," Luis explained. "He came to the school yesterday with the intent to kill us. If we went to the playground this morning, he would likely try again. And probably succeed." A lightning bolt went off in Luis's head—a sudden strike of insight and a horrendous idea. "Paul's only tried to go after people who he thinks have wronged him, right?"

Serena shrugged. "Your guess is as good as mine."

"But from what we've seen, that's been the case. That must mean the only reason he'd kill Mrs. Anderson is if he feels she's wronged him," Luis said. "Now why would he feel that?"

A quizzical look came over Serena's face. "Any number of reasons. The kid murdered his own family, what can we expect from him? And why do you keep bringing this back to him?"

"Because that's the point. Paul targeted her for a reason. What can that reason be except that she had something to do with his death?"

Serena's brows raised in surprise. "Wait a minute. What?" she said. "You think Mrs. Anderson—the sweet old granny teacher with spectacles and gray hair that would give out candy at the end of test days—had something, anything, to do with Paul's murder?"

"I know it seems strange, but that's the only thing I can really think of right now." As soon as he said that, the bell for third period rang. They each grabbed their bags and headed out of the library. "I'll keep thinking about it," Luis said, as he walked off to class.

21

Sitting in world history class with a substitute was a little unsettling for Luis. It was strange to think he'd seen Mrs. Anderson only two days prior, when she was in pretty good health for a woman her age, but he would never see her again. It was such a strange thought. The more he thought about it, the more the idea of death weighed upon his mind. Even though he'd been hanging out with and even holding conversations with the spirits of the deceased, he'd never really thought about death in much depth before.

It was such a final thing. Once something is dead, it can never come back. Even wayward spirits like Alice and Damian were just that—spirits. They could never return to life. And the only reason they're still around in any form at all is because of some unfinished business, and once that's completed, they pass over to the other side and can never come back. And what lay beyond death? Was there anything after death, or was it an end of existence?

The bell rang, and he shuffled out of class, moving on to fourth period and English literature where they were still talking about *Hamlet*—a play written five hundred years ago by some guy who Luis really didn't care much about. What was the point of studying some ancient play when there was a real little girl out there in real danger and a malevolent spirit that was trying to kill him?

Even as Mr. Harding was droning on about *Hamlet's* famous speech, that whole "to be, or not to be" shtick, Luis could only think about that girl, Tamika Little, and what kind of fear and pain she might be in. If only Alice could remember what happened to her, then they could just ask her who it was or what kind of connection Mrs. Anderson had, if any, and get this all sorted out.

Revelation struck Luis again, and it was so obvious to him. Alice couldn't remember what happened to her any more than he could remember about his own father and the accident, but Madam Morgana was able to sort it out. Why not ask her to do the same thing to Alice? Bring up her old memories? It made so much sense! Luis felt almost giddy with anticipation. He now had a plan, and with it, they could find the killer, bring him to justice, and save the little girl.

Luis had to wait until school ended before he could tell Serena, being that they didn't share any classes and their lunch schedules were different. He met her just outside the school grounds where she was waiting.

"Hey, Serena!" he called out as he ran up to her.

"Hey," she said simply. "I was hoping to see you again today."

"Did you think I wasn't going to?" Luis asked, smiling. "I have some good news. I have an idea of how to find out who the kidnapper is."

"Really?"

"Yes." They started to walk toward the playground. "Remember how Madam Morgana looked up my forgotten memories?" Serena nodded. "What if she was to do the same thing for Alice?"

Serena was taken aback by the suggestion. "You mean bring back Alice's memories of her attacker?"

"Yes," Luis said. "If she can do that, then we can save that girl and stop him from hurting anyone else!" His excitement was plain as day. He was rather proud of himself for coming up with this idea.

Serena, however, was a little more reserved. "I suppose that could work, but what could it do to her?" she asked. "Bringing up those old memories of my mom and your dad wasn't that great for either of us to relive, and for her, this would be her remembering how she died. Just think of what that could do to her."

Luis looked up at her quizzically. "Wasn't it just this morning you were getting worked up because I wasn't focusing enough on trying to catch this guy?"

"I do want to catch him, but I don't want to hurt my sister anymore than she already has been," Serena said. "She's been through a lot already. Do we really want to bring that up for her again?"

The point Serena was making started to sink in for Luis. "I think the best idea would be to ask her first. See if she's okay with it," he said.

"Yeah, that's a good idea." Just then Serena's phone started to buzz. She pulled it from her pocket and answered. "Hello?"

"Hello, Serena," a familiar old voice said. "Madam Morgana calling."

A confused look came over Serena's face. She looked down at Luis with pursed lips and scrunched brows. "Uh, hello. We were just talking about you," she said.

"I know," Morgana said. "I called to tell you about Alice. I sense that she's in danger."

"What do you mean she's in danger?" Serena shouted into her phone. Her other hand gripped more tightly around Luis's. "What kind of danger?"

"I can't exactly say," Morgana replied. "The vision was blurred."

Serena rolled her eyes and gave an exasperated sigh. "Can any one of you mediums ever have a psychic premonition that isn't conveniently obscure?"

"I'm sorry I can't give more information. That's not how my powers work. It's not my fault that my visions aren't catering to your specific needs." Morgana snarked. "But you should heed my warning. Your sister Alice is in pain and needs your help."

"What do we need to do to help her?" Serena asked. The tension in her voice was obvious.

"I have a feeling that the best way to help her can be found at Pleasant Hill apartments," Madam Morgana said. "I'm sorry if I can't be more specific than that."

The line fell silent as Morgana hung up. Serena stared at the screen blankly and then shoved it back in her pocket. "Morgana, sometimes I don't like you."

"What?" Luis asked.

"She said something's wrong with Alice," Serena said. "I'd put money on it being Paul. Come on." She tugged on Luis's arm. "Come on, we need to go rescue her!"

"Hold on a minute," Luis said. "That's not all Morgana said. You were on the phone a little longer than that." He dug his heels in, holding her back. "What else did she say?"

"Just something about Pleasant Hill. What about it?" She was anxiously tugging on his arm. "Come on, we have to go!"

"Why would she want us to go to Pleasant Hill? What's there that we need to do?" Luis asked. After a second of thought, "How does she know anything about that?"

"She's a psychic, what does it matter?" Serena shouted. "That's a good enough explanation for me."

"It's not for me. If, as you think, it is Paul again, then I can think of only one reason for us to go to Pleasant Hill," Luis said, holding up his index finger. "Damian."

Serena's eyes widened at the suggestion. "You really think that's what she means?"

Luis nodded. "I think it's time we told Damian the truth. We need to bring him to the playground to confront Paul." He shrugged his backpack straps higher on his shoulders. "Did you bring your car to school today?"

"After your phone call this morning? Of course, I did."

22

The breaks ground the car to a halt when they came to the ruins of the old Pleasant Hill apartments. Once parked next to the sidewalk, Luis could not get out of the car fast enough. He threw open the door and leapt out, almost landing on his face when his foot caught on the seat, but he managed to steady himself and get free, placing a hand over his chest and inhaling deeply. "You drive like a maniac!" He finally managed to say.

"I'd like to see you do better." Serena snapped, slamming the car door behind her. "Now yesterday we had Alice get Damian down for us, how do you expect to do it today?"

"Like this." Luis cupped his hands around his mouth. "Hey! Damian! We need to talk to you!" he shouted at the top of his lungs toward the burnt-out ruins.

Serena winced, holding a hand over her right ear. "You could have warned me."

A light breeze picked up around them, it scattered the fallen leaves and caused a small dust cloud. Out of thin air, the spirit of Damian appeared before their eyes. "Hey, guys.

How's it going? I'm glad you came back. Check this out." He fixed his eyes on a small pebble on the sidewalk. As his stare intensified, the tiny rock began to wobble and finally lifted off the ground. It hovered in midair at Damian's eye level for a good ten seconds before he lost control and it fell back to earth. He gasped for breath, tired out by the ordeal. "Did you see that? I could move it with just my thoughts! Is that cool or what?"

Luis and Serena looked back at each other, worried looks on their faces. They remembered all too easily how Alice had talked about Paul doing the same thing, and for Luis, it sent shivers down his spine. "When did you learn how to do that?"

"Oh, I've been practicing all day. Pretty much since Alice came by to visit yesterday." He looked around a bit, a quizzical look on his face. "Where is Alice?"

"Yeah," Luis said, with a twinge of hesitation. "That's the problem. We think she's in trouble."

Damian's confusion quickly became concern. "What kind of trouble?"

Luis tried to explain. "We think that—"

"We think"—Serena interrupted him—"the vengeful spirit that killed you and burned this place down has now targeted her for some reason."

"What? Seriously?" Damian cried.

Luis glanced quickly over at Serena, silently thanking her. "Yeah," he said. "And we think we might need your help to rescue her."

"Sure. Absolutely." Damian nodded quickly. "I'm all for it. What do you need me to do?"

Well, Luis thought, *that certainly didn't take much convincing.* "Okay, I have something of a plan." Luis pulled open the passenger door of the car. "We think that the spirit has Alice at the playground in the park. Serena and I can confront the spirit head on, distracting him so that you can find Alice and help her escape."

Serena tilted her head and raised an eyebrow at him. "How long did it take you to come up with this plan?"

"The last couple of seconds." He unzipped the front compartment of his backpack and pulled out the bloodstone pendant, which he tossed to Serena. "I still don't know if this thing works, but it's worth a shot at least."

"What's that?" Damian asked.

"A trinket the fortuneteller woman gave me yesterday." Luis zipped his backpack closed and threw it in the back seat again. "They're supposed to protect from dangerous spirits, but we haven't tested them yet."

"As good a time as any, I guess," Serena said, slipping the necklace over her head. "Any other ideas about what to do?" She opened the driver's door and slid back into the car.

"First, let's just try to get there safely. I don't want to be in another accident and possibly die this time." Luis snarked as he climbed into the car. He was expecting a witty remark from Serena, but none came. He looked over at her and saw she was just looking intently down at the steering wheel.

Serena's mind was racing. What Luis just said triggered so many thoughts for her. What if this was what Madam Morgana was talking about? She'd driven here so hastily because she was afraid for her sister, but what if they got in an accident and Luis was killed? Was that how he was supposed to die? Was she going to be the cause?

"Serena?" Luis called, snapping her out of her trance like state. "Are you okay?"

"Huh?" she said. "Oh yeah. Sure. Just thinking, that's all." She turned the key, and the engine started right up.

Damian phased though the door and seated himself in the back. "How do we even know I can leave this place?"

"Alice can wander around without any problem. I'm sure you can too," Luis said. He turned to Serena. "Ready?" She nodded with conviction. With that, Serena drove the car away from Pleasant Hill and across town back to the playground.

Fortunately for Serena, the drive there was uneventful. She was, however, very cautious. As they pulled up to the small parking lot, she parked the car and shut off the engine. Luis, Serena, and Damian sat quietly together in the car, looking out the windshield at the old empty playground. Luis took a few deep breaths, trying to steady himself. He turned back to face Damian and stole a glance at the girl next to him. "Are we ready?"

"As I'll ever be," Damian said.

Serena nodded, her face was stern and eyes burned with anger toward the old playground equipment. "Let's go save my sister."

"Okay. Damian, before we get out, I need to tell you something," Luis said, his hand rested on the door handle.

"What?" Damian asked.

"The vengeful spirit that burned down your apartment complex and who now has Alice," Luis said with a little hesitation. "We think it's the ghost of you brother Paul."

Damian was taken back, disturbed and confused. "You think what?"

Serena slapped Luis on the shoulder. "Way to go, idiot!" she said. "That's exactly what we wanted to avoid."

Luis rubbed his aching shoulder. He gave Serena an indignant look but kept talking to Damian. "We have no proof, but we haven't ruled it out either. His ghost normally resides here at the playground along with Alice."

Damian began to laugh. "Ha ha ha ha ha ha! That's crazy hilarious, man! You really had me going there." He stopped when he saw the serious faces of Luis and Serena face-palming. "You're not joking, are you?"

"Would we have dragged you all the way out here if we were?" Luis asked. "Again, we don't know anything for sure, but we want to find out. My idea is that we go talk to Paul. See if we can get him to say anything to confirm one way or another."

"That's your great idea?" Serena said harshly.

"And when we do, Damian, I'd like you to stand right behind me while invisible. Listen to everything Paul says, and make your own choice. As far as we can tell, Paul doesn't know about you, so you'll be our trump card." Luis pulled on the handle, the door opened, and he stepped out. "Let's see how this works."

"Luis," Damian called from the backseat. "The only reason I'm going to help you is for Alice's sake. I'm not exactly pleased that you knew about my brother and didn't tell me, but I'll let it go for right now. I'll go along with the plan, for now at least." He phased out of the car and vanished from sight. He hovered right behind Luis.

"You still there?" Luis asked.

"Yes." Damian's voice came from right next to his ear, freaking Luis out a bit, but he quickly calmed down from that shock at least.

His heart began to race as Serena stepped out of the car, and they walked up to the chain link fence around the playground. The wind started to pick up as they did, leaves fluttered in the air. This was the moment of truth. Luis took a deep breath and let it out to steady himself. He slipped the bloodstone under his shirt and stepped into the center of the playground. The carousal gave a rusty creak as it slowly turned. To his left was the swing set and two empty swings that shifted in the wind.

"Hello?" he called out. "Is there anyone here? I just want to talk."

The wind picked up, the leaves flew around in a small spiral in front of Luis. He took a couple of steps back as a figure materialized in the midst of the dancing leaves—a young boy with light brown hair, dressed in blue jeans and a gray hoodie with his hands shoved in the pockets. "Hello," the boy said. "You're Luis, right?"

"That's right," Luis said. "And I assume you're Paul?"

"How did you know?" Paul asked, all smiles.

Luis shrugged. "I think I remember when I was here before. Alice pointed you out on the seesaw. I don't think we've ever officially met until now."

"No, we haven't," Paul confirmed. "So what did you want to talk about?"

"Well, I was just wondering what happened to Alice." He gestured his thumb over to Serena. "I brought her sister back so that they could catch up on things, but I we haven't seen her all day."

"That's too bad. I haven't seen her either, so I don't know what to tell you," Paul said, his eyes narrowed and smile on his face. "I guess you'll just have to go looking somewhere else."

"Someplace else." Serena looked down at her extended fingers, inspecting her nails.

"Yeah, someplace else. Because she certainly isn't here." Paul smirked.

"Well"—Luis glanced over his shoulder—"maybe you could help us find her?"

"And how would I know where she is?" Paul asked. "It's not my job to watch her."

"You both hang out together, don't you?" Luis said. "I mean, you're both at this playground all day, right?"

"Except when she decides to run off with you two. You'd probably have a better idea where she is than I do." Paul floated over to the swings and sat down, his hands grasped the chains.

"Yeah, but we haven't seen her since yesterday. We were wondering if you had," Luis said.

Paul kicked his legs back and forth, pushing himself on the swings. "Why would I? It's not like I was at the fortuneteller's place yesterday."

Luis quickly jerked his head over to Serena. She also looked back at him. "We didn't say anything about a fortuneteller," Luis stated, his hands fell in his pockets.

The swing stopped as Paul drug his feet through the ground. His smirk disappeared and was replaced with a deep frown. His brows tilted down; face twisted in anger. "You're annoying. I think you'd better leave."

Luis took two steps closer to Paul. "I'm not leaving until I find Alice."

The wind began to pick up again. Paul levitated from the swing, his hands curled into fists. "Yes, you will." He raised one hand, and a small number of rocks lifted from the ground. They spun around him, like the planets around a star. "Right now."

Luis took a single step back, fear making his heart race. "Hey, there's no need to get crazy now. We're just looking for our friend."

"And you won't find her here," Paul said, the rocks continued to orbit him at faster and faster speeds. "So you'd better leave before I get really mad and do something you'll regret."

"Like what?" Serena shouted, she stepped forward. "Like set a building on fire?"

"So Alice told you about that after all. She's not as smart as I gave her credit for," Paul sneered. "Yes, I set that piece of trash apartment building on fire. They needed to die. I only wish more had died too."

A sly smirk came over Serena's face. "I was referring to the school, you idiot."

"What did you call me?" Paul shouted. "I'm not an idiot, you are!"

A rock flew through the air, aimed right at Serena's head. Seeing the rock come barreling toward her, she held up her arms over her face and winced. But no impact came. Slowly, hesitantly, she opened her eyes and lowered her arms. The rock was hovering in the air only a few inches away from her face.

A look of confused anger came over Paul's face. What was this? He'd wanted to send that rock smash through her brains and out the other side! Why did it stop?

A hand appeared, gripping the rock. As this hand slowly materialized, so did an arm and the rest of a body along with it. And a face Paul knew all too well but never thought he'd see again—Damian.

Damian stared up at his little brother with a look of intense rage and anger. He dropped the rock, and it hit the ground with a thud. "They were right, it was you."

"Big bro." Paul let the other stones fall to the earth. He gave a nervous laugh. "I didn't expect to see you. What's going on?"

"You're a murderer." Damian's tone was cold and filled with hate. He lifted off the ground, bringing himself to Paul's level. "You killed me, and Mom and Dad, and nearly killed everyone else in that building!" he shouted. "Why did you do it?"

Paul scoffed, his hands stuffed back in his pockets. "Because I could. Because you picked on me. Because you never came looking for me after I was taken."

"We did everything we could to find you! Mom and Dad were worried sick when you disappeared!" Damian shouted, tears welled up in his eyes.

"Clearly, not worried enough. I still died, and for that, so did you." Paul closed the distance between him and Damian in an instant and caught his older brother by the throat. "I just wish I could kill you again!"

Gasping for breath, Damian tried to claw at the fingers that held his neck. He grasped Paul's wrist with his left hand and pulled back his right into a fist. Paul had only a second to notice before Damian punched him in the face, sending the younger brother wheeling back.

Paul rubbed his left cheek, his mouth hung open and eyes wide with surprise. That felt real, as real as any punch would have if he were still alive. It was true then, anything one ghost did to another was as real as a person doing it to another. "There you go again. Beating up on your little brother just like you did in real life."

"I never touched you. How dare you try to pin any blame on me!" Damian sneered. "I tried to defend you. When they said you caused the fire that killed me, I didn't believe them. But then you just confessed to it, so what choice do I have?"

"No choice." Paul charged at his brother, grabbed him around the waist, and pounded his fists into Damian's stomach. Damian cried out in surprise and pain. Swiftly, he brought his knee up and slammed it into Paul's face.

"This will only end one way. You can't try to fight me. I'm older and stronger than you," Damian said.

"Yeah," Paul said, rubbing his nose. "But you can't do this!" With the thrust of his arm, Paul sent a barrage of small pebbles cascading though the air at his brother. Damian crossed his arms over his face just in time to be pelted by the small stones.

Why was he getting hit at all? He tried to phase through them, but instead, they just hit him all over! Once they subsided, his arms, chest, and legs were covered in small red welts.

"I imbued them with my own energy," Paul explained, grinning. "There's no escaping those."

23

L uis and Serena watched from below, stunned and afraid as the two brothers fought. A sudden blur of movement from the funhouse caught Luis's attention. Looking in the window, he saw the face of a little girl as she ducked out of sight. "That's the place!" He grabbed Serena's sleeve. "Come on, let them duke it out! I think I know where to look!"

They sprinted to the sideways tilted funhouse, threw open the door, and ran inside. They found Alice forced to the ground on her knees by the other ghost children with her arms held behind her back and a hand clasped over her mouth. Alice's eyes screamed at them with a look of horrible fear but also relief. In truth, she had never been so happy to see anyone in her whole life, or afterlife.

Serena was at first disturbed and horrified by what she saw, but this quickly became anger. She pointed directly at the other ghost children. "Let her go right now!" she shouted.

"Why can't you just go away?" the little girl ghost cried. She huddled on the floor, with her legs pulled up and her face hidden. "You made everything bad! Leave us alone!"

"Give me back my sister and I will!" Serena shouted.

"No!" the little girl screamed. "She's my sissy, not yours! Now go away!" Her voice suddenly grew louder, and the funhouse shook.

Luis had to steady himself as the shaking subsided. This was getting out of hand, and he knew it. Serena was just going to keep shouting and only get the other ghost more riled up. He placed his hand on her shoulder, nodded to her, and stepped forward. Crossing his legs, he sat on the floor and looked at the young spirit girl. "I'm sorry. I didn't mean to cause any problems. What is your name?"

She looked up at him with a worried expression. "Susie," she uttered.

Luis nodded. "Hi, Susie. I'm Luis. I'm a friend of Alice, and you are too, right?"

"She's like a big sissy to me," Susie said. "When I came here, I was scared at first, but then she helped me not be scared. I want to stay with her."

"I don't want to take her away from you. But is this really a good way to stay with her? If someone was holding you down like that, would you want to stay with them?" Luis asked.

"Shut up!" one of the older ghosts said. "Paul said you would try something like that! That you would steal Alice from us!"

Luis looked up this boy, who was holding Alice's arms back. "And what is your name?"

"I'm not telling you, four eyes!" the ghost boy said.

As if to emphasize them, Luis shifted his glasses. "Yes, I have glasses. They help me see." He rested his hands in his lap. "So what did Paul say I would do? Isn't Alice important to you? Do you think she wants to stay here anymore with you treating her this way?"

"But she started running away as soon as you showed up. So if you go away, then it'll just go back to the way it was," the ghost boy said.

"Really? Do you think that's the case?" Luis asked.

"Yes!" the ghost boy shouted. "Alice is like an older sister to all of us. She would never leave once you're gone."

Luis stood back up and walked over to the open window. Looking out, he could still see Paul and Damian in their tussle. "Paul told you all that? Because you can see how much his real older brother means to him." Luis pointed out the window. Just as Luis said that, Paul kicked Damian as hard as he could in the stomach. Damian clutched as his gut as he doubled over in pain. "See? Paul doesn't care about his own real brother. So why would he care about any of you or about Alice?"

"That mean older boy must've done something really bad to Paul to make him do that!" the loudmouthed ghost child shouted.

"Does that mean," Luis said, "that Paul never told you that he killed his own family? That's his older brother who died two days ago in a fire that Paul himself started. He murdered his own family, and just yesterday, he murdered a teacher at my school. What he's doing isn't right and needs to be stopped."

The angry ghost boy looked out the window then back at Luis. He continued glancing back and forth, confused and distraught. "I don't believe you!" he screamed.

"Jason, stop being a meanie!" Susie shouted to the other ghost. The funhouse shook on its foundation again.

Luis waited for a minute as the tension settled. "Now," he finally said. "I know that Alice has been spending more time with us. I'm sorry if it seemed like we took her from you, but if it's at all possible, I want to do the same thing for all you that I did for her. Namely, reunite you with your friends and families."

At this, the eyes of all the other ghost children lit up. Susie jumped to her feet with excitement. "Really? You'll help me find my mommy and daddy?"

Luis leaned down to her level and placed his hand on her head. "I'll do everything I can. But I'll need Alice's help for that, so I need you to let her go."

With only a few seconds hesitation, the other children released their hold on Alice. She gasped for air and fell forward, catching herself with her arms. After catching her breath, she raced over and wrapped her arms around Luis in a deep embrace. She did the same for Serena immediately after. "Thank you! I knew you'd come for me."

"We would never abandon you," Serena said, holding her sister tight. "I'm just glad I got to save you this time."

Holding Alice's hand, Serena stepped out of the funhouse with Luis right behind her. The other ghost children hovered in the air behind them as they did. They saw Damian with Paul in a headlock, his arms looped under the younger boy's shoulders and hands placed behind his head.

Paul gritted his teeth; he stared angrily at Serena and Luis. "Let me go!" he shouted. He struggled against Damian's hold, but his brother held firm.

Alice fixed her gaze on Paul, her eyes filled with pity for him. "Damian," she said. "You don't have to hold him anymore."

"Are you sure?" Damian turned to look at them.

"Yes. He's harmless now," Alice said.

With a bit of reluctance, Damian unhooked his hands, and Paul slipped out of the hold. The younger boy looked around at the other ghosts and people around him. Some angry, others pitying, all staring and waiting for him to make a move or try anything. He just clenched his fists and sneered.

Paul pointed directly at Luis. "You," he growled. "I'm not done with you yet." His form then dissolved, disappearing into thin air.

With his brother now gone, Damian sighed. He descended to the ground below and rested on one of the swings, slouched forward with his arms placed over his knees. His eyes fixed on the dirt below.

Luis, Serena, and Alice watched him in silence. A similar thought ran through each of their heads as they glanced back from one another to Damian. What must he be thinking right now? What must he be feeling? To see the little brother he'd been missing only turn into this violent and dangerous thing, what does that do to a person?

Alice floated over and hovered next to him. She placed her hand on his shoulder, hoping to comfort him, but he brushed her off. "Leave me alone." His voice was low, hushed, and full of sorrow.

She pulled back, her own heart heavy with sadness. As Alice floated back to the others, Susie came up to her and tugged lightly on her shirt. "Alice?" she said in her small cute voice. "I'm sorry we were mean to you. It wasn't nice."

Looking at the little girl's sad and guilty face made Alice smile just a little. She knelt down to Susie's level. "Hey, it's okay. I understand what happened. It wasn't your fault." She hugged the little girl.

"Where do you think Paul went off to?" Serena turned to Luis.

Luis shrugged. "I don't know. But now I guess he's going to be coming after me even more than before." He stepped over to Alice and Susie. "How are you feeling?"

Alice let go and stood up. "Better. Again, thanks for coming back for me."

"Yeah," Luis said, hesitant to get to the next point. "Listen, something happened last night."

"Something happened last night? Like what?" Alice asked.

"Last night, I had another vision. This one about a kidnapping," he said.

Alice's eyes widened in horror. "You mean like what happened to us?" She motioned to the other children around them.

Luis nodded. "I think so. In my dream, I saw a little girl get taken off the street and pulled into an SUV. Then this morning, there was a news report about the kidnapping. I'm fairly certain it's the same person that took you and everyone else here."

"There's something else you need to know," Alice said, her gaze fell. "Yesterday, after I left you, Serena, was when Paul found me and dragged me back here. He said he'd killed one of the teachers at your school."

"We know," Serena said. "Mrs. Anderson. Whatever he did made her have a heart attack."

"What he did, or at least he said he did, was squeezing her heart until it stopped beating." Alice held up her hand for emphasis.

"Ugh," Luis groaned with disgust. "That's kinda freaky."

"I know. And also, he said the reason he did it was because she was involved in his kidnapping and death," Alice continued.

Luis and Serena fixed eyes, each as shocked and confused as the other. Turning back to Alice, Luis asked, "Do you know if he was telling the truth?"

Alice only shook her head. "I don't remember anything about that."

Luis sighed. All this new information was weighing heavily on his mind. His original theory that Mrs. Anderson was targeted for a reason was right, even if it really shook him up inside. Was his old teacher really that kind of depraved person? There was still no real way to be sure, but he knew the only way he could think of to find out. "Alice"—he placed his hands on her shoulders—"I have an idea about how to find the kidnapper and save the girl, but I need you to do something."

"What?" she asked.

"Well, remember how Madam Morgana brought up my memories?"

Alice quickly connected the dots. "You want her to do the same thing to me. Bring up the memories of my kidnapping and murder," she said matter-of-factly.

"To put it bluntly, yes," Luis said. "But if you don't want to do, I can understand. Bringing up those memories, especially after going through something like this, would be—"

"Take me there." Alice cut him off. "Every second we waste here is more time for that predator to hurt or kill his newest victim. Let's just do it so we can stop him as quickly as possible."

Luis blinked, surprised and a little concerned. He shrugged. "Okay. Let's go."

Serena, just as surprised, headed over to her car and unlocked the doors. As they were climbing in, she stopped and looked back at the swing set, where Damian continued to sulk. "Damian?" she called over to him. "Are you coming along?"

"No." He waved dismissively at them. "I think I'll just stay here for a while," he said.

"I just want to say I'm sorry we had to do this!" Serena shouted as she climbed into the car and drove away.

Damian sat on the swing, his head hanging low and arms resting over his knees. He felt empty, lonely, and distraught.

A gust of wind blew around him. It rustled the leaves on the ground and in the trees, he hardly noticed.

What did he have anymore? He was a ghost, trapped to this world by some vague concept of purpose, and his little brother was the one who killed him.

"Hello?" the little girl ghost called to him. She floated over to Damian and stood in front of him. "Are you okay?"

Damian let out a heavy sigh and brushed his hair back, not that he actually had hair. This was just some abstract representation of the physical body he used to have, the one that was now burned to ashes and the bones of which sat in a morgue somewhere. "No. I'm not."

"Is there anything I can do?" the little girl asked. "Do you need a hug?"

"No." Damian's voice remained low and quiet. "I just need to be alone." She didn't leave him alone. Instead, the girl climbed onto the swing next to him and began pumping her legs back and forth. Damian turned his head slowly to look at her, his eyebrow arched. "What are you doing?"

"I'm leaving you alone," the little girl said. "So you shouldn't talk to me."

"When someone asks you to leave them alone, that doesn't mean sit next to them and annoy them."

"I'm not annoying you. You're the one that keeps talking to me," the little girl said. "If you want to be alone, then you need to stop talking."

Damian rolled his eyes and turned away. They sat side by side on the swings in silence, the continuance grinding of the rusty chains pulsating through the air. "What's your name?" he finally asked.

"Susie," the girl replied.

"Well, Susie, I don't feel like being here anymore." He stood up from the swing and stuffed his hands in his pockets. He was walking away when she called out to him.

"Where are you going?"

"Probably back to the burnt-out remains of my old house. I have nowhere else to go," he said as he passed through the gate.

"Why don't you stay with us?" Susie leapt off the swing and floated over to him. "We don't want to be alone."

"Sad fact, kid. Everyone's alone. Most people just don't realize it yet."

"You don't have to be. We can keep you company."

"No, thanks." He waved her away.

Susie stopped and stared at his hand. "What's wrong with your arm?"

Damian held his arm out in front of his face and saw it growing fainter. His hand was now barely visible, and the transparency was spreading up his body. "What in the— what is this?" he shouted with fear in his voice.

"Stand still, maybe it'll stop."

With a sharp intake of breath, Damian froze in place with his eyes wide open. His form continued to dissipate slowly starting from the arms and legs and working its way up. "I can see them."

"See who?" Susie asked.

"My mom and dad." The fear in his eyes changed to happiness, and he smiled. "And my little sister. They're waiting for me. They're calling me." He looked down at himself, which now was little more than a torso and head. "This is crossing over."

"To the other side? To heaven?"

"Maybe." He closed his eyes and waited as the rest of his form disappeared. "Now I can be at rest." He vanished from view completely, leaving behind only an empty swing.

24

The drab-gray Honda pulled up to a small parking area just outside of Madam Morgana's office. The flip-up headlights folded back down as the engine shut off. Luis and Serena stepped out, Alice phased through the roof and floated up behind them.

Luis let out a breath. "Here we are again."

Serena looked back over her shoulder at Alice. "Are you totally sure?"

Alice gave a swift nod. "Absolutely."

With that said, Serena locked the car, and they walked up the steps, stopping only to knock on the door. "Come in," Madam Morgana's voice called from inside. Serena gripped the handle, turned it, and pushed the door open. The smell of incense wafted out to greet them. Stepping inside, they found Madam Morgana dressed similar to before in the same dark room with the same candles and the same incense seated at the same table. "Greeting, children," she said.

"Hello, again." Serena waved.

The fortuneteller placed her hand together on the table in front of her. She leaned on her elbows. "So how have those necklaces done for you so far? Still having trouble with dangerous spirits?"

Luis adjusted his glasses. "A little," he said. "But that's not really why we're here this time."

"Oh?" Morgana tilted her head and arched an eyebrow. "What are you looking for today?"

"Well"—Luis motioned to Alice—"it has to do with her. We want to know if you can do for her what you did for me and look into her memories."

"You want me to specifically look at how she died," Morgana said. She leaned back in her chair, readjusting her dress. "I can't do that."

"Can't or won't?" Luis stepped forward.

"Won't," Morgana replied flatly. "It is more dangerous than you can believe. I remember seeing her the last time, and I can tell just by looking at her that her death and the days leading up to it were not pleasant by any stretch. To bring those memories back would be disastrous. Her very mental stability could be lost."

"Please?" Alice asked. "It's very important. There is someone in danger, and I can save them but only if I can remember."

"I know," Morgana said. "I heard about that girl. But I can't just go through your mind and dredge up everything that you've repressed. It's been repressed for a reason."

"Someone's life is on the line, someone who could go through the very same thing I did," Alice argued. "Right now, my mental stability can go straight to hell if it means rescuing her."

Morgana sighed. The fortuneteller stood, adjusted her dress, and paced around the room. She paused by the window and stared out at the cars that drove passed. "I had the same vision last night as you did, Luis," she said. "I know that's what brought you here, and trust me, I would like nothing more than to stop this man. But I will not force the memories of Alice's death to resurface."

"Oh, come on." Luis jumped to his feet. "You'll pull up the memories of the accident that killed my dad and her mom"—motioning to Serena—"and almost killed me, but not Alice's memories of her own death? We already asked her permission, and she gave it. So why not just go ahead with it?"

"Because your memories weren't traumatic," the psychic said.

"Excuse me? I blocked out my father's death for years, and then you brought it up without a moment's thought! You say that wasn't traumatic?"

"Compared to what you want me to divine now, your repressed memories were nothing. This time, it won't be the death of a family member. It will be her own death and the last few horrific days of her life. Being forced to suffer through them again, years after the fact." Morgana stepped over to Luis and looked sternly down at him. "Imagine telling a person who's just been horribly raped that in order to find the rapist, they have to go through it all over again. Every moment, every little second of pain and trauma, and they have to relive it in all its intensity. That is what you are asking of me, and I will not do it."

Looking up at the older woman with indignation, Luis simply said, "Fine." He sat back down and grabbed the crystal ball himself. "If you won't, then I will."

"You can't be serious," Madam Morgana said, aghast.

"You kept saying I have the same gifts as you, so that means I can do the same things." He placed his hands on the crystal ball and closed his eyes, attempting to focus.

Before he could do anything, Morgana grabbed his wrists and pulled his hands away. "As bad as I said things would be, it'd be far worse to have an untrained child attempt them." She sat back down at the table and placed the ball back on its stand. "You're clearly going to be reckless and try this with or without my help, so I should at least prevent you from doing more damage than it will already cause."

"Thank you," Luis said, leaning back in his chair. In reality, this was what he was hoping for the whole time. He had no real intention of trying any mystical mumbo jumbo himself. Real or not, it just wasn't his thing.

Morgana beckoned for Alice to sit next to her. Once she did, Morgana held her hands over the crystal ball. "Now, Alice, I know you agreed to this, but you do know the risks involved. After I've started, there is no way to stop."

Alice nodded. "I understand."

The fortuneteller sighed, "Very well." She closed her eyes, hummed, and waved her hands around the crystal ball in rhythmic circles. Purple clouds of smoke appeared inside it, as images began to shape.

Alice stood on the street corner across from the elementary school, leaning up against a stop sign. Her arms were folded and ankles crossed. She wore a green-plaid flannel shirt and a pair of faded blue jeans, her red beanie rested atop her auburn hair. Her heavyset backpack hung down from her shoulders.

The final school bell rang, and children began pouring out of the classrooms. They walked, ran, and skipped across the parking lot to their awaiting parents. Alice straightened up when she saw one of the first graders, her little sister Cynthia, come running toward her. "Sissy!"

"Hi, Cindy!" Alice said, scooping the little girl up in her arms and spinning her around. "You're getting too big for me, soon I won't be able to do that." She set her sister back down. "You may have to ask Daddy when we get home."

"No!" Cindy shouted. "He always spins me too fast, it gets scary! I like it more when you do it!"

Alice laughed. She gave her little sister another big hug, squeezing her tight before letting her go again. Taking Cindy's hand, Alice led her away from the school and off toward home. "So what did you do in class today?" she asked.

"Our teacher was silly today," Cindy said.

"Silly how?"

"She made a bird out of paper. And then made it caw at everyone." Cindy looked up at Alice with her cute little eyes. "Can you do that?"

"Make a paper crane? I don't think I know how. I suppose I can look it up," Alice said. "Would you like me to do that?"

The little first grader nodded her head rapidly. "Yes!"

"Okay, okay, calm down." Alice placed her hand on the little girl's head to stop her. "You'll give yourself whiplash if you do that."

Alice took Cindy's hand again. She walked on the left side of the sidewalk, closest to the road. For every step Alice took, Cindy had to take one and a half just to keep up. The younger girl shuffled along to keep up with her big sister.

They turned away from the main sidewalk and entered the town park. Trees reached up to the cloud-filled sky, their leaves now appearing less like foliage and more like autumn fire clinging to the branches. The boughs hung over the dirt path, casting uneven shadows. A stream ran parallel to the path, the water babbling over rocks in the streambed.

A man sat on a bench next to the stream, overlooking the water. He wore a large brown coat with a collar that came up over his face; his hands were stuffed in the pockets. Alice watched him intently, eyeing him with suspicion. The man peaked over his shoulder at them then turned away. Something about that man just rubbed her the wrong way. Alice clenched her sister's hand tighter as they walked past. After they got a little ways away, she ignored him as harmless.

"Sissy, can we stop for a minute?" Cindy whined. "My feet hurt."

"We haven't crossed through the park yet. How can your feet hurt?" Alice said, swinging her arms in the air in an overly exaggerated fashion. She was just messing with Cindy, playing around with her. "Okay then, we can rest for a minute."

Cindy sat down on the pathway, she fell back on the ground with her arms over her head and legs sprawled out. She sighed as if exhausted. "I'm so tired."

"Yeah, I bet." Alice's hands fell to her waist. "When we get home, you'll be bouncing all over the place and driving Mom and Dad crazy. I know what you do." The man on the bench stood up. He kept his head tucked down as he casually approached. Alice saw him but tried not to act afraid for Cindy's sake. "Come on, get up." She reached down and grabbed the six-year-old's hand. "Time to go."

"Can't we stay here just a little more?" Cindy whined.

"No. Mom and Dad are waiting for us." The man continued to advance on them. Alice looked over at him warily. She tugged on Cindy's arm until the little girl stood. "Now come on."

Just then the man grabbed Alice by the arm and shoved her aside. She cried out in shock as she fell down the embankment to the stream. Her feet caught under her, and she tumbled end over end, the rocks dug into her skin and the cold water soaked through her clothes.

"Aaah!" Cynthia shrieked. Alice jolted up and saw the man clutching her sister tightly in both arms, his gloved hand pressed firmly against her mouth to silence her. He took off running down the path, Cindy bouncing with each step. The little girl struggled vainly against his grip, kicking and wriggling. She stared at Alice with fear in her eyes.

"No!" Alice threw her backpack aside and bolted up the stream bank. She took chase after the man, closing in on him quickly. "Let my sister go!" She was upon him, reaching out and grabbing hold of his overcoat.

He wrenched back on the coat, trying to pull it from Alice's grip, but she held firm. The man released his hold on Cynthia and took a swing at Alice, hitting her across the face and sending her spiraling to the ground. "Aah!" Alice cried. She hit the earth with a thud, banging her head against the dirt. "Cindy!" she shouted as she sat up. "Run! Run home now!"

The little girl who escaped the man's grasp ran. She screamed, tears rolling down her face. The man started after her, but Alice jumped back to her feet and threw herself at him, tackling him to the ground. She raised a fist and brought it down against his head, hitting him over and over as hard as she could. After the third strike, the man caught her by the wrist. He shoved her to the ground again and pulled a rag from his coat pocket. He pressed it over her mouth and nose, holding it there long enough for the chemicals on it to take effect. Alice smelled the chemical soaked rag, although she didn't know what it was. Her eyelids became heavy and her vision blurred. In only a few moments, she was unconscious. The man looked up the path, but Cynthia was gone.

Cindy ran as fast as her little legs could carry her. She held the backpack firm against her chest like a shield. She ran so fast she tripped and fell back down, her fall cushioned by the bag. She ran and ran and ran, her legs hurt, and she grew tired. When she stopped and looked back, the man was gone. And so was her sister.

Tears welled up in Cindy's eyes. Her lips quivered. She dropped her backpack, her hands now rubbing the tears away. She cried, wailed at the top of her lungs. Her legs folded up beneath her. She wrapped her arms around her knees and cried, screaming into the air.

"I can't believe you did this again!" a woman's voice shrieked.

Alice jolted awake. Her eyes snapped open, but the room she was in was pitch black with the only light seeping in through the cracks in the doorframe. Her arms were bound to a bed frame over her head with what felt like plastic zip ties. She pulled on them feebly, but to no avail.

"It's just one playmate, Mother," a man's voice said from the other side of the door. "Can't I have just one? I've been so lonely since we moved here."

"The whole reason we moved was to get away from this!" the woman shouted back. Alice heard their muffled voices through the door. She pulled on the restraints around her wrists, tried to use her legs for more leverage only to find her ankles were tied to the bed frame as well. Her heart hammered in her chest. The woman on the other side of the door continued. "I wanted you to stop doing this. People were getting suspicious of you before. We're supposed to start fresh here, but then you grab another child off the street?"

"It wasn't off the street, it was in the park," the man said. "There was no one around, I made sure. I didn't even want to take her. I wanted the smaller girl. But she got away."

"And you let a witness escape?" the woman screamed. "Do you know what will happen now? People will be looking for you."

"She wouldn't have gotten away if you had been there to help," the man said. "If you want, we can go back and try to find her."

"Of course not!" There was a slap. Alice jumped when she heard it. "Are you insane? If people learn about any of this, they'll condemn you. They'll crucify you. And I'm not going to let them take my baby boy," the woman sighed. "Fine. I know you're going to keep doing this, no matter how I try to stop you. I might as well make sure it's done right from now on."

"That means you'll help me?" the man asked.

"Yes. That means I pick out the kids, I decide when me take them, and I choose where. Understand?"

"Yes, I understand, Mother. Can I play with my new toy now?" There was a glimmer of joy in his voice, and Alice began to shake. She knew what that meant and did not like it. Her breathing became quick and shallow, her eyes darted around the dark room looking for anything that might help her, but she saw nothing.

"Go ahead. I just need to sort things out." The woman's footsteps signaled her departure as she walked up a set of creaky stairs.

The doorknob turned, and a pillar of light fell into the dark room. Alice had to turn away from the blinding light as the man stepped in. She could only see his silhouette, but Alice knew it was the same man from the park. "Good. You're awake." He reached into the pocket of his overcoat and revealed a ski mask, which he pulled over his face. "I much prefer when you're awake. It's more fun." He closed the door behind him, cutting off the light.

The man flicked a switch, and the bulb over the bed illuminated the room. It was a plain, concrete basement with only the bed itself and the light fixture and a drain in the center of the floor. With the light on, the man threw his overcoat to the ground and approached the bed.

She didn't want his to come closer. "No!" Alice pulled as hard as she could against her restraints. They didn't budge. "Please don't! Let me go!"

The bed shifted as the man settled next to her. Something was pressed against her lips—another rag. Her mouth was forced open and the rag placed between her teeth. Even as she tried to fight it, her abductor tied the ends together around the back of her head. Her protests now became merely muffled noises. The bed shifted again as the abductor crawled on top of her, one arm placed on either side of her body. His rank breath brushed against her face, the stench filled her nostrils, and she turned away.

He grabbed her face with his thick fingers and pulled her head back. Forcefully, and even with a gag in her mouth, the man pressed his chapped lips against hers, sliding his slimy tongue against her lips and even passed the gag into her mouth.

Alice felt sick, her stomach lurched, and she wanted to vomit. The taste was disgusting, but worse was the feeling of being violated. Her whole body revolted. She tried to back away, but the struggle only made him more forceful. He pushed her back down against the bed, grabbed the edges of her shirt, and tore them open. The buttons popped off, flying through the air in random directions.

With a pair of scissors, the man cut along the seam of her sports bra and pulled it away. She lay exposed on the bed, gooseflesh appearing on her skin, and the cold air lingered against her chest. Alice breathed shallowly through her nostrils, trying not to gag on the retched stench of the man's sweat or breath. Her heart raced like mad. The man placed his hands over her small, budding breasts. His calloused fingers scratched against the sensitive skin, and Alice winced.

She turned away, her eyes clamped shut and tears beginning to slide down her face. This wasn't happening;

it couldn't be happening. She dared not to even think the word, only feel it—rape. She was getting raped. Very soon, he would force himself upon her even more than he was now, and nothing she could do would stop him.

The woman rested on the couch in the living room upstairs. The television was on, but she was hardly watching it. The woman rubbed her fingers against her temples as if she had a headache, but really, she was just annoyed. The door to the basement staircase was left open, and she heard her son open and close the cellar door.

After everything she's tried to do for her son, he still falls back to his old habits. The woman knew this was not going to be the only child he would abduct, and they would only get younger. The only thing she could hope for was to protect her son and keep the authorities away from him. No one was going to take her son from her.

Alice's muffled screams rang throughout the house. There was a rhythm to the yelps and cries emanating from the basement, along with the squeaking of old springs from the mattress. A twinge of pain shot through the woman's heart in sympathy for the young girl. She turned back to the TV and raised the volume, draining out the sounds below.

25

How long has she been here now? A few days? Weeks? A month? She had no idea. She never left this room. Alice remained trapped in this single bedroom. The door was always locked from the outside. There were no windows here, and the only other place she could go was a tiny bathroom, which didn't even have a door—only a jutting sink without a cabinet, a toilet with a single roll of toilet paper, and a small shower without a curtain. As for this room, there was nothing in it aside from the bed itself, which didn't have any sheets or blankets, and the plain light fixture on the ceiling.

She didn't even have clothes anymore; they were taken on the second day.

A knock came at the door. Alice knew it was the woman. The man never knocked, he simply barged in. Alice didn't move, there was no need. She remained on the bed, her legs pulled up, so her arms wrapped around them and face rested on her knees.

The door clicked as it unlocked, and the woman stepped in. She held a paper plate of macaroni and cheese with a plastic fork and a paper cup of water. "Alice," the woman said, her voice was sickeningly sweet. "I brought you some food. I hope you're hungry." She set the plate down on the bed behind Alice and stepped out.

Alice remained motionless as the door locked again. She hated the woman just as much as her abuser. The woman always put on a kind face, spoke softly and gently, and it made Alice sick. Slowly, she turned around and took the plate. Steam rose from the mac and cheese, and her stomach gurgled at the sight of it. She was hungry, as it turned out, and she wanted to eat, but their hands made this food—the same hands that tore her clothes away and hurt her.

Shaking with anger, Alice threw the plate against the wall. The food splattered in a gooey mess. She broke down and cried again, burying her face in her hands.

A loud crashing came from the other side of the door. Alice jumped, startled by the sound. Voices started shouting on the other side.

"Royce, stop! Put that down!"

"Get out of my way, Mother!"

A gunshot went off. Alice screamed a little. She crawled under the bed, curling up in the fetal position with her hands clasped over her ears.

"Move before I shoot you too, Mother!" the man's voice growled. The cocking of a gun was heard. "If I get caught, you'll be arrested too. Get out of the way!"

Alice hid under the bed, trembling in fear like a frightened rabbit. The man had a gun! What was happening out there? The door clicked unlocked again, and the man kicked it open. From under the bed, Alice watched his large brown boots stomp into the room.

He stormed over to the bed, hooked his fingers under the frame, and flipped it over. The bed crashed around the room. Alice screamed in terror at the monster standing over her. For the first and only time in her life, Alice saw the face of her abuser.

He lifted a pistol, aimed it at her face, and pulled the trigger. The muzzle flash was the last thing she saw and the gunshot the last thing she heard. The world became dark. Blackness.

Nothing.

Nothing.

Nothing.

Her eyes snapped open suddenly. Where was she? What just happened? It was bright; the light was golden yellow. Alice looked and saw the sun setting to her left, its light casting beams through the trees and catching the dust that danced in the air. The leaves were changing color to reds and yellows and oranges.

She was dressed in her green flannel shirt and blue jeans. Her beanie rested atop her head. Looking around, she found herself in the old playground, the one in the town park. She was sitting on the swing, her hands folded in her lap and feet lightly scrapping the ground.

But how did she get here? She couldn't remember anything, except that she was alone. With her head hanging low and shoulders slumped, she pushed herself slow back and forth on the swing until the sun fully set. Then she faded from view, leaving only an empty swing.

The images in the crystal ball dissipated. Madam Morgana pulled her hands away and placed them softly on the table. The room was silent; everyone had the same look of shock and horror upon their face. Everyone except Alice. Like the last image in the vision, her head was hanging low with her hair obscuring her face. She was trembling, her shoulders quivered with each breath.

Luis noticed this. A part of him felt sick. Slowly, he pushed his glasses back into place and reached out to comfort her. "Alice?" he said hesitantly, placing his hand on her back.

"Don't touch me!" she screamed. The room shook, the trinkets and objects on shelves all rattled from the power she evoked. "Don't you fucking dare touch me!" Her voice was lower but still just as forceful. A powerful energy radiated around her; the air in the room twisted and shifted all around, blowing in random directions. Alice's hair flew about in the wind, revealing her face.

It was twisted and grotesque. Her lips pulled back in a rage-filled sneer, and her eyes were full of hate. She gritted her teeth, her brows furled, her fists clenched. Curtains and window drapes tore from their racks, candles snuffed out. Alice levitated in the air, the energy swirling around her.

Luis held his arms over his eyes, trying to shield himself. The force of the wind pushed him back, his chair fell over, and he landed with a painful thud against the floor.

"Now you know why I didn't want this to happen in the first place!" Madam Morgana was on the floor as well, under the table and clutching the legs.

Serena stood, looking up at her sister with a look of profound shock and horror. As her hair and clothes fluttered around in the wind, tears formed in the corners of her eyes. Alice, her big sister, had to suffer so much. All that pain and all that misery, only to be killed at the end. Nothing in the world could make up for it now. And all that repressed rage was being unleashed.

A chair flew across the room and crashed through a window, the glass shattered all over the room. The chair smashed against the pavement outside and crumpled, scattering all over the parking lot. Serena watched, visibly shaken. If Alice didn't calm down soon, the entire building was likely to be destroyed.

"Alice!" Serena shouted at the top of her lungs. Her voice barely managed to rise above the swirling winds. The ghost girl contorted her body in a painfully unnatural fashion, her neck twisting backward and head lying on its side. Alice's face was even more monstrous than before, hardly even recognizable as once being human.

Serena had to fight back her fears. That face turned her blood cold, but she had to do something. This was her sister. "Alice, please, you need to calm down!"

"How can you tell me that?" Alice's voice was low, violently distorted and incredibly powerful. Her eyes radiated an eerie yellow glow. "My life was stolen! My innocence— everything I had is gone! I will kill him for what he's done to me!"

Demonic was the thought that came to Serena's mind. Right now, the thing in front of her was a demonic twisted shape of what was once her sister. "Alice, I know!" she cried out. "I was there, I watched you get taken! And I never forgot. I missed you every day you were gone! But we have each other again!" A shard of glass flew through the air. It sliced across Serena's right cheek, drawing a thin line of blood. "Please, don't go away again." The tears flowing from her eyes mingled with the blood on her face.

Alice's features softened. From her perspective, Serena faded away and was replaced by an image of Cynthia, the tiny little first grader, only six years old, with her arms clutching her backpack and sadness in her eyes. She missed her big sister, longed for her to return.

Looking down at her hands—which had now become misshapen with her fingers becoming long and boney—and her skin turning gray and thin, Alice trembled. She placed her hands against her chest, pulled her legs up, and folded her head down.

The twisting air slowed and eventually subsided. Alice floated down to land safely in her little sister's arms. Serena wrapped her up and held her close, brushing the hair from her face. She watched as Alice's features softened, her face returned to normal.

With ruffled hair and his glasses askew, Luis peered over the tabletop. He adjusted his spectacles and stood up, brushing off his clothes. "Alice," he said, his eyes still turned away from her. "I…I just want to say I'm sorry I asked you to do this."

Alice buried her face in her hands. She still felt like crying. "I'd forgotten," she said with a shaky voice. "I forgot what he did to me. And not just to me but to all the other children there. Susie, Jason, and even Paul—he did that to all of us!"

Serena held her sister tighter, clutching Alice to her chest. Her own tears still flowed. The things she had just seen, the experiences she'd watched her sister live through and later die from had left Serena disgusted, mortified, and heartbroken. Alice didn't deserve that, no one did.

"But," Alice said, wiping her tears away. "We got what we wanted. We have his name."

"That's right," Luis said. "The woman called him Royce."

"And that woman was Mrs. Anderson," Alice said. "She was a teacher when I went to school." She had a difficult time saying the words. "And brought me food and tried to stop him."

Luis snapped his fingers. "And she was his mother! That's why Paul killed her!" He placed his hand to his chin. "That's why he took another victim so quickly. His pattern broke because the person holding him back is no longer there!"

"Good, you've got it all figured out." Serena snarked. "Now can we concentrate more on dealing with the psychological ramifications this has had on my sister?"

"Serena, I knew the risks. I agreed to this, knowing what might happen," Alice said. "I just need some time to work it out."

Madam Morgana got up off the floor and readjusted her dress. "This little episode you had was because you never took the time to work it out." She looked past them at her shattered window. "I don't think my insurance is going to cover this. It's surprisingly hard to get insurance coverage when you're a psychic."

Luis shoved both his hands in his pockets and felt around. "I need some change and to find a payphone."

"Why?" Serena asked.

"So I can call the police and leave an anonymous tip. If I use my cell, they'll just backtrack it to me, and then they'll have a bunch of questions about how I know all this and explaining this will be very difficult," Luis said, he turned his pockets inside out and found nothing. He sighed in frustration when a sudden shock hit his body. He froze; his eyes glazed over and empty. His arms became limp and mouth hung open dumbly.

"Luis?" Serena called to him. "Hey, what's going on now?"

"He's receiving a vision," Morgana explained. "What I believe has been happening is a sort of feedback loop. His exposure to Alice has awaken his gifts and made her more versatile. The longer they stay together, the more they influence each other." She motioned to Alice. "I'm assuming she never had an episode like that one before?"

"No, I haven't," Alice confirmed.

Morgana pointed at Luis. "And he's probably never had a vision outside of a dream before."

Luis suddenly perked up. His face became alert once again. "Huh?" he said. "What just happened?"

"You disappeared, kinda zoned out on us for a second," Serena explained.

"Oh." Luis pushed his glasses back up. He stopped, his eyes wide with shock. "Fire. There's going to be another fire. I just saw it."

"Where was this?" Madam Morgana asked.

He rubbed his fingers against his forehead. "Uh, I can't quite remember." The image or numbers appeared in his mind, numbers on a house. An address. "619. General Way." He said.

"That's Mrs. Anderson's house," Serena said. "And with this being the third fire in three days, I'd think it's safe to say that it's Paul causing it."

"We need to go there right now!" Alice screamed. "Even if it is Paul and he does kill the serial killer, there's still that girl there too!" Her hands trembled, voice shaking. "And Paul won't care about her in the slightest."

26

The house was a single-story, three-bedroom home. It sits at 619 General Way, a fairly normal looking house—if only that were the case.

Inside this house, there was a man by the name of Royce Anderson—a tall man of six feet and two inches, about thirty-five years old, with short light-brown hair and piercing blue eyes. To most people, he would look like an average Joe, slightly overweight and with thinning hair on top, but other than that nothing spectacular. Right now, he was in the kitchen. He was preparing some instant macaroni and cheese, watching the water boil in the pot before adding the noodles.

He was making this food for the girl in the basement—a young black girl, no older than ten, not that he cared so long as she was under fifteen. Once they got too old, it just didn't do it for him anymore, and no amount of pictures or video could compare to the real thing. The texture, the resistance, the screaming—it made him excited just thinking about it.

And his useless mother would always hold him back. She never approved of him; she even used to call him a freak and a monster. Every day, his mother would force those sedation pills down his throat to keep him in line, and when those ran out, she kept him from taking more than one playmate a year.

But no more. Now the old bat was dead. It was unfortunate, Royce thought, that he didn't kill her himself. He would have done just that a few days later if she hadn't been struck down by a freak heart attack yesterday, but that was fine with him. As soon as he got the news, he instantly went out to find another playmate. Now that playmate was waiting for him in the sealed off basement, just waiting for him to make her a woman.

The water in the pot boiled. Steam popped and hissed as it spilled over the sides onto the heating ring. He turned the dial down a little, tore open the instant macaroni box, and poured it in.

"Mac and cheese again? Don't you people know how to make anything else?" a sly voice said.

Royce froze in place. He slowly turned his head and peered over one shoulder then the other. There was no one else in that room. So where had the voice come from?

Just as he turned back to the macaroni, the voice came back. "You didn't look very much. How about we try again?"

The air in the kitchen kicked up, as if someone had just opened a window during a gale force wind. Royce spun around, spoon in hand, and came face-to-face with a young boy. He recognized this child easily as his previous playmate, but that boy was supposed to be dead and buried along with all the rest. What was he doing here?

"You look a little shocked. Can't say I'm surprised, I'm sure you never expected to see me again," the boy said. "You never even bothered to learn my name, did you?"

Royce placed his palm against his forehead and closed his eyes. It must be the medication. After his mother died, he stopped taking it, so the weird effects must be taking hold. This was all just a figment of his imagination, best to ignore it. He turned back to the stove, dismissing the boy.

The boy frowned and clenched his fists. "Don't turn your back on me!" A cabinet door flew open hard enough to twist the hinges, and a plate came flying out like a Frisbee. It struck the countertop next to Royce and shattered, the fine pieces of china scattered all over the floor. Royce jumped back, the spoon dropped from his hands.

The boy levitated into the air and grabbed Royce by the collar, shoving him back into the wall. "Listen to me. My name is Paul, and you are the man that killed me after doing a few other things to me first. Normally, I would kill you right now, the same way I did your old crone of a mother, but I need something of you first."

Royce gulped, confused and afraid. "Like what?"

Paul loosened his grip slightly. "Soon, the cops are going to come for you."

"What? But I covered my tracks, how did they find me?" Royce asked.

"I'm getting there," Paul hissed. "They're going to tear this place apart and find everything you've been doing here. And the one who set them off is this little twerp named Luis."

"Luis? Who is that? What does he have against me?"

"You rape kids, what do you think? Anyways, if you want to get out of this, you will do exactly as I say, got it?"

Royce was hesitant. This freaky figment was holding him by the neck inches away from a hot stove. He had only one choice out of this. He gulped. "What do you want me to do?"

A wicked grin came over Paul's face. "First." He grabbed the boiling pot of water by the handle and swung it, dumping the scalding water across Royce's face. The man screamed in pain, clutching at his face. Steam rose into the air. "That was for killing me, you bastard."

Paul floated to the paper towel rack. He grabbed the entire roll and unraveled it, laying one end on the heating ring of the stove and the other end across the carpet in the living room. Instantly, the paper caught fire. The flames spread down the roll of towels in a matter of seconds, igniting the carpet ablaze.

Fire spread quickly throughout the front room of the house. The couch was covered in flames, the television began to melt. Paul watched with eager and sadistic delight. He turned back to Royce, who still held his hands over his disfigured face. "Now if you want to live, you will get out of here now."

Smoke filled the air; the alarm started to blare like a desperate siren. Still in pain and with the smoke burning his eyes and nose, Royce ran out the back door. He jumped into the front seat of his car, a forest-green SUV, and fumbled desperately in his pockets for the keys. He found them and started the engine. Throwing the car in gear, he drove away as fast as he could make the car go, leaving his kidnapped victim in the basement alone.

A column of smoke rose up into the air. Serena and Luis saw it easily from the front seat of her car. "There it is!" Luis shouted, he pointed out the windshield.

"I can see!" Serena jerked the steering wheel to the side, turning the car toward the fire. Her old Honda really wasn't used to this kind of driving; it screeched as she drove.

Luis pressed the buttons frantically on his phone, trying his best to dial the number correctly with the car bouncing all over the place. Finally, he got it done and held the phone to his ear.

The operator picked up. "911, please state your emergency."

"There is a house on fire!" Luis shouted into the phone. "It's at 619 General Way. I can see the smoke from here!"

"Okay, sir. I'm contacting the fire department right now. They will be there shortly," the operator said.

"There's a girl inside that house, she could die if you don't save her!" The car turned again, and Luis braced in his seat.

"The officials are on their way, sir. You don't need to worry. We have the situation under control," the operator said.

Luis clicked off his phone and stuffed it in his pocket. "They say the firefighters are already on their way."

"They won't get there in time." Serena grimaced. They came upon the burning house. Smoke billowed from the few open windows, the fire blazing away inside Serena pulled the car up to the sidewalk and shut it off.

Sirens of a fire truck blared in the distance as it raced through the town, but it was still too far away. "She'll be dead before they get here," Luis said.

Alice emerged from the back of the car; she hovered in the air. "What are we supposed to do?"

Serena yanked off her coat and tossed it back in the car. Using a hair tie from her pocket, she pulled her hair back and fixed it in a bun. "I'm going to save her." She lifted up the collar of her shirt over her mouth.

"Serena, hold on a second!" Luis shouted. "If you rush in now, you'll only get yourself killed too. We need a plan."

"We don't have time to plan!" she retorted.

"I have one!" Alice interjected. "I can go in and scout the place out, find where he's been keeping her, and then lead you there directly and get her out. Sound good to everyone?"

"That's what I was going to suggest," Luis said. "Okay, let's do it!"

Alice flew into the house as fast as she could make herself. She phased through the door and found the living room completely ablaze. Fire was everywhere, reaching up the walls and all over the furniture. There was no way anyone could hope to get through the front door.

"Hello?" she called out. "Where are you?"

A small voice called back, "Help me!" It sounded quiet, distant, and drowned out by the roaring flames. But Alice heard it unmistakably. And it was coming from below her.

She dove into the floor. Once she phased through the floorboards and house structures, Alice found herself in a very familiar room. She saw the uncovered bed, the bare walls, and the total emptiness of it. This was where she was held and the place she died.

A small face emerged from under the bed. Although she had never seen her before, Alice new this must be the missing child. Sweat was dripping down the girl's face, soaking her hair. It must be excruciatingly hot in here, even though Alice couldn't feel it.

The house above her groaned; its support weakened. Any second now, it could collapse on top of them, dooming the kidnapped girl. There was no time to get Serena. Alice was going to have to lead the girl out herself.

Alice floated down to the girl, whom she noticed was completely nude, and knelt down next to her. "Hey." Alice said, startling the girl. "What's your name?"

Taking deep, labored breaths, the girl answered, "Tamika."

"Tamika, listen to me and you have to stay calm." Alice placed her hand on Tamika's shoulder. "The house is on fire, it could collapse soon. I can get you out of here, but you have to do everything I say. Okay?" Terrified, Tamika nodded. "Good. First, I need you to go into the bathroom and turn on the shower."

Tamika crawled out from under the bed and did just that. Turning the shower knob, cold water began to flow. "Now what?" she asked.

"Now take that toilet paper and clog up the drain," Alice said. Tamika did as she was told, the drain clogged with toilet paper, and the tub quickly filled. "Climb in the water and wait. Put your head underwater."

Tamika climbed into the tub. She shivered as the cold water splashed over her. She lay down until the water was covering every inch of her body except her head. Just as Alice left the bathroom, Tamika took a deep breath and submerged herself completely

Alice phased through the door. Coming out the other side, she found a hallway with a water heater, washing machine, dryer, and a staircase that lead upward to another door. The fire hadn't yet spread down here, but it was only a matter of time.

Turning back to the bedroom door, Alice found it locked, just like when she had been here. She quickly unlocked it and threw the door open. Then she flew up the stairs, grabbed that handle, and opened the door.

There was a sudden blast of flames as the oxygen starved fire burst through the door. It ignited again, roaring all around her. Alice threw her arms over her eyes in reflex, shielding her from the blaze. After a minute or two, the inferno returned to its previous burn rate.

Alice raced back down the stairs and into the room. She flew past the bed and into the bathroom, where Tamika was still hiding underwater. She reached in and grabbed the younger girl, pulling her out. Tamika gasped for breath, choking and coughing up water. "Sorry I made you do that, but I needed to. Now come on! We have to run!"

Pulling Tamika by the hand, Alice ran out of the basement bedroom and up the flight of stairs. The heat must've been excruciating because the water on Tamika's body was starting to steam. Faint wisps of vapor rose from the girl's skin as the water evaporated. They ran out the doorway and into the main house, the fire roared all around them. Tamika coughed as the smoke filled her lungs.

"I know it's bad, just hold on!" Alice shouted. She pulled Tamika along, directing her to the back door. They were almost there, just a few more steps and they'd be free.

A loud crashing sound came from overhead. Alice had only a second to see the ceiling break apart above her and cave in. A support beam smashed through the ceiling and crashed to the floor right in front of them, blocking the backdoor.

Shocked and terrified, Tamika doubled over with another cough. She would have collapsed to the floor had Alice not grabbed her. It was too hot—the air was filled with smoke, and all around them, the fire burned closer. It was all over now, there was no way out.

A loud crash came from the front door. The wood around the handle splintered and cracked. Another and another, the door was breaking further each time. Finally, on the fourth try, the handle broke off, and the door flew wide open. Outside, Serena lowered her boot-covered foot. Her hair was still tied back, and she had a scarf around her mouth and nose.

"Come on!" Serena shouted, her voice muffled. She raced into the burning building past the flames, scooped up

Tamika with one arm under the younger girl's legs and the other around her shoulders, and turned to run.

Serena burst out from the doorway, smoke trailing behind her. In her arms, she carried an exhausted and unconscious young black girl. As Serena ran across the yard, the house behind her buckled under its own weight and collapsed in a cloud of smoke and flames.

Standing on the sidewalk, Luis watched filled with tantalization. His mouth hung open, and eyes were wide with shock. Seeing Serena now, standing almost triumphant with the smoke and fire burning behind her, Luis had a newfound respect for her. Right now, covered in soot and ash, she looked amazing—even he dare say, heroic and beautiful.

The ringing sirens of the fire trucks screamed as they pulled up next to the scene. Firefighters jumped off the large red trucks and began unraveling the hoses. Huge bursts of water flew from the nozzles and sprayed over the still burning wreckage that used to be a house.

Two firefighters ran up to Serena, one carried an oxygen tank and mask. "Miss, are you okay?" the first one, a tall blond man asked.

Serena pulled down her scarf and coughed. "Yeah, I'm fine. But she needs help." She rocked the girl in her arms.

"Set her down for us," the second firefighter, a black man with a thick mustache, said.

Serena complied, placing Tamika on the ground on her back. The black firefighter placed the mask over her face and started the oxygen flow while the blond one began chest compressions. After the third compression, Tamika's eyes snapped open, and she regained consciousness.

Tamika jolted up and coughed, ash and soot flew from her lips. She placed a hand over her chest as she gasped for air. With the mask over her face, she drank the air as if it was water. As she inhaled and with her hand still against her chest, Tamika began to realize she was still without clothes. She pulled her legs up and wrapped her arms around them, attempting to cover herself. Her cheeks flushed red with embarrassment.

Luis came over with Serena's jacket. He draped it across Tamika's shoulders, and she pulled it tightly around her. Luis sighed with relief. "You don't have to worry, you're safe now."

"What is your name?" the black firefighter asked, addressing the girl wrapped in Serena's jacket.

After taking a few more breaths, she answered, "Tamika." She paused and followed it up with, "Little."

The firefighters exchanged glances. They knew that name. There was an AMBER Alert out for her this morning, and she was all over the news. The fact that she was found so quickly, and at this house no less, was amazing.

"Tamika," the blond firefighter said. "There is an ambulance on its way that will take you to see a doctor. He's going to make sure you're all right. We'll call your mom, and she'll be there waiting for you."

The ambulance showed up not three minutes later. Tamika was loaded in and taken to the hospital. Luis, Serena, and Alice watched as they drove away. Luis placed his hand on Serena's shoulder. "You did it. You saved her life."

"Only because you knew where we needed to be." Serena rubbed her hand over Luis's hair, messing it up. She smiled at Alice. "And I couldn't have done much without you, Alice. You did all the hard work. I just kicked down a door and pulled her out."

"Don't sell yourself short," Alice said, folding her arms. "You ran into a burning building without a seconds thought. I couldn't be hurt by it, you could."

"Excuse me, miss." The black firefighter from earlier called over. "I just wanted to say that was a very brave thing you did today." He smiled and stepped back to the fire truck, continuing his conversation with the police officers who had also just arrived.

A police officer came over to them, holding a pen and pad of paper. "Excuse me," he said. "I'd also like to give my appreciation for what you kids did today. That was very brave. But I need to get a statement from you, if you could."

Luis readjusted his glasses. "Sure thing, officer. Whatever we can do to help."

27

The interview didn't take as long as Luis thought it would. They simply told the officer that they were driving home from school when they saw the smoke, called 911, came to investigate, and heard a voice inside. Serena jumped in to rescue, and that was it. And for the most part, it was true. They didn't mention anything about Alice or anything else supernatural.

"Thank you," the officer said as he finished the interview. He tucked the pen and notebook back in his jacket and stepped away.

"Come on." Serena hit Luis's arm with the back of her hand. "I'll drive you home."

Once they were back in the car and on their way to his house, Luis adjusted his glasses as an automatic gesture. He glanced over at the girl seated next to him and suddenly felt flustered. The back of his neck felt warm, and his cheeks turned bright pink. "Um, Serena?"

"Yes?" Serena turned to face him.

"I, uh, wanted to," he stammered over his words, unsure of what to say or how to phrase it. "I just wanted to tell you."

"Before you start, just let me apologize first," Serena interrupted. "I'm sorry for yesterday—leaving you like that and screaming at you. That was uncalled for, and it was wrong of me." A strand of hair fell in front of her eyes, and she brushed it back nervously, her own cheeks had a pink tint to them.

Luis smiled, adjusting his glasses again. "Well," he said, as his eyes moved away and placed a hand on the back of his head. "It's okay. Don't worry about it," Luis responded. "I mean, it's understandable why you'd be mad."

"Understandable but not justifiable," Serena said. She fell silent for a moment as she built up her courage. "I want to do something to make it up to you."

"Oh?" Luis asked, his neck felt warm and palms became sweaty. "Like what?"

"Like, maybe we could do something together on Halloween if you aren't busy?" she said.

Luis's heart pounded like mad, a drop of sweat rolled down his temple and splashed on the collar of his shirt. "You mean like as a date?" He managed to say without choking on his words.

"Yes, if you want it to be," Serena said. "Like a date."

Luis felt uncomfortably warm and dizzy. Never had any girl asked him out on a date before and certainly not one he liked. Wait a minute, a girl he liked? Did he really just think that? That was unexpected. Could he actually have romantic feelings for Serena?

Alice watched silently from the backseat. She smirked, looking back and forth from Luis on the passenger side to Serena in the driver's seat. It was a little interesting how, just like with the car, Serena was the one in control while Luis was merely along for the ride.

"Hello? Luis? Are you still there?" Serena snapped her fingers by his ears.

He blinked in surprise, almost forgetting where he was. "Um, yeah."

"You've been quiet for a while, and you haven't answered. Do you want to go out with me or not?"

"Well, um," he stuttered his words; his tongue felt like it had literally been tied in a knot. "Since, um, you asked so bluntly. Yes, yes, I would." His heart raced so fast he was almost afraid it would explode right out of his chest.

"Great," Serena said and pulled the car to a stop. They'd been driving so long they were upon Luis's house before he noticed. He got out of the car, but before he could close the door, the car engine shut off, and Serena stepped out. "I'll walk you to the door," she said, as she walked around the front of the car.

"Oh." Luis's face felt flushed and warm. "Thank you." They climbed the steps to the porch, and just as Luis was about to unlock the door, Serena moved behind him and encircled the boy in her arms. He froze in surprise, almost dropping his keys. "Luis," she said, whispering in his ear.

He audibly gulped. "Yeah?"

"Have you ever kissed a girl before?"

The question almost caused the young man to pass out. His legs felt weak, and his pulse raced. Finally gathering his words, he answered, "No." With Serena's arms wrapped around him and being held so close to her, Luis was very well aware of her breasts as they pressed against his back. Nervous sweat poured down his face.

Serena pulled him closer, leaning over his shoulder with her face right next to his. She could almost feel the heat coming off from him. "Would you like to?"

Still incredibly nervous and full of anxiety, Luis slow turned around to face her. The taller girl delicately pulled off his glasses and held them between her fingers when she placed her arms over his shoulders. With her free hand, she ran her fingers through his hair and caressed his cheek.

With eyes half-closed and the corners of her mouth perked into a smile, Serena leaned down to him and pressed her parted lips against his. Luis's eyes shot wide open with surprise but slowly closed. Tentatively, his hands grasped Serena around the waist and pulled her close. They held each other in embrace, mouths pressed together in a deep kiss. Golden rays of the setting sun fell upon them, casting them in glorious light.

Finally, after what seemed like an eternity of bliss, Serena pulled away. Her heart was filled with exhilaration. She wasn't used to it, but it was a pleasant surprise. She noticed the goofy smile across Luis face and giggled. "Did you enjoy that?" He could only nod, not having the ability to speak now. "Good." She placed another small kiss upon his lips. "I did too."

"Um," Luis stammered. "Would you like to come inside for a bit?" He took his glasses back and fixed them on his face. "I mean, just until my mom gets home."

Serena smiled. "Absolutely." She followed Luis, as he stepped into the house. "I'd like to see your room again. More intimately this time."

Thursday, October 30

Excavating continues at the playground in the town park. So far, the remains of five children have been identified, all between the ages of seven and ten, and all previously considered missing persons. But with how everything is, the police are expecting to find more. The main suspect in this case is

Royce Anderson, a man with a history of mental illness. He was last seen driving a forest-green Ford Expedition. The police are asking anyone with any information regarding this man to contact them.

The news continued on to other events. Luis and Serena sat next to each other on the couch in the living room. Madam Morgana had left an anonymous tip to the police from a payphone after the trio left her office the day before and then told them about it this afternoon.

Luis clicked the TV off and set the remote aside. "How do you like that?" he said. "It's finally over. He can't hurt anyone again."

"It's not really over. He's not arrested yet," Serena said, her arms folded, and legs crossed at the knees.

"Yeah, but now there's a manhunt out for him. It's only a matter of time, and he's not our problem anymore." Luis reached over the couch to Serena with his hand out. "Lighten up a little, it's a good thing."

The corners of her lips perked up slightly as she took his hand in hers. "I know it is," Serena said. "I just wish he had been caught."

A slight click signaled the front door unlocking, and Luis's mother stepped inside. "I'm home!" she called out, as she took off her shoes and set them on the rack by the door.

"Hi, Mom," Luis said.

Serena waved. "Good afternoon, Mrs. Chavez."

Mrs. Chavez paused by the door with a look of mild surprise on her face. "Oh. Hello, Serena. I didn't expect to find you here."

"I wasn't staying long," Serena said, as she stood up from the couch. Her hand slipped from Luis's, an action Mrs. Chavez noticed. "I was just giving him a ride home from school and thought I should wait for you to get back."

"That was nice of you." Mrs. Chavez readjusted the purse on her shoulder. "I guess that was your car out front. I was wondering who that belonged to."

"Yeah, that's mine." She turned back to Luis. "So I'll see you at school tomorrow?"

"Of course. And then on Halloween?"

Serena gave him a small wink. "Absolutely." She stepped past Luis's mother and stood in the doorway on her way out. "It was nice to see you again, Mrs. Chavez."

"Nice to see you too." The older woman closed the door behind Serena as she walked out. "So," she said, as she turned back to her son. "Want to tell me about it?"

"About what?" Luis adjusted his glasses.

"About the two of you. Are you going out now?" she asked.

"Mom!" Luis said, annoyed.

She smiled, stealing a quick glance over at her son. "I just wanted to know. I saw the two of you holding hands just now."

Luis smacked his hand against his forehead. Of course, his mom saw them. Why would he think she had not? It must've been so obvious to her what was going on. He groaned with irritation.

His mother chuckled. "I guess that means I'm right."

"Yes, Mom," Luis said. The aggravation dripped from his word. "We're dating now."

"That's nice," his mother said. "Does she share more of her poetry with you?"

"She has yet to do that," Luis responded in a sarcastic tone.

"I see." His mother set her purse on the floor by the edge of the couch as she sat down. "I take it she's not mad at you anymore?"

"No, she isn't. We talked it out, got everything sorted," Luis said.

"Now I have to ask. Did you kiss her, or did she kiss you?"

"What?" Luis almost jumped from the couch. "Mom! Why would you? We haven't."

"Her lipstick smear is still on your mouth," Mrs. Chavez said with a sly tone, her index finger pointed at his lips.

Hunching his shoulders and folding his arms, Luis turned away from his mother, his face already turning red again. His mother just smirked.

A buzzing in his pocket alerted Luis to a text message. He pulled out his phone, and the screen lit up, shinning light across his face. The message was from Serena.

Serena: *Do you have any idea what you'd like to do tomorrow?*
Luis: *There's this movie that just came out I'd like to see.*
Serena: *Great. Then it's a date.*

He put his phone back in his pocket. "Was that her?" his mom asked.

"Yes," he replied. "Just talking about things we plan to do tomorrow."

"Haven't even been apart for ten minutes, and you already have to text each other." His mother shook her head in amusement. "Kids these days."

28

Friday, October 31

Butch slammed his locker shut with a metallic clang. He tugged his backpack straps over his shoulders as he headed for class. Dark bags hung under his eyes; he'd gotten almost no sleep last night.

Other students swarmed and clamored around him, the rabble of their various conversations assaulted his ears, and he caught vague portions of some of them. One girl was upset that her boyfriend wasn't celebrating their two-week anniversary; another was going to the mall to buy the cute top she saw in the window; and a jock was talking about joining the basketball team.

Butch let out a groan of annoyance as he waded through the crowd. As he came around a corner, he froze dead in his tracks, his eyes bulged open with shock. He quickly backtracked, pressed himself up against a wall, and held his breath. As quietly as he could, he peeked back around the corner of the building to confirm what he thought he saw.

It was Luis and Serena. The older girl had pressed Luis up against the wall. They were locked in embrace with their mouths pressed together and hands running all over each other's bodies. Butch watched with morbid interest.

Serena pulled away, her face flustered and sweaty. She smiled and ran her fingers through Luis's hair. "I didn't expect you to like my outfit that much."

"Are you kidding?" Luis huffed between breaths. "You look stunning."

"Thank you," Serena said. She wore a pair of red-and-black stripped thigh-high stockings under a black mini-skirt, which fell halfway to her knees. Her hair was done up in long pigtails. She had a pair of fingerless gloves with spiked bracelets and purple nail polish. Her shirt was a black low-cut tank top that showed off her cleavage, which she wore under an open vest with chains hanging from the shoulders. "I dressed up for our date tonight. I'd hoped you'd like it."

"I do. A lot." Luis planted a small kiss on her lips.

Serena smiled. She pulled a tissue from a pocket on her vest. "Here." She dabbed the corner on her tongue and wiped away the lipstick on Luis's face. "Shouldn't go to class with smudges all over you."

The bell rang. Luis and Serena shared one last kiss before they separated and heading to class. "Still on for the movie tonight?"

"Absolutely," Serena said. "Seven thirty, right?"

"Right." Luis waved to her, as he stepped into his home-room class.

Butch watched silently from a distance. He glanced around the hallway, up and down in each direction, as the other students steadily filed away into the classrooms. Once they were all gone, he ran off to the bathroom and locked himself in one of the stalls.

"So what did you see?" an all too familiar voice said.

Butch jumped in fear. He'd expected to hear it, but even so, the voice startled him. "Huh?"

Paul's face appeared on the tiled floor. The ghost rose up from the ground gradually, the same sinister look on his face. "You saw them. I told you to come back only if you found something for me. What is it?"

Butch nodded swiftly. "I saw them," he whispered in a hushed voice. "They said they had plans for tonight. A movie date or something like that."

"When?" Paul hissed.

"They said at seven thirty. That's all I know," Butch whimpered. "Are you done with me yet? Can I go now?"

Paul rolled his eyes and sighed. He waved his hand dismissively in the air. "Fine. Get out of here." As he watched Butch try to leave, he fixed his gaze on the stall door and slammed it shut. "One last thing—if you try to tell that four-eyed freak anything about me, I will do to you what

I did to your teacher. Got it?" With horrified terror, Butch gave a small nod. "Good." Paul released his hold on the door, and Butch ran out.

Luis stood in the bathroom facing the mirror. He wore a black long-sleeve dress shirt that his mother had ironed for him and a pair of off-gray slacks. His hair was slicked back; he ran his fingertips over it to make sure it was just right. On a hanger behind him was a dress jacket the same color as the slacks.

"Are you ready?" his mother called from outside the bathroom.

"Almost," Luis called back. He took off his glasses and set them gently down on the sink countertop. The moment of truth was here. With a tug, he pulled open the medicine cabinet and took out his contact lens case.

He hated putting these things in. It always felt like he was going to poke his eye out if he did it wrong. He unscrewed the cap, placed the first lens on his fingertip, and with his left hand, he held his eye open while using his right hand to slowly placed the lens against his bare eye. He blinked to squeeze the air out and then repeated the process for his right eye.

With his contacts in, the last thing he did was take the bloodstone pendent, the one Madam Morgana gave him, and fastened it around his neck. He then grabbed the jacket off the hanger and left the bathroom, shutting the light off as he did.

"Well," he said, as he slipped the coat over his shoulders, "how do I look?"

His mom smiled proudly. She placed her hands on his cheeks and squished them together. "Oh, you look wonderful. My little boy looks so grown up now."

Luis rubbed his face once his mom pulled away. "Thanks," he said. "I think," he muttered that last part to himself under his breath.

A knocking came from the door. His mother opened it and found Serena standing outside under the porch light. "Hi," she said, her hands placed on her hips. "You ready to go?"

"Yeah"—he buttoned the jacket up—"I'm ready."

"Wait, hold on a minute." Mrs. Chavez ran off to the other room and came back a few seconds later with her camera in hand. "Okay, come on both of you." She motioned to Luis and Serena. "Stand against that wall please."

Embarrassed, his face bright red and feeling warm, Luis stepped with Serena over to the plain white wall, a space separating them.

"No, no, no," Mrs. Chavez said. "You have to get closer. Here, like this." She took Luis's left hand and placed it in Serena's right. She then took her son's free hand and set it on his girlfriend's waist, while taking Serena's left arm and draping it over Luis's shoulder. "There, that's better."

Sweat accumulated at Luis's hairline. His heart pounded like a jackhammer in his chest so fast he almost thought he saw his shirt moving with it. For her part, Serena was just as nervous. The fact that her boyfriend's mother set them up this way was strange enough on its own.

Holding the camera up, Mrs. Chavez snapped several photos of her son and girlfriend. She thought they looked adorable this way. "Okay, kids. I got it," she said, lowering the camera. "Now hurry up, you're going to be late."

"Okay, Mom," Luis said, almost running for the door.

Serena waved over her shoulder. "Bye, Mrs. Chavez. I promise to bring him back in one piece."

"You'd better," Mrs. Chavez said jokingly. She watched them as they climbed into Serena's car and drove off toward the movie theater.

"I like your mom," Serena said as she drove.

Luis wiped the sweat from his forehead. "I'm glad. She sometimes bugs me."

"Well, just be glad you have a mom," Serena said solemnly.

"Sorry, I didn't mean it like that." Luis apologized. "Come on. Let's not do that. We're supposed to enjoy tonight, right?"

"Yeah, let's just have fun." Serena gave him a short sweet smile.

"You got really dressed up for this, didn't you?" Alice poked her head up from the backseat. "I must say, you look nice, Luis."

"Alice?" Luis swiveled around in his seat. "What are you doing here?"

Serena glanced back, annoyed at her sister. "Don't you have anything else to do?"

"Nope. Not a thing," Alice said. "I want to make sure my little baby sister enjoys her first date."

"What makes you think it's my first date?" The corner of Serena's lips turned up to form a sly grin.

"The fact that you've told me you've never had a boyfriend," Alice replied.

"Yeah, never had a boyfriend. That doesn't mean I've never been on dates." She looked up at Alice floating above her. "And besides, what if I had a girlfriend?"

Both Luis and Alice did a double take. "You haven't, have you?"

"Hm." Serena only smirked and looked away.

They arrived at the movie theater a little after seven. Serena parked the car and was about to step out when Luis held up a hand to stop her. "Hold on a minute." He climbed out of his side before walking around the car and holding the door open for Serena.

"Aw, that's sweet. A regular gentleman." She took his outstretched hand and stepped out of the car.

"My mom always told me to hold the door for a lady." He closed the car door behind her. They walked together to the front entrance, which Luis held open for Serena, letting her walk inside first. As she walked, Luis noted her swaying hips under the short skirt and quickly averted his gaze, his cheeks burning red. Need to try being a gentleman, not a voyeur.

"So which movie did you want to see?" Serena asked.

A line of movie posters were hung on the wall next to the box office, each one trying to sell themselves as being worth ten dollars a ticket. Luis scanned right and left across them before finally making his choice. "Let's see that one."

Serena looked at the poster he pointed to. "*The Last Stand of the Dragon*?" she said, reading the title. It was a picture of a large green reptilian eye surrounded by sharp brown scales with flames reaching out from the sides. Looking at the poster, she had to admit it looked interesting. "That's the one?'

"Yeah." Luis nodded. "I almost forgot they were making a movie of that. I read the book, it was pretty short but okay."

"Wow, what a glowing endorsement." Serena snarked. Together they walked to the office, got their tickets, and moved up to the snack bar to buy a large popcorn, large soda, and a package of gummy worms. With these in hand, they went into the theater and took their seats just as the previews started.

The pair sat next to each other in the center seats of a relatively middle row. The theater was completely empty aside from them. The bag of popcorn was placed on the armrest between them next to the large soda from which two straws protruded from the lid.

As the lights went down and the movie started, Luis found himself paying less and less attention to what was happening on screen and more to the girl sitting next to him. The way the light from the movie screen fell across her face just mesmerized him. Had she always looked so nice? He shifted uncomfortably in his seat, crossing his legs and leaning away from her, as if he was afraid if he got too close she might hear his thoughts. She did look pretty, though. The more he thought about it, the faster his heart raced and the deeper he had to breathe just to keep himself calm.

Serena's eyes kept moving over to Luis; his constant moving around made it next to impossible for her to ignore him. With the shadows dancing over his face, she noticed for the first time the small dimples on his cheeks, which only added to the appeal. Catching herself again, she crossed her legs and clasped her hands together, resting them on her knees.

In the movie, as knights and dragons fought with one another, he reached for the popcorn just as Serena did, and their fingers briefly touched. They each pulled back, their cheeks turning pink.

From above at the ceiling, Alice occasionally switched from watching the movie to watching Luis and Serena below. Their awkwardness was somewhat adorable from where she stood, or hovered as the case was. It was kind of cute and a little weird for her. Alice couldn't get over the fact that this was her sister, her younger sister, in a dark movie theater with a boy and less than three inches away from trying to hold his hand or maybe more. Alice giggled as she watched them.

As the movie played on, Luis and Serena began to move closer toward each other. They exchanged looks and just as quickly turned away trying to hide their mutual blushes. He had never been more exhilarated or more anxious in his life.

Luis tentatively took a small handful of popcorn and ate them one at a time. He wasn't much fond of it, but he would take anything to distract himself. He grabbed the soda and absentmindedly drank nearly a fourth of the cup.

"Wow," Serena said as she watched him. "You must be thirsty."

"Just a little bit," Luis replied as he set the cup back down. He burped and placed his hand over his mouth, again filled with embarrassment.

Serena chuckled. "You think that's impressive?" She grabbed the soda herself and downed two-thirds at once. She let out a loud belch, catching Luis completely off guard. "That's how it's done."

Luis couldn't help but laugh. It was completely ridiculous but absolutely hilarious at the same time. Serena opened the package of gummy worms and held one out. "Did you want to try one?" she asked.

"Sure." Luis reached for it, but Serena pulled it away.

"Ah, ah, ah. You have to let me give it to you," she said. "Now open your mouth, and close your eyes."

"Oh no. The last time someone told me to do that, I wound up with a ghost pepper in my mouth," Luis said.

"Come on, trust me. I promise not to put anything in your mouth you won't like," Serena said with a smirk.

Luis sighed with defeat. He closed his eyes and opened his mouth. With his eyes closed, Serena placed the gummy worm in her own mouth. She leaned down to him, her mouth open as well, and the candy resting on her tongue. Her lips pressed against Luis's, her tongue slipped into his mouth, catching the younger boy by total shock. The gummy worm slid easily down his throat, but still Serena did not pull away. Their tongues danced together, leaving Luis in a sea of ecstasy.

Finally, Serena stepped back. She smiled, looking down at her much-bemused boyfriend. "There," she said. "Now was that really so bad?"

Luis could only shake his head dumbly. He was still lost in the moment, unable to form a coherent sentence if his life depended on it. But if he were to die right now, he would die happy.

What finally snapped him out of it was the embarrassing physical reaction he got, forcing him to turn away with his legs crossed.

Alice watched the whole event transpire right before her eyes, and it made her simultaneously want to burst out laughing and angrily intervene. She was more than a little shocked by Serena's behavior and now realized it wasn't Luis she needed to be worried about. It was her own sister.

29

Once the movie was over, Alice descended upon Luis and Serena as they came walking out of the theater still holding hands. She came up behind them, her arms held behind her back and ankles crossed as she floated in the air. "So did you enjoy the show?"

"Aah!" Luis jumped, startled. Popcorn flew from the bag he was holding and kernels scattered all over the floor. "Alice!" he shouted. "What did you do that for?"

"Fun," she said. "And you don't have to answer. I was watching you," she said with a coy smile. "It seems you enjoyed it a lot. I know I did."

"Wait a minute." Luis held up his hands in irritation. "You were *watching* us? Why? What were you hoping to see?"

Serena crossed her arms and turned away, hiding her burning red face behind her long hair. "That's a very good question. What were you hoping to see, sis?"

"The two of you, duh," Alice said as if it was the most obvious answer in the world. She moved in close to Luis and looked him dead in the eye. "I just wanted to make sure you didn't try anything risqué in there with my sister, all alone in that dark movie theater with no one else around."

"I wouldn't have done anything like that! I'm not that kind of person!" Luis vehemently protested.

Alice smirked. "Yeah, anyone can say that when they're alone, but put them in a stimulating situation and things will get heated." She turned away from Luis and fixed her attention on her sister. "But it turns out I had more to fear from *you* trying something, didn't I?"

Serena brushed her hair back behind her ear. "Well, for future reference"—her shoulders hunched and arms crossed again—"could you not do that ever again? Nothing kills the mood like having your sister's ghost follow you around on dates."

"That was kind of my goal, you know," Alice said.

Serena sighed. Her hips jutted out as she shifted her weight. "Yeah, I know." Grasping Luis's hand, Serena led him toward the exit. "Come on." She checked the time on her phone. "It's not that late yet. How about we go some-place else tonight? Somewhere a little more private." She shot a dirty look over at Alice.

"Um, yeah." Luis stumbled over the bright red carpet as Serena dragged him down the hall. "That might be a good idea." He took the soda cup again and finished it off. "If you'll excuse me." He managed to say. "I need to go use the bathroom." He scurried off, leaving Serena behind in the lobby.

In the men's room, Luis stood by the sink and stared at himself in the mirror. The cold water was running, and he occasionally cupped his hands under it and splashed the liquid across his face. He panted, desperate for air. His heart beat so fast he thought he might pass out. "Okay, Luis. Come on, you're all right. Nothing really to be freaked out over. It's a natural reaction, completely normal for a guy my age."

"What's completely normal?"

"Aaah!" Luis freaked out, slipping in the water on the floor and almost landing flat on his back. It was Alice, hovering right over his shoulder with her hands behind her back, ankles crossed, and head slightly tilted. He groaned with exasperation. "Why do you keep doing that?"

"It amuses me," Alice said with a smirk. "And you still didn't answer. What's a natural reaction?"

Luis pulled his legs up, resting his chin on his knees. "I don't want to talk about it."

"Oh really." Alice rolled her eyes. "You're fine just to stare at a mirror and monologue to yourself, but the minute you have an audience, you clam up. Come on, just tell me what it is."

Luis's face turned beat red. He turned away from Alice. "It's just the you know. That thing that happens when guys like someone."

"That thing that happens?" Alice realized and almost burst out laughing. "My sister turns you on, does she?"

"Dressed like that, playing weird games, French kissing me, how am I not supposed to be?" Luis shouted. "And why are you so nonchalant about it?"

"I'm not concerned about you," Alice said. "Really, I think she's the one who might try something. And I think if she really wanted to, she would have done something already. Like, I don't know, drive off somewhere secluded and have her way with you like she threatened to."

"You're not helping," Luis hissed between his teeth.

"I know." Alice grinned. "Now clean yourself up already, she's waiting for you."

Luis sighed. He grabbed some paper towels and dried his hands off then tossed them in a nearby trash can. He stood up and straightened out his shirt and jacket as he stepped out of the bathroom.

As he walked back toward the theater lobby, he spotted some guy standing right next to Serena. It was a tall person, close to six feet with broad shoulders and light blonde hair. A football jersey was this guy's most distinguished feature. He was leaning against the wall with a cocky grin, and it looked like he was trying to hit on Serena. Luis quickly concluded this guy was not succeeding.

Alice hovered in the air next to his ear. "That guy's trying to make a move on your girl," she whispered.

"And it doesn't look like it's working," Luis responded.

"Want me to check it out?" Alice asked.

"Nah. I think I can sort this out." He grabbed his jacket by the edges to fluff it up slightly, the strolled back over to Serena. "Hey," he said. "I'm back."

Serena placed her arm around his shoulder. "Glad to hear it. You feel better now?"

"Yeah, a little," Luis answered.

"Dude," the football shirt guy said. "Seriously, uncool. You interrupted my story. And also, who do you think you are, moving in on my girl like that?"

"I'm sorry, I was unaware she belonged anyone. I thought she was just herself, and no one else's," Luis responded snidely. "Besides, that story couldn't have been that interesting since she was yawning not five seconds ago."

Football guy stood there dumbstruck. He could hardly believe his ears. Who was this little twerp, and what made him think he could speak to him like this? He didn't have to listen to this; it was time to teach this kid a lesson or two. "Hey, buddy," he said. "Let's go for a walk and chat a little."

"Josh," Serena said, "give it a rest already." She waved him away. "Just get out of here."

"I will just as soon as shorty here and I have a talk out-side," football guy, or Josh as his real name was, replied.

He even has a stereotypical football player's name, Luis thought. "If you'd like to tell me something, I'm sure it would be fine for my girlfriend to hear it too." He gestured to Serena.

"Wait, huh?" Josh did a double take and shook his head. "You think that Serena here is your girlfriend?" He laughed and slapped his knees. "There's no way this babe would go out with a little squirt like you. Besides, you don't look like her type."

"Oh," Serena crossed her arms and pursed her lips. "And what exactly is my type, since you seem to know so well?"

"Yeah, you're type is me," Josh said. He looked down at Luis with a mocking grin. "Didn't she tell you? Before she decided on this little getup"—he motioned to her clothes and makeup—"she and I used to be an item."

Luis's brow wrinkled in confusion. His eyes widened. "Excuse me?"

"Oh, you mean she didn't tell you about it?" Josh quipped. "I don't blame her. She probably didn't want to make you upset. After all, how can a little boy like you ever measure up to a man like me?"

"Very easily," Serena interjected. "Talk all the smack you want, Josh, but Luis is five times the man you claim to be. And as I recall, I broke up with you over a year ago. Get over it already, you big wuss."

Josh scoffed and rolled his eyes. "Now don't play games, Cindy. You know you want me back. Just dump this little snot right now, and we can forget about all—" Serena swung her fist and punched Josh right in the face. There was a sickening crack as her knuckles made contact with his nose. He recoiled and stumbled back while holding his hands over his now bleeding face. His voice was muffled as he groaned in pain. "Ow, what the ever loving—" he was cut off again when Serena grabbed him by the collar and forced him against a wall. She stomped her boot down on his toes, making him wince again.

"Try to make a move on me again," she said through gritted teeth, "or insult my boyfriend again, and I will kick your ass so hard you'll be wearing it as shoulder pads. Got it?" Her voice was low and harsh. Blood fell from Josh's broken nose and landed in small droplets on her hand. He audibly gulped and nodded. "Good." She let him go and stepped away.

Luis watched with shock and bemusement. Alice hovered over his shoulder and was likewise stunned. He leaned over to her and whispered, "Remind me never to get on her bad side."

"Don't get on my bad side." Serena shook her fist. "I'm sorry I had to do that. Now where were we?"

Luis gazed up at her with an eyebrow raise and lips pressed together. He jutted his thumb over his shoulder to the front door. "About to go have a little talk." Without another word, he turned around and began to walk away.

Serena watched him, confused. "What did I do?" she asked herself. She followed a few steps behind him, her arms folded.

30

Standing outside on the sidewalk, Serena propped herself up against a wall with her arms still crossed. Luis stood facing away from her with his hands in his pockets and gaze fixed on the cement. Serena blew the hair out her face. "Well, you wanted to talk. Let's talk. I'm guessing it's about Josh, isn't it?"

Luis let out a heavy sigh. "Yeah." He turned to face her, a look of hurt in his eyes. "Why didn't you tell me you'd been with other guys?"

"Is your ego hurt?" Serena commented. "I know how the mind of a teenage boy works. If I had told you, then you would have felt insecure thinking about how you could never measure up to my ex. And if I didn't tell you and the truth came out, like it just did, then you would feel betrayed and not trusted because I didn't tell you."

Luis looked back at the floor. "Well, you're right about that," he said, his voice hurt. "I don't care that you've dated other guys, in fact, I kind of expected it. But I just thought you'd respect me enough to tell me."

"What did I just say?" Serena said with a hint of irritation. "And besides, that was all before I'd chosen my current lifestyle choice. So you can figure anything going on with Josh was a long time ago." She stepped over to him and placed her hands on Luis's shoulders. "And I wasn't lying when I said you were five times the man he pretends to be."

Luis placed his hand over hers and smiled up at her. "You really mean it?"

She ran her free hand over his cheek. "Absolutely." She kissed him on the lips again. "Come on, let's get out of here." She took him by the hand and led him out to the car. After unlocking the door, she turned and headed back to the theater. "Just let me go back and clean this stuff off my hand." She twirled her fingers in the air, which still had blood on them.

"Sure," Luis said. As Serena ran back inside, he climbed in the passenger side of the car and locked the door behind him. Storm clouds were moving in overhead, and Luis could hear the sounds of distant thunder. He remembered vaguely hearing the news reporter talk about thundershowers for this Halloween.

Alice appeared in the backseat, her arms rested on the headrests of the two front seats. "You know, she didn't tell me about that guy either. In fact, I remember she said she never had any boyfriends."

"She probably doesn't consider him ever being her boy-friend," Luis said. "And besides, it was most likely not the best experience of her life."

"I'm sure of that." Alice chuckled.

As they laughed, Luis looked out the windshield across the parking lot and saw a lone figure. He tilted his head in confusion. The person was standing motionless in the middle of the street, their face obscured, and hands stuffed in their pockets. Luis climbed out of the car, still looking over at the person in the street. "Hey!" he shouted. "Are you okay over there?"

The figure did not move. Overhead, the clouds moved closer, and thunder rumbled. Luis closed the car door behind him and stepped out toward the boy. "You should probably get out of the street and go inside. It looks like a storm's moving in."

A pair of headlights appeared from down the road. They grew brighter as the car approached. Luis watched as the beams of light fell over the kid in the street. Still the figure did not move or even seem to notice. Luis cupped his hands around his mouth and shouted, "Hey, kid! You'd better move!"

Still the boy in the street remained motionless, even as the headlights flooded over him. Luis knew he couldn't just watch this happen. He threw off his jacket, pulled together his courage, and raced out into the street. His arms pumped back and forth in time with his legs, charging forward as fast as he could go. The car, an SUV, drew closer with each second. It was less than fifty feet away. In another second, it would hit them both and likely kill them.

Luis threw his arms open and hurled himself at the kid. He tackled him to the ground and rolled end over end out of the way of the car just as it sped past. The sound of screeching tires was heard as the breaks of the SUV locked, and it came to a grinding halt. Luis lay gasping for air on the ground, his body ached all over from rolling on the pavement, and he had a small cut on the side of his head from scraping the ground.

Slowly, he pushed himself up. He gingerly touched the cut on his head, winced from the pain, and looked down at the blood now on his fingertips. "You know," he began to say, "you could have been killed just now."

"That would be quite difficult," the young boy said. "Considering I'm already dead." He lifted his head and met eyes with Luis, a sinister grin across his face. It was Paul. "Nice to see you again."

Luis jumped to his feet. He tried to run, but to no avail. A man jumped from the front seat of the SUV and charged. He grabbed Luis by the arm and slapped a rag soaked in chemicals over his mouth and nose. Luis struggled, he kicked and tried to pull away, but the drugs took their effect quickly, and he lost consciousness.

Alice witnessed everything from the parking. "Luis!" she shouted. "Hold on, I'm coming!" Just as she began to fly to his aide, Paul intervened. He caught her by the throat and held her in midair.

"Not this time, Alice," he said. "He's coming with me." The man picked up Luis's limp body and placed him in the back of the SUV. "Do you recognize him?" Paul motioned to the man. "Probably not, I did scald his face with boiling water. That is Royce. You know, the man who killed us after raping us."

Alice watched in horror, and Royce slammed the door shut with Luis inside. She struggled against Paul's grip, but it was no use. "Why?" She pleaded. "Why are you working with him?"

"He and I have similar goals. I just had to tell him that Luis was the kid that ratted him out, and that did the job," Paul explained.

"But he's a murderer. He killed you, why help him?" Alice asked.

"Don't worry about that. Once Luis is dead, I'll finish Royce off myself." Paul smiled wickedly. "Watching a person die, to see their life slipping from their eyes is quite enjoyable. It's the ultimate high. I've done it before, quite a few times. I can understand him killing. But he decided to kill me, and that was his only mistake."

Royce climbed back into the driver's seat of his SUV. The engine rumbled back to life, and the wheels spun, leaving tracks on the pavement as it drove away. As it disappeared into the night, Paul finally released his hold on Alice's throat. "Good-bye, I trust we won't see each other again."

"Where are you taking him?" Alice demanded, rubbing her throat.

"Someplace close to us all," Paul whispered and faded away into the darkness. He was gone again, leaving Alice alone and helpless. Thunder rumbled overhead as the first few drops of rain fell from the sky and splashed against the cold ground. It wasn't long before the light sprinkle became a downpour and soaked the earth. Alice couldn't feel the rain, but she was cold anyways.

Serena came back out of the movie theater to find her car empty. "Alice?" she called, seeing her sister staring off into the black night. "What's going on? What are you looking at?"

"Luis is gone," Alice said, her voice low.

"Gone?" Serena sighed. She slumped against her wet car, disgruntled. "Don't tell me he was still upset over that thing with Josh and ran off home, did he?"

Alice shook her head solemnly. "No. It was Paul."

Serena froze in place, her breath caught in her throat. Her blood ran cold with fear. The truth began to set in for her. This must've been what Madam Morgana had predicted.

"And not just Paul, either," Alice said. "It was also Royce, the man who killed me and Paul and all the others. For some reason, Paul was using him."

"Oh no," she said. She threw car door open jump inside. "Alice, get in! Tell me where they went!"

Alice phased through the roof and landed in the backseat again, her legs folded up to her chest. "I don't know. Paul didn't tell me. He just said it was someplace close to us all."

Serena gave a quick nod. "That's good enough for me. I think I know where he's going." She turned the key, pumped the gas pedal. The engine sputtered and then roared to life, the headlights flipped up and blanketed the area in front of them in light.

"Where?" Alice asked.

"The only place that we all have in common." Serena slammed the car in reverse, and the tires spun on the wet pavement. "The playground."

31

Royce turned off the headlights as they approached. Yellow caution tape and police barriers were set up all around the playground equipment. There was a police car stationed next to it as well, with two officers seated inside. Royce quietly shut off the engine. He wore black work gloves on each hand, which he wrung nervously over the steering wheel. The car was parked still half a block away. Paul descended in from the roof of his car and sat in the passenger seat. "What are you waiting for?"

Royce rubbed his forehead just above his eyes. His face was disfigured from the scalding water Paul threw on it; the skin was blistering and peeling in places, revealing the red raw flesh beneath. One eye was half closed from the swelling. "There are cops over there," he muttered, saliva dripped down from his drooping lips. He wiped it away and winced when his sleeve brushed a blister.

"So what?" Paul dismissed it as if it was nothing. "I can deal with them. Just drive over there already, you fat bastard."

With a twinge of fear, Royce complied. He restarted the SUV and drove it, so its headlights shined directly through the windshield of the police cruiser. Rain pelted the first officer as he got out of the passenger side.

Officer Frank Brisbane was a twenty-five-year-old man, slightly balding on top and a little overweight from too many doughnuts but with a thin mustache and otherwise powerful build. He ran a thumb over the brim of his hat to wipe the water away as it collected. "This area is a designated crime scene." He called over to the SUV parked in front of him. "I'm going to have to ask you to leave this area now."

The other car didn't move, and the driver made no sign he heard Officer Brisbane. The police officer peered back into the cruiser and nodded to his partner. Junior detective Jake Freeman returned the gesture and grabbed a hold of the radio communicator in preparation.

With his Mag-Lite in hand, Officer Brisbane stepped cautiously over to the vehicle. His other hand rested firmly on the gun holstered at his waist, just in case. He moved over to the driver's side and tapped the Mag-Lite against the window. It rolled down, revealing the disfigured face of the driver. "Sir," Officer Brisbane said, "may I ask you to step out of the vehicle?" The driver complied. He stepped out, instantly soaked in the pouring rain.

Once out of the car, the driver held both of his hands over his head. "Walk over this way please," Frank said, motioning with the hand not holding the Mag-Lite. The instant he took his hand away from his gun, the clasp unsnapped, and the pistol lifted from its holster. It floated through the air until it came to hover right between him and the disfigured driver.

Officer Brisbane saw the gun hovering in midair and stole a quick glance at his belt. It was gone. He shot a look to his partner in the car and reached quickly for the pepper spray on his belt. He wasn't fast enough. The gun came up and fired three shots, one after another in quick succession. Officer Brisbane fell back as the lead slugs buried themselves in his chest, his face twisted in pain. The bullets pierced though his lungs, and one struck his heart. This last sight as he fell was the flash of lightning overhead. His blood mingled with the water and mud beneath him as he died.

In the cruiser, Junior detective Freeman frantically took the police radio and held it to his mouth. "This is One-L 19!" he shouted. "Officer down! Repeat, officer down at the town park, the old playground crime scene! Three direct shots, center of mass! Suspect—" The gun turned in midair and fired another four shots into the cab of the cruiser.

The bullets struck the glass of the windshield, smashing straight through it and leaving spider web cracks behind as they hit the junior detective in the face and chest. The radio flew from his hand as he slumped down in the chair, blood oozed from the holes in his body. He was already dead as the radio buzzed, and the dispatcher continued to try to contact him.

Paul lowered the gun, smoke rose from the barrel. He threw it to the ground where it splashed in a mud puddle. The thing must be empty anyways, no use in keeping it. He looked back over his shoulder to Royce. "I told you I'd take care of it. Now prepare the kid. The drugs will wear off soon."

Royce moved to the back of the SUV and opened the hatch. He climbed inside and found Luis still unconscious. He took the white plastic zip ties he'd kept back there and strung one set around the kid's ankles, with another around the wrists after he pulled the boy's arms behind his back. Royce then took a long piece of cloth and fit it in Luis's mouth, tying the ends together behind his head.

It was at this point Luis started to regain consciousness. His eyes fluttered open, and he had a horrible throbbing in his head. He groaned and tried to move but found his arms were stuck. His heart began to race; his breathing became rapid. What was going on? Where was he? How did he get here? His legs were likewise bound together, and there was a gag in his mouth. He tried to scream, but only muffled sound came out.

"I was right, you are awake." Paul hovered into view, his hands stuffed into the pockets of his jacket. "I hope you had some pleasant dreams because you will never have any ever again."

A plastic sack was pulled over Luis's head and tied in a knot around his neck. His breathing only quickened out of fear. Even as he tried to thrash and get away, he was pulled from the car by the collar of his shirt and drug through the mud. The pendant around his neck snapped off and fell away, landing in the mud behind him.

Luis struggled and tried to run, but each time he did, Royce would just lift him up and throw him back to the ground. He couldn't run anyways, his legs were zip tied together. The situation was hopeless, and Luis knew it. Sweat and tears rolled down his face, the air inside the bag was becoming hotter and thicker the more he breathed. This was the end. No matter what, there was no way he was going to get out of this.

Finally, Royce stopped dragging him. For a split second, Luis was filled with some renewed hope, but that quickly faded as he felt himself being lifted off the ground and then tossed back down. He landed in a hole, at least three feet in the ground, face down in the mud.

It was then he heard another sound, which utterly terrified him—metal scrapping against mud and rocks. A shovel. A slopping sound was heard as the shovel lifted a chunk of earth into the air and tossed it in the hole, which landed with a splat right on Luis's back.

"Quite fitting, isn't it?" Paul's voice reached his ears. "That you would die here in the same place where you met Alice and caused so much more trouble then you're worth. It's quite amusing, I must say."

Another pile of mud fell from above and splattered right on his head. He cried out again. He was growing tired now. The air in the bag was too thick, the wet dirt being piled on him was too heavy, and it was becoming too difficult to breathe. This was the end; his life was over.

But wasn't it over anyways? He should have died in that car accident with his father and Serena's mother years ago. He had just been living on borrowed time since then, and now that time was up. No one was coming to save him. He was simply going to die.

Royce pushed the shovel into the ground and lifted another clump of dirt on it. He dropped it on Luis in the hole. Paul watched everything with delight, almost giddy at the sight of it. As each new shovel full of dirt fell, Luis got that much closer to death.

The rumbling of another car engine caught Paul and Royce's attention. They stopped and turned. Even in the dark and in the rain, Paul knew who it was. That was an old Honda with flip up headlights, and that was Serena driving. "Keep burying him," Paul ordered. "I can take care of this." He faded and disappeared.

32

Serena drove through the rain into the park. Water from puddles splashed as she drove through them. Her wipers swished back and forth at a crazy speed to keep her windshield clear. Her heartbeat was almost as frantic as the wipers. Paul had Luis—that was all she knew.

Ahead of her, there were two cars. One was a police cruiser with its door wide open, and the other was a forest-green SUV with its headlights on and shining into the playground. She couldn't see the make and model, but she was sure it was a Ford Expedition, just like the one the kidnapper drove. In the unnatural white lights of the SUV, she saw a lone figure standing among the playground equipment. He turned occasionally, swinging a shovel around and throwing clumps of dirt in a hole.

That was him, the man who killed her sister—Royce. Her foot pressed harder against the gas, and the car sped up. Suddenly, it lurched and sputtered. The engine coughed and died, smoke billowed up from the hood. "Oh, come on! You piece of—" She turned the key off and stepped out. The rain soaked through her clothes and chilled her to the bone almost instantly.

Paul stood on the hood of her car with a bundle of wires and rubber tubes in his hands. "I don't think you'll need these anymore." He tossed them to the ground in a jumbled mess. "I hope you're not planning on helping your boyfriend because then I just might have to—"

Paul trailed off as Serena walked right passed him. He scowled viciously. "Hey!" he shouted, raising his hand in the air. "Don't you dare ignore me, you little bi—"

"Shut up!" Serena spun around and shouted in Paul's face. The ghost boy recoiled in shock.

She marched forward, shoulders hunched, and her hands stuffed in the pockets of her heavy black coat. She ignored Paul, instead fixing her angry gaze on the man dropping shovel after shovel of dirt on her boyfriend.

It was him. No doubt about it, that was the man who killed her sister. For the first time in her life, she could see the face of the man who ruined her life and destroyed her family. Her nails dug into the palms of her hands as she clenched her fists tighter than she thought possible. That man had filled her thoughts for years, a deep burning hate that had festered underneath her normally expressionless exterior and was now boiling to the surface.

In the light cast by the car's headlights, she saw the fallen police officers and the gun lying in the mud. She grabbed it without thinking and aimed at the man with the shovel, the gun wobbled before her eyes as she grasped it with shaking hands.

She could do it now and end it all. Just pull the trigger, kill him where he stands, and it would all be over. Yet as she stood in the rain with the water both from the sky and her tears flowing down her face, she found herself unable to do it. Why did she hesitate?

Alice emerged from the roof of the car. "Serena?" she called out. "What's going—" Her voice fell away when she saw the gun in her sister's hands and the person she pointed it at. As her eyes fell upon him, a mixture of emotions boiled up within her. She suddenly became terrified, frightened, angry, resentful, and wrathful all at once.

"Hey, asshole!" Serena shouted. The man dumped the shovel of dirt and turned to face her. His face was disfigured, and one eye was almost swollen shut. There was a look about him of fear and a little sadness, but also cold and emptiness.

Royce saw the gun. Instantly, he dropped the shovel and held his hands up over his head. "Hey, hold on now," he stammered. "I know this looks bad, but I was coerced! It's not my fault."

"Not your fault?" Tears streamed down Serena's face, mixing with the rain and making her mascara bleed. "You're the fiend that murdered my sister! Destroyed my family and ruined my life! Give me one good reason why I shouldn't kill you right now?"

"Because," he said, blubbering, "I don't want to die."

She placed her thumb on the hammer and pulled it back until it locked in place. "That's not good enough." Her finger rested on the trigger. Just pull it already, end it now. He doesn't deserve to live. Put a bullet in his brain.

"Go ahead," Paul said. "Shoot him, I don't care. I was going to kill him afterward anyways."

"Serena, don't!" Alice shouted. "Luis wouldn't want you to."

"This isn't about what Luis would want, this is about getting closure." Paul smirked. "Isn't that right?"

"No," Serena said. "Alice is right. If I kill you, then I'll be no better than you." She kept the gun aimed Royce. "I'm going to take the handcuffs from one of those cops, and I'm going to cuff you to the swing set. Then I'll just let the police sort it."

Lightning streaked across the sky, followed by a thunderclap. Serena jumped, and her finger twitched. The gun went off. The last bullet launched from the barrel. It crossed the distance between her and him in less than a second and buried itself in his chest.

Royce convulsed as the hot lead burned into his heart. He cried out, doubled over in pain, and clasped his hand over his chest. His punctured heart shuddered as it tried to beat and then stopped completely. He fell to the ground, his faced buried in the mud, his breathing stopped.

Serena could hardly believe what she had just done. She looked from the still smoking gun to the man lying dead in the rain. Her brows scrunched, and lips quivered before she fell to her knees and sobbed. The gun splattered in the puddles when she threw it away. Rain pelted her body. Her fingers dug lines in the mud as she clenched her fists.

"Well, would you look at that. I didn't think you had it in you, but I guess I was wrong." Paul gloated. "Congratulations, you're now a murderer. How does it feel to take a life? Feels good, doesn't it?"

"Shut up!" Serena screamed so loud her throat hurt. She leapt to her feet, raced to the hole in the ground, and jumped in.

She found Luis quickly, his arms were bound behind his back with zip ties and a plastic bag covered his head. "Luis! Luis, I'm here! You're safe!" She slipped her arms around his and dragged him out of the pit. His body was heavy and limp. Fear filled her heart and mind when he didn't move. "Come on, say something." She tore at the bag, and it ripped away. His eyes were closed, face calm looking. His mouth was taped closed with a rag in it. Without hesitation, she ripped the tape off, hoping the pain might wake him up. Still he didn't move. She pulled the rag out of his mouth and placed her lips to his, breathing for him.

His lips were cold. His whole body was cold. Lacing her fingers together, Serena started chest compressions. Still Luis was unresponsive. He didn't breathe, and his heart didn't beat.

"You're too late." A familiar wicked grin came over Paul's face. "I've won. Your little boyfriend is dead."

Serena couldn't even bring herself to say anything. She could only weep while still pressing her hands into his chest. This could not be happening, it just couldn't be. She threw herself over his body and sobbed.

Paul chuckled. "I guess that takes care of that."

"You're a sick monster!" Alice shouted.

Paul closed his eyes and nodded. "Say what you will. But it seems now I have only one person left on my hit list."

Paul flew toward Serena with his arms outstretched, too fast for Alice to intervene. He reached out for her, prepared to tear into her chest and pull her heart out. Just as his ghostly form touched her, a powerful jolt of raw energy surged and threw him back. Paul cried out in pain, steam rising from his hands.

Alice stared with confusion. She had been terrified that Paul would kill her sister, but then something forced him back. What was it? She caught a glimmer of something hanging around Serena's neck and recognized it instantly— the bloodstone pendant.

She noticed the other one lying in a mud puddle in the SUV's headlights.

Tentatively, he picked it up and held it up between her fingers. "It wards off evil spirits," she whispered to herself.

Clenching it in her fist, she flew at Paul as fast as she could. He looked up just as Alice thrust her arm out and pressed the pendant into his chest. A powerful surge of energy burst from the bloodstone and coursed through Paul's form. He cried out in agony; the force shoved him away.

His hands clasped over his chest, steam rose from the place Alice hit him. As he pulled his hands away, Paul saw what looked like scorch marks. His body began to glow red and then turn black like burning paper. "Wha-what's happening to me?" he screamed in terror.

Alice held up the pendant. "Bloodstone is harmful to poltergeists. It forces them away," she said. "You're now crossing over to the other side."

"What?" Paul screamed, suddenly terrified. "I don't want to! I want to stay here, I want—" His voice faded along with the rest of his form, crumbling away like dust in the wind. The last thing to go was his eyes. He looked at Alice, and for a brief moment, she saw a frightened child. He was absolutely petrified of what fate awaited him on the other side. Then he was gone.

Serena continued to weep over Luis's body. Alice hovered over to her sister and knelt down in the rain next to her. Paul might be gone, along with Royce, but they had done plenty of damage. And now the thing that brought Serena joy had once again been taken from her.

A thought came to Alice just then. Something Paul had said a while ago, about the way he killed a person. "Serena, move for a bit."

"What?" Serena's face was stained with tears as she looked up.

"I have an idea. It's a long shot, but it might just work." Alice placed her fingertips on Luis's chest and closed her eyes. Her hand sank into his body. It didn't take long for Alice to find what she was feeling for, and her hand closed around Luis's still heart. With it in her grasp, she started to manually pump his heart.

Serena watched enraptured. Slowly, color started to come back to Luis's face as his blood once again began to flow. His eyes snapped open, and he lurched off the ground with a sharp intake of breath. He gasped and coughed, his whole body ached. But he was alive.

Alice released her hold on his heart and pulled her hand back. A part of her was still in shock that it even worked. Luis sat up, hunched over, and panted for breath. After a few seconds, he finally managed to regain his composure. His eyes shifted up to Serena and Alice. He cleared his throat. "Hey." His voice was weak. "What's up?"

Serena nearly tackled him to the ground, her arms wrapped around him. She wept into his chest. "You were dead!" She managed to say between her sobs. "You're heart had stopped, but Alice brought you back."

"I was dead?" Luis asked. "And Alice did what?"

"What's the last thing you remember?" Alice leaned in close.

"Um, I was drugged," Luis said. "I remember being picked up and dropped in a muddy hole and then having dirt piled back on top of me. It started getting really hot, and I got tired. Then it suddenly got cold and nothing, I was just surrounded by darkness. And then I woke up." He quickly realized. "Oh, God, I really was dead. Wasn't I?"

"But she brought you back somehow." Serena finally loosened her hold on Luis and pulled back, the corners of her lips perked up in a smile.

"Alice, how did you do it?" Luis asked.

"It was something Paul said earlier," Alice explained. "He said he killed that teacher by stopping her heart. I just thought maybe I could restart one the same way."

"I'm glad you did," Serena said. She reached out to hold her sister, but her arms passed right through Alice. "Come on now. You don't want me to hug you?"

"I'm not doing it." Alice held up her hand and saw as her fingers began to dissipate. She was dissolving, but unlike

Paul's transition that was quick and violent, she was fading slower and more gracefully.

"Alice." There was a tone of worry in Serena's voice. "What's going on?"

"I'm passing over," she said, her form was getting weaker by the second. "I think I realize now what my unfinished business was." Alice tilted her head back to look up at the cloud-filled sky. The rain fell, but she couldn't feel it anymore. "The last thing I did before I was kidnapped was push you out of the way," she said, meeting eyes with her sister. "My unfinished business was to protect you and make sure you were safe and happy.

"And you made that possible." Alice moved her gaze over to Luis. "With my murderer gone, Paul gone, and you alive, I've done everything I needed to do."

"No!" Serena shouted. "We just found each other after all this time. I don't want to lose you again!"

"But this time, I'm not leaving you alone." Alice looked back from Serena to Luis. "Luis is here now, and he can take care of you. Right?"

Tears formed in Luis's eyes as he nodded. "Absolutely."

"I'm going to miss you, both of you," Alice said, she could barely keep herself from choking up. She smiled at Serena. "Promise me, if you tell Dad how much I love him and miss him, I'll tell Mom. Agreed?"

"Agreed." Serena dried her eyes and smiled.

"Good. I love you. Both of you. Take care of each other." Alice's form dissipated completely, and she faded away into the night, gone forever.

Epilogue

Saturday, November 8

"My sister was Alice Thomas. She was the first victim taken and—" Serena paused to compose herself, using a tissue to wipe away her tears and bleeding mascara. "She died to protect me."

Luis sat in the back row of a church pew in St. Michael's Cathedral. His mother was beside him and a short distance away was Alice and Serena's father. They were all dressed in black. Serena stood up at the podium overlooking the small crowd of people who had gathered for the memorial. The service was being held for all the victims found in the playground, a total of ten children. Their most recent photographs were framed and displayed in a row just beneath the podium.

"Alice let herself get captured so that I could get away. I was only six years old at the time. I have no doubt in my heart that my sister loved me dearly. I only wish I could tell her again." Serena stepped down from the podium; the tears flowed down her face fiercely no matter how she tried to dry them. She sat down between her father and Luis, who took her hand in his as she did.

Another woman stood up and made her way to the front of the church. She introduced herself as Susie's mother and proceeded to talk about her little girl. She broke down sobbing and left the podium in tears. One by one, a different relative of each of the victims stepped up to talk. The only child who didn't receive a eulogy was Paul, as he had no living family left. The ghost children had all come too. When Luis told them about the service, they begged him to take them. After each person spoke, their corresponding child would start to dissolve just as Alice had on Halloween. He knew some of the children better than others. Some like Alice and Paul, of course, and others like Susie and Jason, but most he had never really met by name—James, Elizabeth, Marion, Jeffery, Mathew, and Katie. They were all names, but also so much more, and he never got to know them.

The memorial concluded with the church bells ringing eleven times, ten for each of the victims who died and once for the girl who lived. As they were leaving, Luis and Serena were approached by an older black woman. "Excuse me," she said as they stepped out the door. "You're them, aren't you?"

"Who?" Luis asked.

"You're the pair that rescued my little girl. I'm sorry, I didn't introduce myself. I'm Michelle Little, Tamika's mother," the woman explained.

"Oh," Luis said. "Yes. We were the ones."

"I wanted to thank you in person for everything you've done. I don't think I can ever repay you." She turned to address Serena in particular. "And I'm sorry for your loss. I understand what you must've gone through."

"Thank you," Serena said. "I thought I was over it until today. Now I realize she's truly gone."

"Mom!" The woman's daughter, Tamika, came ran up to her. "Mom, I see her! That's the girl who saved me!"

"Yes, Tamika. This is, um, I'm sorry. I didn't get your name."

"Serena Ravenwood," she said with a smile.

"Yes." Michelle turned back to her daughter. "Tamika, this is Serena. She's the girl who ran into the fire and saved you."

"But, Mom, that's the other girl." Tamika pointed to the framed picture of Alice. "She's the one that unlocked the door and lead me out of the basement."

"Tamika, that's impossible. She's been dead for ten years," her mother said.

"But I saw her. It was real."

Michelle sighed, "I'm sorry. She's convinced someone else was there to save her."

N. J. HANSON

"No, it's all right," Serena said, shooting a knowing smile to Luis. "Maybe Alice was there in spirit."

After the service, Luis and Serena went back to the playground. The police barricade was still in place around it. Even after Royce's body was taken to the morgue and the case closed, the playground was still off limits while being repaired. With the deaths of two police officers, there was a little apprehension about the area. The officer's deaths were considered to have been committed by Royce, and Royce's death was an act of self-defense on Serena's behalf by the police. The vandalism of her car was also lumped in with Royce's other crimes.

Luis rested his hand on the fence as he stared out over the equipment. It was still hard to believe that Alice was really gone for good. Any second, he expected to see her sitting on the swings. She would wave and smile, before jumping up and running over to greet him. There was nothing but a breeze of cold November air and a flutter of leaves.

Serena stepped up next to him, her fingers laced with his. "I miss her too."

"Probably more than I do, I bet," Luis said.

"Probably." Serena squeezed his hand.

"It's strange. I didn't know her for very long, but I'll never forget her." Luis adjusted his glasses again. "I can honestly say she changed my life, and I'm better off for having met her."

Serena gave him a light kiss on the lips. "Come on, my dad is taking us for lunch if you want to come."

"Sure. I'd love to." They walked down the path together back to her dad's truck. The wind picked up slightly, and the swing started to move, letting out a metal groan as if someone were on it, but now it was just an empty swing.

CPSIA information can be obtained
at www.ICGtesting.com
Printed in the USA
FSOW04n0125040716
22269FS